The Last Time I Saw You

JO LEEVERS

LAKE UNION
PUBLISHING

Published by Lake Union Publishing, Seattle

www.apub.com

Amazon, the Amazon logo, and Lake Union Publishing are trademarks of Amazon.com, Inc., or its affiliates.

ISBN-13: 9781662506390
eISBN: 9781662506406

Cover design by Emma Rogers

Cover images: ©GiorgiN, ivan_kislitsin, Erik Svoboda, Anna Kucherova, Kriengsuk Prasroetsung / Shutterstock; ©Natalia Ganelin / ArcAngel; ©Eugene Sergeev / Alamy Stock Photo

Printed in the United States of America

PRAISE FOR
TELL ME HOW THIS ENDS

'A fabulous book . . . Really moving.'

—Zoe Ball, *BBC Radio 2*

'A pleasingly complex narrative, flecked with reflections on the healing properties of storytelling . . . this promising, poignant debut concludes with that vital ingredient: a well-crafted twist.'

—Hephzibah Anderson, *The Observer*

'An engrossing mystery.'

—Hannah Holway, womanandhome.com

'This poignant mystery is beautifully written.'

—*Candis* magazine

'An incredible story of regret, grief and the gift of time, all wrapped up in a heart-rending package.'

—Ashley Tate, author of *Twenty-Seven Minutes*

'I was totally hooked. A moving and deftly written story of loss and friendship, with a protagonist who reminded me of Eleanor Oliphant. Bravo.'

—Kate Maxwell, author of *Hush*

'A heartfelt exploration of how the secrets we carry shape our lives. The quirky, endearing characters and the mystery at its heart had me hooked.'

—Mikki Brammer, author of *The Collected Regrets of Clover*

The
Last Time
I Saw
You

ALSO BY JO LEEVERS

Tell Me How This Ends

For A, T & M, who I love very much

Prologue

Now she has her own front door key, Georgie worries a little less. At school, she keeps it safely zipped inside her sequinned pencil case and, any time she needs to, she can reach inside and touch the soft leather of the fob to make sure it's still there. It means that even if her mother doesn't answer the door when Georgie gets home, everything will be OK.

Getting that key was all part of starting secondary school, along with the scratchy uniform, dinner money instead of a packed lunch and a whole new set of rules, decided by the other kids rather than the grown-ups.

It's a Monday, the first day back after the Easter break, and the girls in her class have been talking about where they went for the holidays: a caravan on the Isle of Wight, a villa in Spain. Georgie had no desire to tell anyone about hers: a disastrous week in Wales, in a damp cottage where her parents had shouted at each other downstairs and she and her brother stayed out of the way until it was over.

But Georgie is hoping that when she gets back to the messy, warm chaos of their house in St Luke's Road, things will be back to normal. Maybe she'll walk in to find her mum already making their tea, stirring one of her too-bitter tomato sauces on the stove, the smell of garlic drifting down the hallway. Music will be playing on the radio, her mum swaying as she sings along, and that awful holiday and the things that were said will be forgotten.

But when Georgie gets home from school and turns the key in the wobbly lock, she knows something is wrong. Even as she pushes the door open, the air feels loose, as if the house has been empty all day. She calls out anyway – 'Hello?' – and goes through to the back garden.

On her mother's bad days, this is where Georgie will often find her, slumped into the sling of a deckchair, too far away to hear the doorbell. She'll sit there for hours, sunglasses on, a cigarette hanging loosely between two fingers, a small pile of grey ash gathering on the roughly shorn lawn. Georgie sees the back of the deckchair and her heart soars. But then a gust of wind lifts the stripy seat, turning it inside out into a big, billowing flag that tells her that nobody is home.

Upstairs, Georgie runs her fingers over the rumpled clothes in her mother's wardrobe. Dabs some Body Shop perfume on her wrists, twists a dry lipstick up then back down again. Everything is still here. Perhaps it'll be OK.

Back in the kitchen, she makes a jug of orange squash, tries not to wobble as she pours it into two cups. Then she puts four digestive biscuits on a plate. She wants to make it all right, because Georgie knows she is to blame for all this, in more ways than anyone can guess.

Later, her brother, Dan, gets back from rugby practice and they sit at the kitchen table and wait to hear the click of the latch on the front gate. When it comes, followed by the careful wiping of shoes on the mat, they know it's their father. And as soon as he walks in, Georgie feels her insides gathering into a hard knot because she knows what he's about to say.

'Your mother has gone away for a while,' he tells them, licking his dry lips. 'She's not well and a break will do her good. It'll do us all good.' Then he presses his mouth into the shape of a smile.

In return, Dan does his best to switch on his sunny grin, but Georgie can't bring herself to play along. She's thinking about everything that happened on last week's holiday and the words she said that set it all in motion.

Georgie goes over to the sink, tips away her squash and watches the orange liquid spread across the white porcelain. She has so many questions that only her mother can answer. But, she supposes, she'll have to wait a little longer to hear the truth.

Chapter One

NANCY

Standing in her doorway, Nan can tell it's going to be a cold one tonight. Already, a glistening has formed between the ruts of the path and a sheen lies over the bare branches. Her dog joins her, but then slinks back to the warmth of the fire. Bree is a dog that will usually keep going in all weathers, her tail a plume of white as she follows old trails through the bracken. But this afternoon, she's making her feelings clear: this is not good weather for a walk.

Except Nan knows she has to get out. She can feel her thoughts stirring, winding themselves into a ball of restlessness. A rising panic that means she has to get moving, otherwise those thoughts will drag her down to the dark place she fears.

So she pushes her feet into the hard leather of her boots, fumbles at the frayed laces. Winds a scarf twice around her neck and buttons her coat, the heavy wool one that's seen her through more winters than she cares to remember. Its dank weight feels like a comfort of sorts.

She stamps once, twice, on the ice-flecked ground, to bring Bree to her side, then locks the bothy, although really there's no need. No neighbours for miles. Looking up, already the trees are sharp outlines against the darkening sky.

The air is a slap of cold. She draws it into her lungs in increments, imagines it as a white cloud that fills up her insides. Cleansing; purging. Once she gets going, the ache in her knees lessens and the steady crunch of her boots sets a reassuring rhythm. This is a walk she could do with her eyes shut; Bree too, who is loping ahead with her nose to the ground.

Just to the brow of the hill, Nan decides. Enough to clear her head, stop her thoughts going back to that old pain deep inside her. Living in this bothy has been a sanctuary, after too many years of moving on, a figure on the fringes of life that people barely noticed.

With her long grey plaits, her greatcoat belted with twine and her heavy boots, she knows how she must appear to the locals: a loner. A vagrant. A witch. Nan has been called those things and more. On her rare trips down to the village, the shopkeepers are civil, but they keep their eyes lowered as she counts out her grubby coins.

As Nan reaches the top of the hill, she notices an odd glow below. At first, she wonders if it's bonfires – but Burns Night has been and gone. She looks harder, blinking in the gloom. No, not fires – beams of light that are moving in a line, like segments of a snake.

Nan stops. All she can hear is the sound of her own hard breathing. Next to her, Bree waits, and they watch as the line of torch lights makes its jagged way across the field, panning the lumpy heather.

Then the wind must change because she can hear them. Deep male voices that make her stomach tighten; calls from women that sound more desperate. 'Es-ee . . .' they seem to be saying. Then a buzzing, swooping noise fills the air above – a helicopter, with its huge beam criss-crossing the land. Dusk is turning to darkness and if someone is lost out there, every minute counts.

It looks like the search party is heading towards the marshy wetlands to the east, an area that appears from a distance to be lush grass but conceals icy water. She turns away. Too many people, too much light and noise. It's a relief to know that, this time, it's not her tragedy, not her fault.

The lights and the noise mean Nan and Bree can't take their usual path, so Nan loops round the other way, heading west. Bree doesn't like this route: it's more exposed and it takes them past the big crag people call Hound Rock.

As they pass under the lee of the rock, the wind disappears and the dog stops, stands still. Then, before Nan can call out, Bree is off, waving her feathery tail like a taunt. At this hour she could be after a rabbit, but there's also a chance she's caught the scent of carrion. Bree has a habit of rolling in long-dead carcasses and the stink will be terrible if Nan doesn't catch her first.

Nan climbs the low ridges of rock, smells wet moss and iron. But Bree has scampered up to the next level, where there's an opening. It's a place where walkers sometimes shelter from the rain, leaving behind sweet wrappers or, worse still, wads of toilet paper.

'Bree, down. Now!'

Bree doesn't listen and her white tail has disappeared into the gloom. Nan knows going further is foolish, so she stops. Eventually, Bree will come home, probably reeking of something long dead.

And then she hears it. A whimper that isn't Bree, because she knows every noise her dog makes. At first, she thinks it must be a sheep that's strayed to higher ground. But it's different, more like a mewling.

Nan holds her breath, strains to listen. All she hears is the blood pounding in her ears.

And then the sound comes again. It's fainter this time, closer to a sob. And in that horrible, hollow moment, Nan knows it's no animal and she drops to the ground and she's climbing and crawling as fast as she can towards it. Her knee hits something hard and she swears, remembers she has a voice.

'Hello? Is someone there?'

Nan keeps going, stretches out one hand, then the other. Her fingers close around an object. It's a single shoe. A child's shoe.

She's frantic now, patting the ground inside the cave, moving forward, but there's nothing but twigs and earth. Then her fingers brush against something solid and she feels the shape of one small foot and then the other. Her heart tightens into a single, sharp pain and she doesn't think twice, she reaches out both arms to find the child – because, yes, it is a child – and bring it out of its hiding place.

She knows she's doing all the wrong things because there could be fractures, but it's instinct that makes her unbutton her own thick coat and pull the bird-boned child to her. There's a lurch in time as she remembers this feeling, alien yet so familiar.

'You're OK,' she manages to say. 'I've found you.'

For a terrible moment there's no movement and she can't feel any breathing. Just the cold sheen of a too-thin sweater, the wetness of the child's jeans. Nan wraps her coat tighter and rubs the child's back, keeping up a firm, regular rhythm.

She's stuck in this moment with no way forward or back, just doing what feels right. She feels the bony nubs of the child's spine, holds her breath again. And then it shifts just slightly, lets out a whimper.

And all at once, Nan knows they need to move. She has to go down to the village for help, face the noise and people she's hidden from for so long. Because this isn't about Nan, it's about saving the child – something any mother would do.

Nan hardly notices the crack in her knees as she rises – the child is heavier than she'd first imagined – and then she steadies herself and starts to put one careful foot in front of the other.

Nan carries her bundle down the hill, one step at a time, with Bree by her side. They walk in the dark and the cold until the fuzzy glow of light below separates into a line of single beams, and then one bright beam breaks free. A figure is running towards them, a light juddering and blinding Nan so that she has to stop, and then a voice calls out: 'Someone's coming – I think she's got her. My God. She's found.'

Chapter Two

GEORGIE

She would never admit this to anyone, but the antenatal clinic is swiftly becoming Georgie's least favourite place to be. It should be a place of joy, but sitting in this too-hot waiting room is making Georgie deeply uncomfortable. Wilf's been called away for work, so she's here on her own. But there are several other dads-to-be here, all of them looking shifty, glued to their phones, averting their eyes from the row of swollen bellies that say, 'Yes, I had sex.' 'Me too.' 'And me!'

The first scan had felt so special. Seeing that pulse of a heartbeat, those floating limbs and even the outline of a nose – all incredible. But then came the questions and Georgie didn't know answers to half of them so she plumped for whatever sounded best. Now, every time she comes back to the clinic, she worries she'll be caught out. She might be asked all over again if there's a history of gestational diabetes, pre-eclampsia or postnatal depression and she honestly can't remember what answer she made up last time around.

This morning, Georgie is here for her final check-up – 'Getting close now,' Serena the midwife reminds her. 'Two weeks and counting!' She does her measurements – quaintly old-fashioned, with a dressmaking tape measure – and then presses a warm, dry hand around the edges of Georgie's huge belly to check where the baby's lying.

Then there's the blood pressure cuff – the reassuring pump-pump as it inflates, then the sad hiss of detumescence before her arm is released with a rip of the Velcro. It's only then that Serena frowns. 'Remind me: low blood pressure – runs in the family, does it?'

'Yes, it does,' says Georgie. Because it's simpler than admitting she has no idea what health issues she might have inherited from her mother.

By the time Georgie leaves the clinic, she's missed the bus home and the next one isn't for two hours – one of the quirks of country life. Georgie sets off walking, a decision she regrets as soon as she gets to the edge of town and remembers how the pavement tapers away to a thin point and then disappears completely. Another aspect of rural life she's getting used to.

So for the rest of the walk, it's a matter of pressing herself, big belly first, into the high hedges when cars whizz by. Disentangling her hair from a particularly prickly bush, Georgie is reminded how much easier life would be if she could drive.

It's another fifteen minutes of stop-start walking along a busy A-road before Georgie reaches the turning to the eco development where she and Wilf now live. Their house is one of only three that are finished and is at the end of Orchard Drive. It's not a proper road yet, more a wide, muddy track, riven with deep tyre marks from the lorries and earthmovers that come and then, like the workmen, disappear for weeks on end.

'Supply-chain problems,' a foreman in a yellow helmet told her, arms crossed, feet firmly planted. Georgie suspects money-chain problems is closer to the mark, but she doesn't say this to Wilf, who remains resolutely upbeat about living on a building site. He says things like *It'll be great when it's finished* or *We're bound to have neighbours soon*, as he scrapes the claggy mud from his shoes each evening.

Until they do, she and Wilf are the first and only residents of this pioneering eco development, where every home is built with sustainable materials and efficiently insulated with wood fibre. Wilf says projects like this are the future, that we all need to wake up to climate change. But Wilf is abroad for ten days, so right now it's just Georgie living here, in a house that might be helping to save the planet but feels rather lonely.

Georgie scrapes her boots along the edge of their step to get off the worst of the mud and gives the front door a good push. It sticks a little, needs a bit shaving off the edge, but the carpenter hasn't been seen for weeks. Rather like the tiler, who went to get something out of his van and never returned. Georgie stands in the hallway and tries to identify the still unfamiliar smell of the place: there's a whisper of this morning's toast but mostly it smells of damp plaster.

Sitting on the bench in the hallway, Georgie consciously breathes out. Wilf will be home in five days and then they will be on the home straight – the countdown to her due date. She doesn't want to be the woman ticking off the days until her man is back, but when Wilf is around, things feel so much more doable. It's as if Georgie steps into a parallel world, one where she's a better version of herself and makes sensible decisions. She doesn't make things up to her midwife or set off walking along busy main roads with no pavement.

Maybe it's because Wilf never knew the old Georgie. They met when she was doing her job, calmly and competently, and ever since he has taken her at face value. And that's how Georgie is determined to keep it: she never wants him to meet the Georgie that came before, the woman who was a blurry mess, blundering through life, damaging people and ruining lives.

This hallway bench, like most of the furniture in this house, is a hand-me-down from Wilf's parents. His mother is a play therapist and his father is a headteacher at a special needs school and they live nearby, in the Victorian farmhouse where they brought up their three sons. The whole place has an elegantly knackered feel, rooms piled high with furniture picked up in country auctions over the years. 'Cheap as chips. It's all firewood, really,' his mother, Ruth, had said, wiping her hands on her smock as she watched Wilf and Georgie loading her rejects into a hired van.

As a consequence, Georgie and Wilf's new home is an odd mix of styles: hulking wooden blanket boxes, a 1970s sideboard and saggy armchairs of indeterminate ages. The furniture that was part of a characterful boho jumble in that family farmhouse sits uneasily within these echoey rooms, much like Georgie.

In the kitchen, she opens the fridge and grabs handfuls of lettuce straight from the salad crisper. Right now, Georgie craves anything fresh and crunchy: wet iceberg lettuce, chunks of dewy cucumber and just washed carrots. Sometimes, she pops ice cubes out of their rubbery tray and bites down on them, savouring the hard crunch.

Then, with a little more decorum, Georgie arranges the remaining salad on a plate and adds a hunk of cheese for protein. Afterwards, she flicks through the selection of teas, which live in a diddy kitchen drawer specially designed to hold such sachets. Camomile, she decides, is the least offensive. She twists the hot water tap and it splutters into life.

Georgie misses the routine of putting the kettle on and waiting for it to boil, but apparently this tap is more energy efficient. She dunks the teabag, lifts it out by its string and adds it to yesterday's dried-out bags, pressed together on a saucer like a nest of grey baby mice.

Georgie is not officially on maternity leave yet, but her work as a wedding photographer has tailed off. She'd built up a good circle of contacts and word-of-mouth recommendations back in London, but now they've moved she'll need to start all over again. Wilf says she should visit all the local wedding venues and introduce herself; put adverts in the newspaper. Georgie can see how that would work for Wilf – he's Mr Outgoing and Positive – but she's not that sort of person. Most of the time, she appreciates Wilf's can-do attitude – the way it balances out her glass-half-empty approach to life. But on this occasion, she thinks he's wrong. Her style of photography went down well in London, but she's not sure people in this corner of Devon will get it.

Because Georgie doesn't do the standard wedding shots. She knows most people prefer a glossy version of their day, the sort of pictures that get put inside silver frames and set on a mantelpiece, but Georgie's photos feel more like snatched memories. She'll snap the bride whispering something to her best friend or capture the couple's first dance as a joyful blur – images that convey the atmosphere of the day.

'Tell them it's wedding reportage,' Finn used to say. 'It'll make them feel cool.' Even now, she can hear his voice, picture the way his face would light up when he hit upon a good idea. Later, he was less enthusiastic, calling her work 'a sell-out'. But he never complained about the way it paid the bills.

She shakes her head, horrified by the way her mind has circled back to him, here of all places, in this new house that's all about her and Wilf and the future. It feels like an infidelity. Worse still, she knows what Finn would think of this place. 'Faux rustic for country wannabes,' he'd say. Or, 'Into cutesy cottagecore are you now, Georgie?'

But Wilf isn't fake or faux or a wannabe anything. He's the most genuine person Georgie has ever met. He's the opposite to Finn and all he represented and that's the whole point of being here.

It was Wilf who suggested moving to Devon. He wants their baby to have the carefree sort of childhood he enjoyed: 'Playing on the village green, walking to school – all that stuff.' And it made sense, he pointed out, to be near at least one set of grandparents. The alternative – moving closer to Georgie's father and stepmother in Surrey – was far less appealing. And Georgie definitely doesn't want her baby to have the same childhood she did, living in a cul-de-sac on the outskirts of Redhill, in a house that had high levels of hygiene but little in the way of love. In fact, the more distance Georgie can put between herself and her family's past, the better.

She feels herself drawn upstairs to the baby's room, which has become a centre point for her, an anchor. Here, everything is laid out, ready and waiting: rows of washable nappies, boxes of biodegradable wipes. Drawers full of sleepsuits and muslins, all freshly laundered and folded. And in the middle of the room is the crib: an oval design with a canopy. Gleaming white, it reminds Georgie of a spaceship that's waiting, just like her, for signs of life.

Beneath the skin of her belly, Georgie feels the churn of her baby moving. 'This is our new home,' she whispers, but it doesn't sound convincing, not yet. She hopes everything will fall into place when Wilf gets back.

'It's bad timing, but I'll only be away ten days,' he'd said. When she and Wilf met, he told her how he was going into business with his friend Mehdi, running eco walking tours in remote parts of the world, starting with Morocco. 'We want to take visitors to these places without destroying the landscape or exploiting the people who live there. And half of our profits will go to community health projects in the villages,' he'd explained. Georgie had nodded along, thinking this sounded like your average greenwashing, but it turned out that Wilf and Mehdi were genuine – and this first tour is a make-or-break moment.

Mehdi had been lined up to be the guide for this group, which includes journalists and an important local politician. Except, at the last minute, Mehdi broke his collarbone playing squash. There was no way he could put on a rucksack, let alone lead a tour. 'It'll be a disaster if we cancel,' Wilf told her. 'Without press coverage, we won't get bookings for the rest of the year. I have to go, Georgie. But I'll be back soon.'

So Georgie had smiled and said 'Of course', but inside she was screaming. She watched him carefully pack his clothes and equipment and she wanted to pull it all out and shout, 'No, don't go, don't leave me', because what if Wilf never came back?

It might happen, she wanted to tell him. *It did happen.* She didn't go to the front door when he left, but watched from upstairs as he carried his rucksack over the rutted ground to the waiting taxi. 'I don't like goodbyes' was all she said.

That was five days ago and ever since, Georgie has been trying to relax into the country life in this sleepy corner of Devon. She's tried, she really has, to be friendly since they moved here. She smiles at the other women at the clinic until her cheeks hurt. And although it would be cheaper and easier to do an online supermarket shop, she resolutely buys her groceries from the farm shop, loading up her wicker basket with jars of overpriced jam, floury loaves and mud-caked vegetables. She always makes a point of saying a bright and breezy 'Morning!', but the woman on the till still treats her like a stranger.

'It takes time for people to accept incomers,' Wilf had told her.
But how long? she wanted to ask.

She looks out of the window at the churned furrows outside the house, the sodden fields behind. Beyond that, the grey strip of the main road and the glint of cars and lorries. Georgie is clear about why she's moved here, the things that she needs to leave behind. It's just that her future here still feels hazy, as unfinished as the mud-clogged road, the gappy bathroom tiles and the ill-fitting doors.

One of the faded armchairs that Ruth gave them is in the corner of this room. 'Perfect for night feeds,' she'd said. Georgie lowers herself into it, hears the muffled twang of an old spring. She gets out her phone, does the usual flick through: Twitter, Instagram, WhatsApp. Not that there's much to catch up on.

She deliberately unfollowed all her London friends when they moved here, left her WhatsApp groups – too many reminders. Now, she just checks the news and a few accounts of professionally pregnant women, 'mum influencers' who spend their days whizzing up smoothies and advertising stretch mark creams.

But today, those mums-to-be are all talking about the same thing. A story has gone viral, with the hashtag #lostgirl. A child has gone missing on a Scottish island and a search has been mounted. Georgie skims through the posts. Someone has uploaded a blurry photo of the village where the seven-year-old girl was staying and a school photo of her smiling a gap-toothed smile.

Georgie's own baby shifts again and she moves her hand over her stomach, feeling the nub of a foot or an elbow. It's OK, hers is safe inside her, but someone else's child is lost. A little girl who went out for a walk this morning wearing her favourite sweater, jeans and a flimsy pair of plimsolls and now everyone fears for her safety.

She watches as, before her eyes, the online mood starts to shift – concern morphing into thinly veiled accusations. *How terrible, but how did the little girl wander off? Where were her parents? Is she really lost or has she been abducted? What are the police doing? Actually, what do we really know about the parents?*

Georgie must have dozed off because she wakes to darkness. Her phone is still in her hand and she can't help going back to that story, even though she knows it's wrong, feeding on someone else's pain. But as she starts to scroll, her heart lifts. Already, the story has changed: *Missing girl found! She's safe! Miracle rescue!*

Georgie leaves the shouting on social media and looks for a local news feed. She walks downstairs, makes a hot drink and sits down on the sofa to read it. But by the time she's finished, Georgie has forgotten all about her camomile tea.

Missing child saved by island loner

The search for seven-year-old Jessie Lucas has been called off – for all the right reasons. Jessie was staying with family when she went missing on the morning of Monday 7 February.

Volunteers rallied to search for the child around midday and a Search & Rescue helicopter added assistance in the early evening. With overnight temperatures expected to drop well below freezing, hopes were fading fast. Local shopkeeper Andrew McNabb says: 'We had no idea which direction the little girl had gone in.'

Little Jessie was carried down from Hound Rock by a woman who had been out walking her dog. She is known locally only as 'Nan' and islanders say she is something of a loner.

Tim Lucas, the child's father, says: 'We cannot thank this woman enough for bringing our daughter back to safety. We are incredibly relieved that she's home.'

Jessie is being treated for mild hypothermia but is expected to make a full recovery. The local woman 'Nan' could not be reached for comment. This is the ninth rescue operation in the past twelve months and visitors are urged to heed advice on walking and climbing in the area.

At the end of the story is a photograph and the caption reads: *Little Jessie, her mother, Alice, and 'Nan', who brought the girl to safety.*

Georgie reads those words several times because when she looks directly at the picture, it feels as if someone is cracking open her chest.

In the photo, the little girl is sitting between two women. One is clearly the girl's mother, but the other is an older woman. In comparison, she looks dirty and unkempt.

She's wearing a big overcoat and a scarf that's wound around her neck several times. Her grey hair is parted in the middle and two long plaits frame a ruddy, wind-beaten face. There's a mole above her lip, a crackle of lines around her eyes. But her eyes are as bright as ever and her mouth is caught half open, as if she's trying to say something.

As a photographer, Georgie knows that expression well – it's the one she sees when someone doesn't want their picture taken. But Georgie recognises that face for another reason. It's older, plumper and more weathered than Georgie remembers. But there's no mistaking that the woman in the picture is her mother. The mother she hasn't seen in twenty years, who she had long since given up for dead or having run so far away that she'd never be found.

Georgie feels a dizzying lurch and she leans forward to rest her head in her hands. The twisted wreckage of her childhood is rushing back in, all the chaos she's worked so hard to leave behind. She remembers her mother as the woman she was in the days before she left: a storm of gritted teeth and sharp nails that blew through the house, rattling doors and windows with her tears and her angry words. Georgie and her brother, Dan, sitting upstairs, waiting for the storm to die down.

Then, Nancy standing at the front door, waving Georgie off to school like nothing was wrong. Pretending she'd still be there at the end of the day – and all over again, Georgie feels the betrayal.

Nancy had walked away from the ruins of their family life, leaving her children to piece things together and mend their father as best they could. But as Georgie blundered through the years that followed, her anger was tinged with guilt, as she wondered how much she, too, was to blame for the mess they were living through.

Back in the bare living room of her eco cottage, Georgie tries to take deep, long breaths, like Serena the midwife taught her. In two weeks' time, Georgie will give birth to her own baby, a child she already loves with such a ferocity she can't imagine how a mother could leave and never look back.

But now her mother has returned, risen from the dead. And, more than ever, Georgie needs answers.

Chapter Three

NANCY

She hadn't realised the man was going to take her photograph. All she saw was a flash, a dazzle of white dots, and by the time she'd blinked them away, it was too late to say anything. The man was gone.

Then there was the deafening roar of the air ambulance circling above and, with everyone shouting over the noise, Nancy decided it was best if she slipped away. So she had edged into the shadows, given a small stamp on the ground to call Bree to heel, and together they had melted into the darkness. They walked side by side, leaving the hubbub and bustle behind until it was just the steady crunch of Nan's boots and Bree by her side. The way they both liked it. And by the time they reached home, the events of the past few hours felt like a dream.

Now, back in her bothy, Nancy crosses her arms over her chest, to that already cooled place where the little girl had fitted so easily. Nan had carried her down on tracks that were bumpy and frozen, her heart thumping, worried she was already too late. To keep herself calm, Nan had hummed. Such a silly tune, an old lullaby she thought she'd long since forgotten, about mockingbirds and diamond rings, but its rhythm helped her put one foot in front of the other. And, if she wasn't mistaken, the girl recognised it too, burrowing in that little bit deeper.

The way the child's limbs fitted into hers was so familiar. Her head was pressed to Nancy's chest and if she tilted her chin down, Nancy could feel the tickle of fine hair, breathe in that biscuity smell. She pushes the memory away.

That sensation comes from a lifetime ago, when Nancy was a different person. She's lived in so many places since then, changing her name, changing her accent, doing whatever it took to fit in or to get by. There have been dark times, when she slept in hostels or shop doorways, loading herself with blankets to disguise her female shape.

Then the beginnings of a recovery, in a place far from home. She'd returned to England to work in warehouses and on production lines before finding a peace of sorts in Ireland, where she'd looked after animals, discovering they were better company than most humans. Then she'd moved to the wilds of Scotland.

But now, in the narrow bed of her bothy home, Nancy remembers the flash of the camera and she starts to think about what it could mean. While she has no need of a phone or the internet, she knows that other people chatter non-stop through the ether, how pictures and stories zip from phone to phone and pop up on screens in homes all around the country.

Nancy sits bolt upright in bed. How could she have been so stupid? Running and moving on have become second nature to her over the years. But living on this island she's got too comfortable, let herself stay in one place too long. Made the mistake of telling locals a too-close version of her name. And today, she's blown her cover.

Sleep won't come now. She can feel the adrenaline spreading out from her core, setting every part of her on alert, like an animal ready to run. Because who knows where her picture will have travelled to by now. He could be looking at it this very minute, smiling that private smile.

When morning comes, Nancy will pack her few belongings and she will have to leave the island. This place has been a balm for her soul and she'll be sad to say goodbye, but running away is hardwired into her now. She takes a small comfort in knowing that nothing will ever feel as bad as the first time she left.

Nancy sits up in bed for a long time, barely noticing the cold night air. Soon, she will forget the feeling of how that small child cleaved to her. Everything fades, if you wait long enough. She stares at the window, waiting for dawn.

Chapter Four

GEORGIE

It's a stroke of luck that she already has an overnight bag packed and ready to go. The pregnancy books advise doing this in good time and hers has been waiting beside the front door for a month: all Wilf's doing. Georgie removes a few things she won't be needing yet: a thick wodge of maternity pads; an electric essential-oil diffuser. She replaces the bulky dressing gown with a second pair of maternity leggings and a sweater: her current dull but practical uniform. She keeps her sponge bag, the portable charger, the water bottle and a multipack of cereal bars that she suspects will taste like sugar-frosted cardboard.

It's only 5 p.m. but outside the darkness is complete, and it feels later. On Google Maps, she finds the Scottish island she saw on the news, uses the satellite version to comb over expanses of heather and rock. It really is the back of beyond. The sort of place a person could hide for a long time. But for twenty years? It simply isn't possible. And it certainly isn't the story that she and Dan were told as children. Georgie calls a taxi, locks the door to their faux cottage behind her.

The taxi driver is a chirpy sort who can't seem to get past the fact that Georgie is pregnant. He keeps trying to catch her eye in the rear-view mirror and he says three times how he won't charge for 'the extra passenger' and each time Georgie ignores him.

She needs to get the 17.41 to London Paddington, then the Tube across to Euston where she'll catch the Caledonian Sleeper up to Scotland. If this bloke puts his foot down, she can make it. 'Yes, an extra passenger, ha ha,' she says. 'Please could we speed up a bit? I really need to catch this train.'

She makes it on board with seconds to spare. Trying to run when heavily pregnant really doesn't work well: her belly feels like an appendage, one that throws her centre of gravity out of whack.

Once she's sitting down and her breathing returns to something approaching normal, Georgie gets out her phone. She should let Wilf know where she's going. Although that's tricky because, as far as Wilf knows, Georgie's parents are called Irena and Frank and they live in a house on a 1970s estate in Redhill in Surrey, where they have a fine collection of bonsais and are founding members of the local Neighbourhood Watch scheme.

She starts to type out a message:

> *Things have gone a bit mad here. Turns out that my mum – my real mum, not Irena – is living up on a Scottish island. Been there for a while, by the sounds of it. I mean, I was twelve years old when she left us, but it definitely looks like her and she has a similar name. So I need to go and see her. Get a few things sorted in my head before the baby comes. Then you'll be home and I can put the past behind me and we can start our new life together.*

Then she holds her finger on the screen and watches those difficult words disappear.

Hope it's going well, she writes instead. *I'm just off to visit an old friend but I'll be home before Friday. Can't wait to see you then.* She adds two exclamation marks to make it look more upbeat and presses send.

She hasn't exactly lied to him; she just hasn't got around to telling him about her messy family history. Still, by the time Wilf flies back from Morocco, Georgie will have this all sorted. She'll have the answers she needs and Wilf can walk in and hug her and say how much her bump has grown and then tell her lots of stories about his work trip. By then, Georgie will have buried the past for good and she and Wilf can get on with their future, counting down to her due date, just two weeks away.

Admittedly, it was a surprise when she discovered she was pregnant but, as Wilf said, it's just speeded things up a bit. She loves the way Wilf sees the positive side to everything. And leaving London, starting over with Wilf, has made her happier than she's been in a long time. So the last thing she needs is this – the past spreading into her present like a swirl of dark paint in a jar of clean water, threatening to pollute everything.

As she moves her hands over the tight, shifting shape of her own baby, Georgie can't help but wonder what her mother felt at this point in her pregnancy. Was she excited, or was she filled with fear and dread? Did Nancy already know a restless sickness lay inside herself?

Because, if that was the case, Georgie worries something equally corrupt is lurking inside her that will eventually force its way out. Back in their eco cottage in Devon, things could not look more perfect. There are tiny sleepsuits, a designer cot and a pristine steriliser waiting for the new arrival and Georgie already loves her baby with a primal urgency. But is love enough to overcome her bad blood and make her a good mother?

Maybe it was having babies that was the tipping point for Nancy. Or was Georgie culpable in other ways for pushing her mother into leaving? Twenty years on, Georgie still has no idea how Nancy would answer these questions. But then, she wonders, how much did she ever know about the woman who was her mother?

Chapter Five

Nancy, 1984

'Don't get yourself in trouble'

Nancy grew up in a house that never felt like her own home. That's because it was a pretend home for other people, guests who paid good money for a stay at The Beaufort Bed and Breakfast. 'Never enough money, though,' her father, Mike, would sigh, pushing his glasses up his nose as he went over the books every Sunday night, tracing a thick finger down the rows of numbers that determined whether they would eat scrag end or chops next week.

The guest rooms are at the front of their semi on the out-skirts of Stamford, while Nancy and her parents, Theresa and Mike, are confined to an extension at the back of the house. This is also where old and tired pieces of hotel furniture end up, along with the chipped plates, blunt knives and forks with wonky tines. Surrounded by second-best, Nancy is never under any illusion as to who matters the most at The Beaufort – it's the paying guests.

For a brief time when she was little, living in a hotel made Nancy the envy of other girls at primary school. She would sneak them mini packets of biscuits and tiny tubs of long-life milk from the guests' tea trays. And sometimes she'd bring a friend home and show off the best bedroom, the one with the silky peach bed cover and a view over their suburban street. 'It has a private toilet and bath,' she'd tell them proudly, and they would admire how the toilet roll was folded into a downward V, sniff the cake of soap in its waxy wrapper.

But that was when Nancy and her friends were too young to know any better. Now Nancy is sixteen, she can see that The Beaufort, with its red carpets and scuffed wallpaper, is a shabby affair. She feels sorry for the people who arrive on a Friday night, expecting the 'family-run welcome' advertised in the Yellow Pages. As she shows them to their rooms, she sees the way their faces fall and she sympathises because, if she could, she'd like to check out of this place too.

These days, Nancy keeps quieter about where she lives and the en suite is no longer a source of pride. In fact, now it's her job to clean the bathrooms with their unfashionable pink fittings, and no matter how much Vim she uses, Nancy never quite manages to erase the chalky streaks of limescale.

Still, she learns a lot about people from her work. She soon wises up to the travelling salesmen who brush a little too close to her as she carries her cleaning bucket up the stairs. But she also sees the good – and the way bigger families often have an easy banter about them. She watches how children put their elbows on the table, how they joke with each other – even their parents – and yet nobody gets told off. It must be something that comes with having brothers and sisters, she supposes.

But the happy families are few and far between because most guests are disappointed by The Beaufort. They discover the taps that drip and the central heating pipes that knock and bang when the system fills at 6 a.m. The way the TV in Room Three doesn't show the new Channel 4 unless you hold the aerial by the window.

Even couples who come for a romantic break end up bickering, blaming each other for choosing this dump of a place. 'No refunds' becomes her father's constant refrain as he stands at the serving hatch to the kitchen that doubles as his office. *At least you're only here for a weekend*, Nancy wants to say to them. She has to endure two more years of this place before she can escape to university.

Still, no one is more disappointed to be living at The Beaufort than Nancy's mother, Theresa. Back when Theresa was sixteen, she too had been a bright girl. But this was in 1966 and no teachers had even mentioned the word 'university' to her. Instead, like most of her friends, and her parents before her, she went to work at the local factory that made aircraft parts. The only difference was, Theresa was allowed to work in the accounts office because she had done surprisingly well in her O levels. It was a junior job, but one with prospects, and it was noted that, despite her being a girl, Theresa 'showed promise'.

But all that changed when, aged seventeen, Theresa went to a Rotary Club dance. There she met a man called Mike Jebb, rumoured to be in line to take over his parents' bed and breakfast and considered quite a catch. Beneath the silvery shimmers of a hired glitterball, Mike spun Theresa round and round to 'Everlasting Love' and her fate was sealed. Theresa and Mike married in haste, with Nancy born – 'Surprise!' – a short seven months later.

So by the time Nancy is a teenager, her mother does little to conceal her feelings about how her own life was curtailed. Theresa has developed firm views about boys, views she makes known to Nancy on a regular basis. Boys are filthy, they are devious and they will do anything and say anything to get inside Nancy's pants. She must stay away from them at all costs, otherwise her life will be 'ruined, quite ruined'.

Theresa also has a habit of saying spiteful things and promptly walking out of the room, so there is no chance to reply. 'You were an accident,' she remarks to Nancy one Sunday evening, as the two of them sit watching a film on TV. 'Tied me down forever – to that lump.' She gestures to Nancy's father, sleeping in his armchair, then disappears into the kitchen, like nothing has happened.

Nancy, who has heard this before, sighs and goes back to watching Sid James cackling at Barbara Windsor on the telly. Nancy also knows that her own birth – an emergency caesarean – is the reason she remains an only child. 'Doctors were in such a rush, they rummaged around inside and damaged my tubes,' Theresa has said bitterly.

Sometimes Theresa addresses these things directly to Nancy, but more often to Aunty Annette. Theresa and her sister Annette like to sit at the kitchen table, smoke Rothmans cigarettes and talk about their feckless husbands and the price of meat in the market and why polyester sheets are still a thrifty choice for the bed and breakfast.

'You've got opportunities, Nancy,' her mum continues as she breezes back into their living room. 'I never did. So don't get yourself in trouble. Or it'll be the end.'

Nancy turns off *Carry On Camping* and slinks back up to her bedroom, where her books are waiting. If she passes these exams and then her A levels, she could go far – all her teachers say so. But as she trudges up the stairs, Nancy feels Theresa's words following her, nipping at her heels.

On evenings like this, her mother's dark mood can feel like a solid thing, a yellow cloud that billows into the corners of their modest rooms, swirls beneath the dining table and drifts under Nancy's bedroom door. When the house is filled with this yellow cloud, Nancy knows to keep her thoughts to herself because they will only be smothered, extinguished by this heavier presence.

For Nancy, the only thing that helps lift this cloud is when she pretends to be someone else – when she's acting. Living in a bed and breakfast, she is accustomed to putting on a show – *Good morning, what a beautiful day! Oh, I'm sorry, I'll check the TV in Room Three right away. Central heating noises? No, I don't think there's a problem* – but this term her English teacher is getting the class to read plays out loud.

Nancy loves the feeling of shrugging off her old self and trying on a new identity. While her classmates stumble over words or read them in a monotone, Nancy finds it easy. All she has to do is pretend – and she discovers she's pretty good at it.

Tonight, she is memorising quotes from *Othello* for her mock exam in a week's time. In her exercise book, she copies down her favourite line: *O, beware, my lord, of jealousy; It is the green-eyed monster which doth mock the meat it feeds on.*

She suspects that underneath Theresa's snipes, her mother envies Nancy's brighter future. Soon, Nancy will leave this house behind – her cleverness will be her passport out of this mealy-mouthed town. And she has no intention of repeating her mother's mistakes.

Chapter Six

Georgie

The train conductor wears a name badge that says she is called 'Susan' and that she is happy to help. Susan has already checked Georgie's ticket, but as the train starts its lazy crawl towards Paddington, she reappears, leans down to talk to Georgie in a conspiratorial whisper. 'You got somewhere to stay if you get stuck in London?' she asks.

Georgie shakes her head. 'I'm heading over to Euston for the sleeper. Up to Scotland,' she says. Not that it's any of Susan's business.

'Yes, I thought I saw that on your ticket,' Susan says, glancing up and down the carriage. 'But I don't think you'll be getting out of London tonight, love. Strike day tomorrow and services out of Euston and King's Cross are already winding up. Pandemonium over there. Our crew is hoping for a quick turnaround so we can head back to Exeter. My advice would be to stay in your seat, come back with us.'

This can't be happening; Georgie has to be in Scotland by tomorrow morning. She feels a loosening inside. She's barely reached London and already her so-called plan is falling apart.

Five minutes later, as the train enters the dark cavern of Paddington station, Susan makes a more official announcement. 'We regret to inform passengers that there are currently no onward trains from other London mainline stations. Tube trains and buses may also be affected. This industrial action is part of an ongoing dispute. We apologise for any inconvenience to passengers.'

In Georgie's carriage, there's a second of silence, like a mass intake of breath – and then uproar. All around her, people are getting out their phones, ringing people. Pulling suitcases down from racks, standing in the aisle to be first off. There is swearing and groaning and people muttering about taxis and how Uber prices are already twice what they should be.

Someone's hand is pressing down on Georgie's headrest and several strands of her long hair are caught underneath. Georgie sits very still, trying not to tug her hair from its hold. Should she do what Susan said, stay sitting here and wait for the train to refill with a new batch of angry people? Then she can slink back home and forget this stupid idea.

She pictures her kitchen, just as she left it. Her single mug on the counter. Beside it, the saucer of squashed teabags. A four-day wait until she hears the scrape of Wilf's key in the front door.

There's a shifting and jostling as people move towards the train doors, but her hair is still trapped under a stranger's hand. Georgie makes a decision. With a sharp yank she pulls herself free, tucks her hair behind her ears and stands up. 'I'm pregnant, please let me through,' she says. And, amazingly, people do.

An hour later, Georgie is sitting on a bench in Paddington station. On the departures board, rows of flickering orange letters spell out the same message: cancelled, cancelled, cancelled. Susan had been overly optimistic; even her train back to Exeter was cancelled and now the platform is awash with people dragging suitcases and children from café to concourse, platform to taxi rank, shouting increasingly panicked messages into their phones. *No trains – no, none . . . Fights for taxis . . . I told you, there's no Tube trains either. Or buses . . .*

Georgie feels oddly serene, patting her bump every now and then and sipping a hot chocolate so sweet it makes her teeth ache. She queued for fifteen minutes for this drink so she's going to enjoy every moment of it. There's an unexpected comfort in seeing everyone else's lives thrown into disarray – it makes her feel less alone.

Beneath her hand, the baby is awake, nudging at its increasingly tight space. So, as she sits, Georgie hums it a lullaby, one she only half remembers but keeps returning to, about mockingbirds and diamond rings, and it seems to soothe both of them.

But she can't sit here all night, so she scrolls through her contacts, wonders about ringing Tanya, an old drinking mate. Or Lisa, who lives over in Dulwich. But they belong to a different life, one she's taken great care to leave behind.

That odd ringing in her ears is back, a sign that she's tired and dizzy. Pregnancy vertigo, she reminds herself. And low blood pressure – both perfectly normal.

There's a teenage girl at the other end of the bench who is talking into her phone. She wipes away a single tear, nodding at whoever is on the other end of the line. 'Yes, OK, I'll wait out there. Thanks, Mum.' That must be nice, Georgie thinks, to have someone to depend on.

It is 9 p.m. and there is really only one option. She flicks through her contacts again, going back to the start of the alphabet, to D for Dan, the brother she hasn't spoken to for two years.

She's been putting it off because the moment he hears her voice, it'll drag them both back to the events of two years ago, a time she's trying so hard to forget. She can't do this, but she must. She presses the green call icon and draws breath, half hoping it'll go straight to messages.

Dan picks up on the second ring. 'Yeah, hi.' He sounds distracted, as if he's just come off another call and hasn't yet registered who he's speaking to.

'Dan,' she says. 'It's me, Georgie.'

She presses her phone hard to her ear, hears only silence. She knows what will happen in a second – her brother will end the call, then put his phone on mute. The last time she saw him, Dan made it quite clear he didn't want to see Georgie.

Quickly, before he can cut her off, she speaks: 'It's about Mum,' she says. 'I've seen her, Dan. Our mum's come back.'

Chapter Seven

GEORGIE

They have had no contact for two years, but now Dan is coming to get her – or he says he is. Over the phone, she'd started telling him the story of a lost child being rescued and then, because she wasn't making much sense, she'd WhatsApped him the picture of the shabby woman in an overcoat. And then Dan understood.

'Yeah,' Dan had said slowly. 'Yeah, I think you're right. I'll be there as soon as I can.'

The moment she heard his voice it felt like a homecoming, going back in time to when they were a unit; unbreakable. Until Georgie destroyed their bond beyond repair. But now Dan says he is coming and her heart lifts with hope.

Around her, the crowds have thinned out and the empty concourse feels like a fresh abandonment, proof that everyone else has places to go. The girl who was waiting for her mum is probably halfway home by now, her tears dried.

The station clock says 9.30 p.m., but Georgie will give it a little longer before she heads to their meeting place outside. She tries hard not to think about the last time they saw each other, the decisive way that Dan had walked away from her.

He'd been trying to avoid her all of that grim day, but finally she'd cornered him, tried to get him to listen. Dan hadn't said a word, just looked at her in disgust – a look that said *You're drunk at Finn's funeral, really?* – and turned his back. She deserved it – and more. But this gulf that has widened between them, it hurts so much.

She's two years older than him, but Dan has always been there for her. He was the sensible one who rescued Georgie when she messed up. No matter how late, he'd drive out to some station at the end of the Tube line when she'd fallen asleep on the last train home. When she'd gone to a festival and lost all her money, her rucksack, even her shoes, it was Dan who had come to get her. Until two years ago, he'd been her ally.

Georgie walks out to the spot where Dan told her to wait. Her mind is awash with detritus: the sad, grubby times that she and Dan got each other through, clinging together for what remained of their childhoods. Then the good times of their twenties. Before Finn.

She's expecting him to be driving something sleek and dark, a company car with tinted windows and plush leather seats. So when a sky-blue 1970s VW Beetle double-parks in front of her, she ignores it. It's only when a taxi driver behind blares his horn that Georgie takes a second look and realises it's Dan driving. She opens the passenger door, shoves her overnight bag on to the back seat and manoeuvres herself in.

Dan barely acknowledges her, just puts the car into gear and drives off. It's not until the next set of traffic lights that he speaks.

'So. You're looking . . . very pregnant,' he says.

'Yes, thirty-eight weeks and counting,' she says brightly.

'Wow. That's gone quickly.'

She knows Dan will have been told her news by their dad and Irena. She sends them bright and breezy emails that say things like

Baby now the size of a peach. I'm eating lots of leafy greens. Or *Went on a lovely country walk. Wilf is researching off-road buggies.* Sometimes her updates are based on fact; other times, she copies out what more competent mothers-to-be on online forums are saying.

Irena sends back equally upbeat replies on behalf of them both. *Thank you for the news. Frank is looking forward to being a grandfather.*

'Quickly? Yep. Kind of,' she replies. 'But sometimes it feels like I've been like this forever. It's hard to remember what life was like before.'

'Well, that's probably for the best,' Dan says smoothly.

Georgie looks away at the glassy world of the London streets, the late-night grime of the pavements and the rain-blurred glow of shop signs. She'll take that comment because she knows she deserves it and more. In fact, she wishes Dan would rip into her here and now, get this confrontation over and done with. She'd willingly soak up his pain and his grief if it would help him feel better.

Go on, tell me, Dan, she wants to say. *Tell me how much you miss him, how much it hurts. Because you can't make me feel any worse than I do already. Tell me you hate me. Because I stole your best friend and then he died and it was my fault.*

But she doesn't. They can't let what happened to Finn over-shadow why she's here tonight and why Dan has come out to get her.

So instead, she steers them back on track. 'It's her, isn't it? Living up in Scotland?' She can't tell if Dan has heard. Her words feel drowned out by the growl of the car's engine and it doesn't help that Dan is driving like a kid on a fairground ride, all jerky accelerations and sudden stops. It's as if he's not used to driving it and Georgie wonders whether this sky-blue Beetle is some sort of midlife-crisis buy. If so, it's a poor choice for Dan, who is hunched over the steering wheel with his knees almost touching it.

'Dan,' she says, more firmly. 'What are we going to do?'

He glances at her, pulls the car up short and parks on what must surely be a double yellow line – a very un-Dan-like thing to do. He's shaking his head as he gets out his phone. Then he brings up the picture Georgie sent him and uses two fingers to expand it, just as she did a few hours ago.

She's waiting for Dan to go into organised mode, to take control and calmly explain what they do next. In a minute he'll probably say *Now let's not rush into things* and then he will call the local police, to confirm whether this oddly dressed woman is the same one who vanished from their lives twenty years ago. Dan is like that: measured and sensible.

But Dan doesn't do either of those things. Instead, he's typing the name of the Scottish island into Google Maps, balancing his phone precariously on a cup-holder because there's nothing as sophisticated as sat nav in this diddy car. Then he puts the car into gear, gives a quick glance left and right and does a tight U-turn.

'Dan,' she says again. 'If you want to drop me at the coach station, that would be great.' But still her brother won't look at her. He has an air of grim determination and he's speeding along a side street – surely breaking the limit. Finally, when he speaks, he's saying all the things that Georgie thought earlier today, in a too-tight voice.

'She's back – and it looks like she's been back for a while. I can't believe it, living like some hermit up in the back of beyond. Rescuing someone else's child, like she doesn't have children of her own. Christ.'

'I know,' whispers Georgie. She holds tight to the looped leather handle she's found above her seat, runs her finger over the neat bumps of saddle stitching. On Dan's phone, she can see a thick blue line wending its way northwards. It almost makes this enterprise look easy: 11 hours, 20 minutes (551 miles), it says on the screen.

'We need to get there before she disappears again. She could be gone already,' he says. He sounds so steely and sure and she supposes this is how he acts when he's at work, where he sits in a swivel chair in his glass office with a view over the Thames.

'We'll have to drive all night, but we can do that, can't we?' he says.

'Yes. I think we have to.'

This is the first solid information they have had about their mother in twenty years, since that Monday morning when she waved them off to school and then vanished. Georgie barely counts the identical postcards she and Dan received a year later, sent from a country that sounded exotic and distant and with a photograph of a tiger cub on the front. Georgie had snatched her card up, taken it off to her room to read. But the message on the reverse was so short she wondered why Nancy had bothered. It was even more disappointing when she discovered Dan's card said exactly the same thing.

The words were written in letters that weren't even joined up, as if Nancy was learning to write again. None of it made sense. Was Nancy writing in code? Had someone stood over her, dictating what she should say?

The creatures here have been through a lot. Thinking of you back in England. I miss you every day. Hope to see you soon xxx

Georgie had stared at the picture on the front for a long time, searching for meaning. Their father explained it to them: Nancy had gone abroad to help the endangered wildlife. 'She always loved

41

animals,' he reminded them. And her odd handwriting? 'She must have wanted to make sure you could read it. Her writing was never the neatest.'

But Georgie wasn't sure she believed him. Nancy had never expressed much interest in animals. They didn't even have a pet. And Georgie could always read her mother's handwriting just fine. With no one there to offer her a more convincing explanation, Georgie became consumed by the idea that Nancy had been taken to this country called Thailand under duress. And she had a good idea who was responsible.

In the nights that followed, she and Dan whispered and talked and then they came up with a plan. To her thirteen-year-old self, it seemed perfectly reasonable. She and Dan would run away too: they would fly out and rescue their mother.

They got as far as packing a suitcase, which they hid under Georgie's bed. Dan was charged with finding their passports and Georgie was going to steal their father's credit card. They had it all worked out. But weeks passed and somehow neither of them made a move. They agreed the postmarks on their postcards were pretty hard to read, so it was hard to know exactly where to go. Dan pointed out she might have moved on by now anyway.

Then the summer holidays came and Georgie needed her summer clothes so she unpacked their suitcase, replacing Dan's folded shorts and T-shirts in the drawers in his room without saying a word. Their rescue fantasies died because they both knew the truth: their mother had gone and she wasn't coming home.

But now, speeding down the back streets of London in this sky-blue car, it feels as if she and Dan are going back in time, to when they were a unit, bound together by secrets only they could understand. Finally, they are carrying out their childhood mission – to go in search of their lost mother, who, it turns out, didn't die in some mosquito-ridden jungle or at a drug-fuelled beach party. At some point, she came back to this country – it was just that she neglected to tell her husband and children.

As Dan zooms along the Westway, Georgie starts to feel alive again. She opens the window a crack, breathes in the chill, petrol-laced air. It's as if for the past few months she's been wrapped in a weighted blanket – numb to her past and unsure of her future. But now she's racing towards that past and the memories she's kept at bay for so long.

Every now and then, she glances over at her brother. In the glow of the street lights, she can see his chin set at the determined tilt she knows so well. She and Dan are far from friends again, but at least they are doing this together. And for that, she's grateful.

Then Dan speaks and her stomach drops.

'What about Dad?' he asks. 'Should we tell him that she's back?'

Somehow this feels like a step too far – as if it would burst the bubble of their childhood adventure. Telling their father would make this official; it would mean handing over the responsibility.

'No. I don't think so,' she says carefully. 'Let him have his peace for a little while longer. Until we know what's what.' It's unlikely their father will have seen the social media storm – he despises such nonsense.

These days, Frank and Irena lead a nice quiet life in Redhill, the life that he probably always wanted. Golf on Sundays. Trips to the garden centre, where they use their loyalty card to get a discount on mid-week lunches. A life so different to the chaos of the Nancy years that came before.

Georgie has spent so long trying to understand why her mother left. But perhaps the bigger mystery is what brought Frank and Nancy together in the first place.

Chapter Eight

Nancy, 1986

'Well, who do we have here?'

The first time Nancy sees Frank Brown is in the student union bar. It's the end of freshers' week and it is loud and late and everyone is busy forming their cliques. She's mistakenly been swept up into a Sloaney group, girls who have perfect teeth and a well-fed look, softened by pearls and frosted lipstick. Camilla went island-hopping in Greece for the summer and Izzie had fun au pairing in France.

Nancy spent her summer like every other summer before that, working in The Beaufort: making beds, scouring the bathrooms and wiping a damp towel back and forth over the carpets to make it look like she's hoovered. She doesn't tell her new friends any of this. They are from Barnes and Hampstead and look confused when she says she's from Lincolnshire, unsure exactly where it might be.

She didn't think university would be like this. She's fought so hard to get here, to escape small-town people who spend Saturday nights at The Plough, drinking pints, playing the slot machines and then snogging in the car park. But all she's found so far are people who don't seem so different, except they have cut-glass accents and drink G&Ts instead of snakebite.

She'd imagined life as a student would be more exciting: late-night discussions about method acting and breaking the fourth wall. Sitting in a circle in someone's room and being passed a joint, like it's no big deal. But so far, Camilla and Izzie just like to come here, to the student union, to drink gin and eye up the boys.

In fact, they aren't even interested in drama. 'It was the easiest course to get on to,' Camilla explains. 'Better than History of Art. All those dates!' She flutters her fingers in distress.

'In my audition, all I did was think of when our spaniel Monty had to be put down,' says Izzie. 'The tears – they just came.' Camilla nods and Nancy does too – 'Poor Monty' – but she knows she will never fit in with these girls.

So after five nights of this, Nancy is looking at her watch and wondering if it's too early to go back to her room. And that's when she sees him. While everyone else is desperately trying to fit in, Frank is standing on his own at the bar, tapping a cigarette from its box, lighting it as he looks around. He's not pretending to be interested in spaniels or skiing. This is a guy who is fine, thanks, just as he is.

She never told Frank she'd spotted him that night. In the years that followed, the story was that Nancy and Frank had met at a lecture called 'An Introduction to Study', when he'd come in late and the only place left to sit was next to her.

In that too warm lecture hall, where a timetabling error means Humanities and Science students have to double up, people are already shifting in their seats. Plenty are probably wishing they hadn't come because all they can see is an image of an old painting projected on to the screen at the front of the hall. It's a rather over-blown painting of a woman with long auburn hair, her eyes closed.

Beneath the screen, a small man with a pointed beard stands at the lectern, arranging his notes.

Beside Nancy, Camilla leans in and whispers, 'Ooh, I know this one – it's by Rossetti.' But Nancy isn't listening to Camilla. She's trying to sneak a look at the boy who has just sat down on her other side. If she tilts her head, she can see him methodically laying out a notebook and two pens.

At the front of the hall, the lecturer clears his throat, waits for silence. And then he begins. 'Lizzie Siddal. Painted by Dante Gabriel Rossetti,' he says in a high, reedy voice, and Camilla nudges her, hard.

'She was Rossetti's muse. Well, one of them.' The lecturer looks up and surveys the rows of faces. 'His reason for creating. And each and every one of us here – we all need a muse.' He starts taking slow, deliberate steps from one side of the hall to the other. 'A reason to create. A reason to be here.'

Camilla leans into Nancy. 'Gerry Mac, Drama,' she confides. 'Very well connected. Used to do West End plays. Knows people in Hollywood, someone told me.'

Gerry Mac stops pacing. 'We all have our motivations for being here. Some . . .' Here, he pauses. 'Some may be less impassioned than others, arrived here through Clearing, for example.' There is a ripple of embarrassed laughter and Nancy resists the urge to nudge Camilla back.

'Over your next three years, there will be challenging times,' he continues. 'And that is when you must return to your touchstone. Your reason for being here. Your muse or motivation.'

Nancy sits forward in her seat. This is more like it: a rallying call to creatives and intellectuals – people like her, who are here to learn. Who want their lives to change.

'Would any of you freshers like to share your reason for being here?' Gerry Mac is scanning the sea of faces. He raises an eyebrow

46

and a slow smile tickles at his lips, in a way that makes the ends of his moustache quiver. The silence stretches out.

Nancy can't bear it – is no one here interesting or brave enough to speak up? Before she can think twice, she raises her hand. She feels it shaking a little, but it's too late to change her mind because now Gerry Mac is looking straight at her.

He doesn't speak for an embarrassingly long time, not until he's sure he has everyone's attention. And then Gerry Mac says, 'Well, who do we have here?'

'Nancy Jebb,' she answers, her heart beating hard. 'English and Drama.'

'Well Nancy Jebb English and Drama, what brings you to this educational establishment in the fine city of Norwich?'

'I want to learn things,' she says. 'Expand my horizons.'

'And I'm sure there will be plenty of young men happy to oblige there.' There's another polite ripple of laughter and Nancy feels her face flush. She's unbearably hot, she wants to get out of here, but she can't, she's hemmed in. On one side, Camilla is laughing along, a loud horsey laugh that Nancy has already heard too many times in the past week, and on her other side is the guy she spotted a few nights ago.

But he isn't laughing along. He's sitting very still and looking down at Gerry Mac and shaking his head.

Things move on. Gerry Mac brings up a slide of a study plan. Another slide of something he calls a mind map. But Nancy feels too embarrassed to open her exercise pad, let alone write anything down.

When the lecture finishes, she stands up, desperate to escape. Frank stands back to let her pass, but as she's walking towards the library, he catches up and falls in step with her. He's so close she can smell the shampoo he must have used this morning, something astringent and sensible.

She sneaks a glance, sees that he's wearing a rugby shirt with the collar turned down rather than up, a good sign in her book. She guesses he must have shaved this morning too, because he's nicked himself on the chin, a blood-red dent in an otherwise pleasant face.

He clears his throat. 'I just wanted to say, what that lecturer said. It wasn't on.' He sounds as if he's genuinely offended.

'Oh, he was just making a joke. I shouldn't have put my hand up,' Nancy says. She stops walking, twists her hair up into a clasp.

'Still. He shouldn't have embarrassed you. It was unprofessional.' There's a choke in his throat and she feels a rush of gratitude that he noticed. That he's the sort of person who knows the difference between right and wrong.

They go for a coffee and she tells him how much she loves acting, and that studying English and Drama is a compromise because her parents wouldn't let her go to drama school down in London. 'They said it would just be a load of posh eejits showing off,' she says. This way, they thought she'd get an academic education too – something to fall back on when the acting doesn't work out. She's loath to shatter her parents' illusions by telling them that this place also has its fair share of posh eejits.

Frank's parents sound far more sophisticated. His mother works as an office manager, his father runs a company that makes medical equipment, and they support his decision to study computer science. 'They are old-fashioned but in a nice way,' he tells Nancy.

Three weeks later, when she and Frank lie down together on his slim student mattress, Nancy decides that this is also a good description of Frank. Old-fashioned but nice. Afterwards, she is glad to be rid of her virginity, but it hadn't been exactly how Nancy had imagined. She'd been expecting Frank to light a fire inside her, that she'd be consumed in an unstoppable roar of flames. Instead, she'd felt a steady, pleasant warmth and then found herself patting Frank's damp back, as if thanking him for a job done nicely.

Later, Frank helps her practise her lines for an audition – she's trying out for Emilia in a production of *Othello*.

'Well done. Excellent,' he says and claps when she gives a perfect read-through. Nancy smiles back. She has escaped her small-town life and her small-minded parents. The life she deserves is about to start. And she can't wait.

Chapter Nine

GEORGIE

Since they were children, Dan has been the organised, efficient one who goes by the rules and Georgie is the scatterbrained, impulsive one who does things on the spur of the moment. So Georgie knows that at some point, the initial burst of reckless energy fizzles out and you begin to question whether your idea is such a good one after all.

For her and Dan, this happens about thirty minutes into their trip. The silence between them takes on a tentative air and she suspects Dan is starting to regret his decision. Now he has the information about their mum, he's probably wondering if he can ditch his sister and continue this journey alone. Georgie wouldn't blame him: she's already caused her brother enough heartache. But now, inside this tiny car, she can feel the resentment building and she starts to worry about the things that he – or she – might say.

She clears her throat. 'Hey, Dan.'

He doesn't answer, he's busy jabbing at the ancient car radio in an effort to fill the uncomfortable silence. He turns up the volume knob and, as Georgie hears the opening chords of Steppenwolf's 'Born To Be Wild', she remembers how her brother used to play McFly when he was getting ready for school rugby matches and that Green Day provided the anthems for his GCSEs.

He used to play the guitar too – just endless two-chord strumming, but it was his thing for a while. Shyly, he'd shown her his songs. 'They're really good,' she'd told him, as she skimmed over the verses – always about lost love; looking for love; a love who left without saying goodbye.

She didn't ask if they were about a girl or the more obvious yawning gap in both their lives. She pretended not to notice how some of his lines – and his riffs – sounded suspiciously similar to Coldplay. Instead, she encouraged him, because that's what you do for your family. It's what he did for her, too.

When she failed her mock A levels, their father shook his head in despair. 'Oh, Georgie,' he said. Her head of year said things like, 'Well, what did you expect? You're barely here.' But at sixteen, Dan was more help than the lot of them. He went to a different school, a grammar that primed its pupils early in how to pass exams and say the right things in interviews, and he found ways to subtly pass on this information to Georgie.

The day before the deadline to submit her A-level art portfolio, he got lots of her old photos printed, smoothed out her drawings and stuck them all in her sketch book. Later, he gently suggested that a photography course might be a good option, sent off for some college prospectuses and left them on her bed. And then, when she still didn't quite get the grades, he rang the admissions office to plead her case. He said he was Georgie's father, Frank Jebb.

In ways like that, the two of them had limped through their teenage years, siblings but also surrogate parents to each other. She told Dan that yes, his new baseball cap definitely looked cool, and he told Georgie that those girls who were freezing her out were losers. They told each other the things their mother would have said.

Remembering all this, it hurts even more that she and Dan have reached this point of awkward silences and unspoken words. But Georgie knows why. Dan has had girlfriends and good friends.

He is married to Mandy. But in all this time, the only person who really understood Dan was Finn. He was Dan's rock, until Georgie ruined everything.

She turns her head to look out of the car window, but that's a bad idea because she realises they are driving along some kind of overpass. Alongside, she sees a rain-spattered blur of railings, flickering like the trim to a spool of old film. She can't look down because she knows what will lie below – a hard, slick surface that will remind her how vulnerable they are, hurtling along in this little metal box.

And then, for reasons she can't entirely fathom, Georgie is assailed by a deep sense of dread, the certainty that one day they will all be bones and dust; even this baby inside her that's cushioned in flesh and fluid will, eventually, dry away to nothing.

This knowledge lies like a stone in the pit of her stomach. It's getting harder to draw breath, her throat is closing around a thin thread of air. She keeps very still, tries to visualise the muscles relaxing, letting the air back in. Because she can't look down from this bridge, she looks up and concentrates on the street lights, counting each sour yellow rectangle to ward off her fear.

She's vaguely aware of Dan beside her, nodding along as he heads out on the highway, but it's getting harder for Georgie to hear the music. It's not just the rumble of the engine, there's a familiar ringing in Georgie's ears that will soon coalesce into a single high-pitched note. And all the while, she keeps her eyes open because closing them only makes the dizziness worse.

There's the sting of sick at the back of her throat and she thinks *Please, no*, because she can't throw up in Dan's dinky little blue car.

But then it passes. She's aware that the railings are gone and the solid road is back. Her ears clear and the world outside steadies until it looks almost normal again.

Pregnancy vertigo, she reminds herself. Not uncommon, according to Serena the midwife. Possibly made worse by her low blood pressure. *Drink plenty of water* had been her advice at Georgie's last appointment. *And avoid tall buildings and bridges.*

They drive on. The windscreen wipers make their rubbery scrape, back and forth. Every now and then, the driving app pipes up: 'You are still on the fastest route.'

Georgie forces herself to break the silence – to keep them focused on why they are doing this. 'Do you think she'll still be there?' she asks. 'I mean, should we call the local police up in Scotland – ask them to go and check?'

'That's the last thing we want to do. If a uniform turns up at her door, there's a danger she'll bolt. She'll disappear again and we'll have lost our chance.' Dan turns up the radio again, a signal that their chat is over.

As she stares at the black road ahead, Georgie remembers this is what Dan does. When things get difficult, he refuses to acknowledge them. Usually, he goes into jolly mode and pretends bad things aren't happening. Or goes for a run, sweats it out by punishing his body. But this time he's opting for silence.

When Georgie was little, everyone always said how alike she and her mother looked, but now she wonders if it's Dan who has inherited her mother's defining trait: an ability to switch off. Maybe this is how Nancy did it, all those years ago – she simply stopped thinking. Because if you don't think too hard, maybe walking out on your life isn't that difficult at all.

Georgie must have dozed off because she's woken by a sharp swerve and a grinding down of gears. She opens her eyes to see the glare of a petrol station. The inside of her mouth feels crumpled and there's an ache in her neck. It's 11.30 p.m.

Then her bladder wakes up too and she realises she urgently needs the loo and Dan has barely pulled up the handbrake before Georgie is out, walking as fast as she can into the shop. She pushes open a grubby door marked 'Toilet' beside the chiller cabinet, sees ribbons of wet paper on the floor, an unflushed toilet with a seat that's skew-whiff. The air is sharp with the tang of urine.

Georgie tries not to touch anything and braces herself so she can hover just above the toilet seat. But at the last minute her foot slips, her extra weight throws her off balance and her bottom lands on the seat with a wet slap. As she stands, Georgie sees her reflection in the mirror. Knees bent, big pants around her thighs, she looks like an alien life form, her stomach a bulbous globe. She sighs; at least there's toilet paper.

Back out in the shop, day-old Cornish pasties are sweating in the hot cabinet and there's a coffee machine. Georgie buys two pasties and a coffee for Dan, then, on impulse, she grabs a large, overpriced bag of chocolate eclairs. For old times' sake.

Back in the car, she passes Dan his pasty, sets the bag of sweets between them.

Dan lays a paper napkin out on his lap, gestures for her to do the same. 'I'd like to keep the upholstery clean, if you don't mind.'

But then he notices the bag of sweets. 'Ah. Our favourite,' he says, and it feels like the smallest gesture of reconciliation.

'Saturday morning pictures at the Odeon,' she replies.

'Cartoons, then the main feature film. Meant we could escape the house for a whole morning.'

'*Spy Kids*,' she says, getting into her stride.

'*Shrek*.'

'Not forgetting that classic, *Snow Dogs*.'

'Ah, yes. The finest of its oeuvre.'

It had been a brief window when she was fourteen and Dan was twelve, and they would sit in the dark and watch films that had talking dogs and happy endings, a respite from what was happening at home, where their father was trying to make a new life with Irena, pretending Nancy had never existed.

It's nice, reminiscing like this, and Georgie is weighing up whether she can chance a joke about Dan's teenage songwriting skills when she sees something in his face has changed. As swiftly as it arrived, that moment of closeness is gone again.

A muscle in Dan's jaw is twitching, a sign that he's nervous or angry, and he holds out a hand for Georgie's rubbish. 'Long time ago now,' he says curtly. 'All in the past.'

It might just be the lateness of the hour, but now she's looking at him properly, Dan looks older and more worn than she remembers: he has dark shadows under his eyes and his hair is thinning. There's a dark stain on the front of his shirt – the sort of thing that she imagines Mandy would pull him up on pretty sharpish.

Then a thought occurs to Georgie about this cute 1976 baby-blue car with chrome trim and retro dials on the dashboard.

'Dan, is this Mandy's car?' she asks.

Dan is busying himself with folding his napkin and then his paper bag into neat squares. 'It's a long story' is all he says, and Georgie knows she's not going to hear it.

All over again, she feels a sense of loss, remembers Dan turning his back on her at Finn's funeral, his back so straight as he wove his way through black-suited mourners to get as far away from her as possible.

She blinks several times, focuses on the wiggly line illuminated on Dan's phone, the one that tells them they still have ten hours and twelve minutes to go. This is why they are here – not to talk about Finn but to find their mother. And their time is running out.

Georgie puts on her seat belt and waits for the roar of the engine to fill the car again. But something is wrong; the only sound she can hear is a dull click. It comes again: click-click. She looks over and realises Dan is turning the key in the ignition – but the engine isn't turning over.

And suddenly Dan is swearing, running his hands through his thinning hair, and she wants to tell him to stop that because it's not like he's got loads of it to spare. He's letting out an animal sound, a growl of frustration.

'Bloody, bloody hell,' he's saying into his hands.

'What's the matter?'

'It must be the starter motor or something. I think that's what they said, last time it happened. Or it could have been the spark plugs. Something beginning with "s". Mandy would know.'

This is a hitch, but Dan is overreacting. 'OK, so let's call the breakdown service,' she says.

'Can't really do that, Georgie,' her brother says, his voice taking on a detached tone. 'Seeing as it's not my car.'

Georgie's hunch about this diddy car was right. 'OK, so ring Mandy. I know she'll be asleep, but she'll understand if you say where we're going. Just ask for her AA details. Or RAC, whatever.' She suspects Mandy is the sort of person who belongs to both services because, like Dan, she errs on the side of caution.

'Nope. Can't do that, I'm afraid.' Dan has given up trying to turn the ignition key. 'I didn't exactly ask if I could borrow her car, you see. And I'm not insured to drive it.'

Georgie says nothing because this is the sort of stupid, reckless thing that she used to do when she was young, not Dan.

Until this moment, Georgie has been absorbed by all the things she can't say to her brother, things that are off limits. But now she's more worried about the things Dan isn't telling her. What's been going on in her brother's life since she last saw him two years ago? Because something isn't right here.

She looks down at his mobile phone, balanced in the cup-holder, and that optimistic wiggly line heading north. Their long-awaited rescue mission – the trip they both fantasised about as children – has barely started and already it's come to a grinding halt. And Dan, her ever dependable Dan, has given up.

She looks over at him – arms crossed, eyes shut tight, and his legs wedged either side of the steering wheel. Then down at her own bump. Already, the cold is seeping into her toes and her fingers. Sleeping in this car is not an option.

'Dan,' she says. 'Come on, this isn't like you.'

He opens his eyes, but stares resolutely at the roof of the car.

'We need to find a hotel for the night,' Georgie says. 'Then we can work out what to do in the morning. We can see if any trains are running or get a coach. Dan, come on. We can't give up this easily.'

He purses his lips. 'OK, Georgie.' His words are clipped and sharp. 'OK, whatever you say. Because it's always about you, isn't it? What Georgie wants, Georgie gets.'

Chapter Ten

GEORGIE

Tucked away behind the petrol station is a run-down 1980s-style motel, where a morose night porter takes pleasure in telling them all he has left is a twin room. As Georgie wordlessly follows Dan down the long corridor, there's a depressing familiarity about this place with its strip lighting, its carpet tiles and the smell of cigarettes overlaid with air freshener. And as Dan taps the key card on the door, Georgie realises it reminds her of the sort of places their dad used to take them for a Sunday carvery.

After he sold their old family house in London, their dad moved them out to an unleafy corner of Surrey called Redhill. 'A fresh start,' he said, several times a day, about this place with roundabouts and a shopping precinct that wasn't quite the country but definitely wasn't the city. But because of Redhill's proximity to Gatwick Airport, there were several motels nearby, places where people stayed over before early-morning flights and got a fortnight's cheap parking included in the price.

Frank's favourite establishment sat at a junction of three main roads not far from their new house. It had long tables designed to accommodate larger, happier families, a huge TV in one corner and a small play area in another. Sticky stacks of Duplo; a game of

Jenga daubed with greasy fingerprints. Broken crayons and dried-up felt-tip pens. All too babyish for Georgie and Dan, but their dad didn't seem to notice.

He took them to the Sunday carvery as a treat and to give Irena a day off from cooking. 'Day off from microwaving,' Georgie would mutter, too quietly for the grown-ups to hear.

Irena had first appeared in their lives as a cleaner, hired by the hour to make their old messy, crumb-strewn house back in London more habitable. But the task was so overwhelming that she soon stopped trying and, like the rest of them, succumbed to the house's mood of abandonment. Georgie would come home to find a pale woman in a tabard sitting on the still-grubby sofa watching daytime TV and drinking coffee out of their mother's favourite mug, waiting for their father to return.

Then, almost imperceptibly, Irena's hours had changed. She started arriving in the evenings, when it was too late to start cleaning, and she stayed over in their dad's room until morning. The house seemed to resist Irena's efforts, remaining as messy as ever, but that didn't matter because a year after Nancy left, their father announced it was time to move on. He had bought a lovely new house in Surrey, nearer to Grandma and Grandpa Brown. And – ready for another nice surprise? – Irena was coming too.

In this much lauded new house, they soon discovered that Irena's cooking was limited to freshly pinged microwave meals: lasagnes and cottage pies that she emptied on to their plates with a slop. But on Sundays, they ate out.

Irena drank glasses of sweet white wine, politely asking Georgie and Dan, 'Everything going well at school?' Georgie never dignified these questions with a reply. In her view, Irena's efforts at being a stand-in mother were even more lacklustre than her cooking. Their dad smiled away, pleased at how well everyone was getting on. Then he would treat himself to a pint of shandy, raising it to his lips with a slight tremor, and the sight of her father taking that precious first sip always made Georgie's heart squeeze.

He was doing his best, trying hard to make a new life for them, so she and Dan went along with the charade. Dipped thin, cold chips in ketchup; chased scoops of yellow ice cream around a silver bowl with a spoon, all the while delaying the moment when it was time to take their sugar headaches and their sadness home.

Georgie doesn't know how she would have survived those years without Dan. In that bleak house in Redhill, the two of them grew closer, bound together by the shameful secret of their own mother leaving. As if by mutual agreement, neither of them told their new schoolfriends that the woman who laid out plates of after-school snacks – a fan of Penguin biscuits, a circle of Jammie Dodgers – was a virtual stranger.

'Why do you call your mum Irena?' asked Lisa, Georgie's friend, as they painted each other's nails with glittery varnish filched from the make-up counter in Boots. 'Because it's her name,' Georgie said breezily. 'Maybe it's more of a London thing. You wouldn't understand.'

Georgie and Dan went to different schools but lived the same lie. It was easier that way, but it was hard too. After school, when the day's pretending was done, Georgie would slink into Dan's bedroom and sit on the floor, waiting for him to finish playing Nintendo. Then, when the plink-crash noises of his game ended, he would slide down to sit next to her. Staring ahead, each would say the unsayable. *Is she ever coming back? Are we staying here forever?* They never had answers for each other.

Dan soon found his escape in sport – hearty, wholesome games like rugby, where he could bash and crash and roar and it was OK to do that. In more contemplative moments, he strummed his two chords on his guitar and sang his sad little songs. Then he discovered that cross-country running was a better way to drown out the thoughts in his head. 'I just keep going, keep running. I don't think. I'm like a machine,' he said, trying to explain its appeal to Georgie, who refused to do anything that was remotely sporty or involved being in a team.

Instead, Georgie had developed less healthy teenage pastimes. She drank, she dressed in black from head to toe, dyed her hair to match and drew thick dark lines around her eyes that left smears on the pillows. She was always itchy, uncomfortable in her own skin, and took to scratching her sun-starved arms until they bled. She bunked off school with a boy called Carl, came home with a necklace of love bites. Her dad was too busy making his new life with Irena to notice, but to Georgie, this was visible proof that someone wanted her.

It wasn't long before she graduated from nicking nail polish in Boots to sprees in Topshop, where she'd stuff skimpy tops and underwear into her school bag. When she got caught, she turned on the tears, said she came from a broken home with a cruel stepmother.

That was a lie. Irena wasn't cruel, it was just that she had no idea what to say to a sullen teenager who seemed hell-bent on getting in trouble. 'Do you want more pocket money, is that it?' she asked Georgie, who laughed in her face. As if it was money she craved. The only thing she and Irena agreed on was not to tell Frank. 'He doesn't need this, on top of everything else,' Irena said, the closest she came to acknowledging their missing mother.

Any evidence that Nancy had ever existed was thin on the ground since they'd moved to Redhill. The only proof of life was the two postcards with their short, puzzling message, forwarded with other post in a fat envelope by the new occupants of St Luke's Road.

The old London house had been full of her things, from the scrappy shopping lists they found at the bottom of Tesco bags to the tangle of necklaces still looped over her dressing-table mirror.

But then the removal company came. Georgie had watched two men in brown overalls loading up her mother's paperback books, photographs and pictures in dusty clip frames. In the kitchen, they packed away her mismatched plates, blackened saucepans, jars of lentils and spatulas with melted plastic handles. Her clothes went into boxes too, even her slippers, which still bore the shape of her toes. They packed it all up and took it away in their big van.

But at the new house, only a few cardboard boxes ever arrived. Georgie and Dan ripped the brown tape off box after box, but they never found any of her things. Only stuff that belonged to the two of them and their father had made the journey from north-west London to this hushed cul-de-sac in Redhill.

'It was just too painful seeing it all,' explained their father in the gulpy voice that meant he might cry again. 'A fresh start,' he reminded them. Irena rubbed his back and said, 'Frank, don't upset yourself.'

After a while, Georgie couldn't imagine her mum's stuff in the new house anyway. The bobbly scarves she'd knitted, the monstrous cheese plant too big for its pot – none of it would look right in these boxy rooms with cream carpets, plastic-framed windows and polystyrene coving.

Irena, however, suited the house perfectly. While Nancy used to let the dirty dishes pile up, or would drop glasses on the kitchen floor and use her bare feet to kick the shards away, Irena scrubbed the new kitchen until the tang of bleach made Georgie's nose hurt. Appliances hummed all day long and soon their clothes smelt of fabric softener, not their mother's garlicky stews. With Irena's expert help, their dad set about erasing the memory of everything that had come before.

'We all have to move on from difficult memories,' he told them on a regular basis. To prove his point, their father and Irena were to be married. He had filled out some forms to apply for a 'dissolution' of his old marriage, on the grounds that his spouse was untraceable. At her new school, Georgie was studying liquids, solids and gases in science and she imagined her real, once solid mother dissolving, floating away in tiny, colourful particles.

But while the rest of her life evaporated, Dan had been there, a constant. And she'd been there for him. Because while Dan played sport and joked with their dad, at night she knew that he still cried. And when he wet the bed, she stripped the sheets, remade it while he was still rubbing his eyes. Back then, they understood each other without having to say things.

And yet, here they are, finally doing their longed-for trip to find their mother and it's not a bit how she imagined it. For a start, they've got no further than an ugly motel room on the outskirts of Solihull and are barely speaking.

Georgie looks around at the faded lilac curtains and the purple bedcovers the shade of an old packet of Silk Cut cigarettes. She shucks off her boots and, still dressed, slides under the duvet, which smells aggressively of washing powder. The need to sleep is pulling her down and Georgie finds herself imagining her bed is a raft amid a deep purple sea, buffeted by waves and winds. She hopes that if she survives what's left of the night, in the morning she and Dan will find a way back to each other. And then, just maybe, they can find a way to continue on this ill-fated journey into the past.

As she drifts off, Georgie's mind stirs up a different memory. She sees Finn sitting in a window, a quick dip of his head as he licks a cigarette paper, neat as a cat lapping milk. The way the light caught on the shaved pelt of his head and how she'd had to stop herself from reaching out to stroke it.

No, no, not that; she drags herself back and thinks of Wilf. Him hugging her from behind, reaching his hands around to cradle her growing stomach. Leaning back into him, the brush of his stubble on her cheek, and feeling the rightness of it.

63

Then, unbidden, a different scene takes shape and it's one from far longer ago, and it's of her parents, Frank and Nancy. Dan is there too and the four of them are walking along a beach, their parents leading the way. It's the end of a long, sunny day and the sand is deep and Georgie's feet slip-slide into it.

She wants to catch up with her parents and check everything is OK, that they aren't arguing, but her feet won't go any faster. Then she sees Frank and Nancy stop and her dad puts his arm around their mum. She watches as Nancy's thin body sinks into his. It's a quiet, private moment, so Georgie stops and waits. And she lets herself feel a surge of hope, that maybe things will be all right after all.

Georgie opens her eyes because her tiredness has evaporated. Lying under her purple duvet, she realises that this journey into the past isn't just about her and Dan tracking down their mother. It's about finding out what lay buried at the heart of Nancy and Frank's marriage – whether their relationship was flawed from the start or whether it was Georgie's own meddling that had helped destroy something fragile but beautiful.

Chapter Eleven

Nancy, 1986

'I love you – you're so crazy'

Nancy hasn't been back home for months. She knows her mother wouldn't approve of what she wears, what she smokes or what she's getting up to at university. Neither would Theresa like what Nancy does to her hair, coating it in hairspray then clamping sections between the blades of a crimper until she hears it sizzle. Theresa wouldn't like her Dr. Martens boots, her fishnet tights or the oversized chambray shirt she wears belted as a dress. But that's OK because she's not dressing to please Theresa any more.

It's Frank's shirt, of course, the one she picked up off his bedroom floor one morning. 'It looks better on you,' he'd said. 'Keep it.'

So she did. She liked the way it still smelt of him, of them, in bed together. And now, each time she wears it, it makes her feel good. It's proof that she has her first proper boyfriend, someone who loves her and looks after her in a way that no one ever has before.

All through the first term, Frank helped her practise her lines, and when she got the part in *Othello* he came to every performance – sat in the front row and clapped, raising his hands above his head. 'Bravo!' he shouted, a reminder that Frank is already more familiar with the milieu of theatres and curtain calls than Nancy.

Frank is from another world, one where people don't hiss 'Shhh' because she's making a show of herself or committing the worst sin of all – showing off. Frank does everything with a quiet confidence. When he walks into a pub, he doesn't hover by the bar until a table becomes free, like Nancy does; he looks around, then asks people to budge up on a bench or he starts rearranging chairs. Nancy doesn't know if it's a man thing or a class thing, but when she's with him, she also feels a bit more important.

Being on stage helps her feel braver too. 'Owning the space', she discovers it's called. Then there's 'stage presence', which Daisy says that Nancy definitely has. Daisy is on her course – a refreshing change from the Camillas and Izzies – and they have already agreed to share a house next year, along with Polly, who is Daisy's girlfriend. Polly is pushing for it to be a 'women-only space'. She's not keen on Frank, says 'his type' are part of the problem not the solution, and she sneers at his Home Counties accent.

Polly is from Doncaster; she wears a donkey jacket and sells copies of *Socialist Worker* outside the student union. When she talks to Nancy, she stares at her earnestly. 'We're the only working-class ones here,' she tells her.

Nancy doesn't think her parents would like to be called working class – back at The Beaufort, Margaret Thatcher is seen as a local girl done good. But Nancy doesn't mention this to Polly or the Socialist Worker Student Soc meetings they all go to. Instead, she drops coins in the buckets to support the fight against apartheid, and she boycotts Cape apples and the late-night Shell petrol station shop because they are part of the problem too.

When she mentions these things to Frank, he creases his brow and says he's going to give these issues some serious consideration. He has a different set of friends, mostly boys with meaty thighs who row or play rugby and talk in an easy shorthand about Val d'Isère, South Ken and crammers, words that are unfamiliar to Nancy. They also refer to their parents as Mummy and Daddy, without a shred of embarrassment.

They are polite to Nancy, but they prefer girls like Camilla and Izzie, who are 'lots of fun'. When Nancy sees her old freshers' week friends at parties, they flick their hair and avoid her gaze, but that's OK with her. They aren't her kind of people. It's just that she isn't sure who is.

Daisy and Polly are nice enough, but Nancy lives in fear of saying or wearing or buying the wrong thing. She has to throw away a barely used tube of hand cream when Daisy tells her the company is blacklisted. Other times, the rules seem more flexible. Like the fact Daisy has her own car, which is definitely elitist, but people turn a blind eye because it's pretty useful for lifts. That's the thing about drama students – putting on a show comes easily to them.

In the end, she decides that's what she likes about Frank – at least he's sincere. When the student union organises a coach down to London for an anti-apartheid demonstration, he comes along too. But they soon lose Daisy and Polly in a crush in Trafalgar Square. The police move in and there's a scuffle nearby. There's shouting and Nancy trips over, feels grit under her hands and a terror of being trampled underfoot by this crowd that moves as one.

Frank grabs her under her arms, hoists her up and finds a way through the crowd. They are soon in a side street and then another, until they reach a station. 'Getting a bit hairy, wasn't it?' he says, sitting opposite her on a train that will take them away from the noise and crowds and shouting. He gives her his white handkerchief to dab at her bloodied knees and her still-smarting palms. As Nancy sits back, even the sound of the train engine chugg-chugging feels reassuring.

By teatime, they are in Surrey sitting down with his parents, Lorna and Charles, for cups of Earl Grey tea and a Victoria sponge cake. Nancy accepts a second slice, eyes darting around the home where Frank grew up. It is impeccably respectable, every bit as normal and reassuring as Frank. There are framed family photographs, bone china shepherdesses in a glass-fronted cabinet. A silver cup engraved with Frank's name from a grammar school tournament.

It is all so very civilised, as if no other world exists beyond their garden gate. The marching students and South Africans being murdered with burning rubber tyre necklaces are of no concern to Mr and Mrs Brown and their Surrey village. Here, the talk is of the summer fete and rumours of a hosepipe ban.

Of course, Nancy's own parents are equally oblivious to politics, but they do it in a cowed way, as if they know their opinions do not count. Sitting in Surrey, Nancy thinks of her parents' living room, with its shabby carpet and tired G-Plan suite; the fake roses in a vase on the mantelpiece, petals silvered with dust. The chipped Beryl Ware cups deemed unfit for guests. And she feels ashamed.

On the way back, Nancy darts into the train loo because the inspector is coming and she doesn't have money for a ticket. Frank squeezes in with her. 'I love you – you're so crazy,' he whispers into her ear.

He also tells Nancy she's crazy when she does stupid, drunken things. Because by the third term, Nancy still hasn't really found her people. She doesn't fit in, but she discovers that it matters less if she drinks. After a few drinks, she doesn't worry whether Frank's posh friends see through her, or what to say when her political friends ask where she stands on neo-Marxism. Everything is easy and dreamy and all she has to do is laugh and look pretty and have fun.

Admittedly, things sometimes get a little out of hand. She lobs a whisky bottle at the window of a BMW car showroom because it represents capitalism, watches in horror as the glass shatters in a slow-motion snowfall. At 5 a.m., she calls a taxi because she wants to go to the beach to watch the sunrise and then does a runner without paying.

Sober Nancy worries about everything: if the bus will come on time and whether the driver will be cross if she doesn't have the right change. If people will laugh if she walks into her seminar late and if her accent sounds funny. At times, it feels like her head might explode with all the thoughts that churn around inside.

Drinking makes all those worries go away and it dampens down the noise in her head for a while. And even if it comes with a hangover of shame, letting out her emotions is a new experience for Nancy. Away from Theresa's disapproval, Nancy lets herself shout and laugh and cry.

And the next morning, Frank is there to hold her hair as she's sick, bring her glasses of fizzing Alka-Seltzer and tell her, no, she wasn't that bad last night, not really. Nobody minded about the scratched LPs or the stolen bike or her idea to dig up the flowers on the main roundabout. Actually, most of the guys think she's pretty funny.

He comes to her performances too. Because the only other time Nancy feels a similar sense of release is when she's on stage. While everyday Nancy gets nervous about the smallest things, all that changes when she's acting. That's when the weight of being Nancy falls away.

At the start of her second year, she tries out for a bigger role in a university production: Nora in *A Doll's House*. She doesn't get it; instead, she's given the smaller part of the nanny and performing gives her such a buzz. As she takes her bows, she knows this is what she wants to do. The elation of being on stage, the liberation, the adoration – there's nothing like it.

After she and Frank go to the cinema to see the new film everyone is raving about, Frank takes to calling her his Betty Blue. She's not sure how to take this, because it's not like the film has a very happy ending, but Frank says it's a compliment.

Nancy decides to go with it. She buys a new lipstick in a deep shade of red, practises her Béatrice Dalle pout in the mirror. She starts to understand that she can be anyone. She could be the nanny or Nora or Lady Macbeth. And if Frank wants her to be Betty Blue, she can do that too. She will gladly play any of these roles because they seem easier than the role Nancy struggles with the most: being herself.

Chapter Twelve

GEORGIE

Georgie is sitting by the window in what the motel optimistically calls a restaurant, tearing her paper napkin into long, thin strips. Her foot taps the ground impatiently. Dan has messaged to say he's coming down, but there's still no sign of him. What on earth is he doing? Already, it's 7.30 a.m. and they have a long way to go.

Still, it's only Tuesday, she tells herself. As long as they get to this far-flung Scottish island tonight, it'll be fine. They can find Nancy, travel back home on Wednesday and then Georgie will be back in her eco cottage with time to spare for Wilf's return on Friday.

She's watched the other motel guests come and go – truck drivers, a family of four and lone men in saggy suits. They eat their fill of dry croissants and drink the bad coffee and leave and there's still no sign of her brother. She's holding off texting him again – she and Dan are only just back on speaking terms, and she doesn't want to ruin their tentative truce.

She'd slept badly, then found herself wide awake at 6 a.m. with an idea. As quietly as possible, she'd eased the door open and come downstairs to make a phone call. It had felt exciting because she had a secret plan forming, but now the tiredness is swooping back in. Her skin feels itchy and she wants to wash every residue of this place from her.

But she can't leave her window seat yet. She's keeping an eye out for a man called Kevin, who will be driving a dark-blue pick-up truck and might be able to rescue them. Or, more specifically, rescue the dinky, useless car that Dan is driving.

Georgie allows herself a small smile. For once, it's her who is doing the grown-up thing and it feels like a small peace offering to her brother. A way to help get them back on a better footing.

But as soon as her brother pushes open the door to the restaurant, her excitement fizzles out because she can tell he's in a bad mood. His face is puffy with tiredness, and he runs a hand through his wet hair as he walks towards her. 'Didn't bring a comb,' he says. Then he scans the room, looking in vain for a waiter. 'And I haven't got a toothbrush – had to use my finger and a bit of your toothpaste.'

'Coffee is in the machine,' Georgie says, hoping this might help. 'It's all self-service.'

Next to the machine, a paltry breakfast buffet is laid out on a side table: three pots of yoghurt stand in a bowl of iced water; another bowl contains vivid chunks of tinned fruit. The cereal choices are beige and no-nonsense: Weetabix, Corn Flakes or Rice Krispies. A white cloth is folded over a tray of mini pastries, long since cooled.

Dan frowns, then plumps for the pastries. Waits while the coffee machine chunters through its stages and delivers a dribble of brown liquid and soapy foam into his cup. From here, Georgie observes the back of Dan's head, a circle of shininess peeping out from underneath the wet strands. His fashion sense has deteriorated since she last saw him: he's wearing high-waisted jeans and trainers that were bought with practicality rather than fashion in mind.

Maybe they are his running shoes, which were to hand when he rushed out of the door and drove to Paddington last night.

Outside the window, Mandy's bubble-shaped blue car stands out from the more sensible silver and black hatchbacks. The way it is parked at an angle, transgressing the white lines of the parking bays, is a reminder of how urgent their mission felt last night – and the fact that this car is stuck, going nowhere.

Georgie can't contain her excitement any longer. She leans across the table: 'Guess what?'

Dan is dissecting a pain au raisin, picking out the burnt nuggets and dipping the edible bits in his coffee. He takes a sip, slams the cup back down too fast. Coffee slops into the saucer. 'Crap. Burnt my mouth.'

He narrows his eyes and looks at her. He's had years of Georgie's 'guess what's and knows they rarely bring good news. 'Go on then – I know you're dying to tell me something.'

'The car,' she says. 'I think I might have solved our problem.'

Dan chews, looks at her sceptically. 'You nipped out and fixed it first thing, then?' He blows on the surface of his coffee. 'With your mechanical skills.'

Georgie feels a rush of frustration. It's not like Dan's doing anything to help – Dan, who pretends to be the Big I Am, but definitely isn't telling the truth about why he's driving Mandy's car. Or why, as far as Georgie knows, he hasn't spoken to Mandy yet.

'No, not me.' She tries to keep her voice light and breezy. 'But I know someone who can. They're on their way.' She reaches out for one of his pastry crusts. 'An old friend. Well, friend of a friend.'

Dan saunters over to the breakfast bar shaking his head, returns with a pot of yoghurt, an obscure brand with a picture of a peach on the side.

She clears her throat. 'I made a call to Kevin a couple of hours ago.'

Dan looks up. A blob of yoghurt slides off his spoon.

'Yes, that Kevin,' she says. 'In the circumstances, I thought it was our best option. He works out of a garage near Watford, so it shouldn't take him long to get here. It's all off the books – no need for insurance documents. And we can settle up with him later, too.' She nods towards the car park, where a battered truck is pulling up next to Mandy's car. 'I think that's him now. Key?'

She holds out her palm and Dan hands over the black fob without a word. As she walks across the car park, Georgie looks back and catches sight of Dan hovering at the window, but he doesn't come outside.

Kevin was one of Finn's mates, one of those shady characters that everyone knew in a vague sort of way, who played guitar but could also fix lighting rigs and sound systems and cars and vans and most other things. But she suspects Kevin and Dan didn't have much in common. Finn was like that: he had an ever-changing circle of instant friends, but he'd always come back to Dan, his oldest, best friend.

They had met at university, where Dan studied Statistics and Finn was doing some catch-all subject like Humanities. 'I've been hanging out with this really interesting bloke,' Dan told her when they both came home for the Christmas break. 'He's easy to talk to. Kind of cool, actually.' Then he laughed. 'No idea what he sees in a square like me.'

But somehow Finn and Dan hit it off and they soon became inseparable. Even after Finn dropped out of uni, they stayed in touch. 'He's the first person I've talked to about . . . you know, Mum, all of that stuff,' Dan told her. 'He's unusual. He really listens, you know?'

Georgie didn't really, because she couldn't imagine opening up like that to anyone.

'You should meet him sometime. I think you'd get on,' Dan told her.

But somehow Finn was never around when Georgie visited her brother. And on the few occasions when Dan came out with her, Finn was always busy with some band or other. Mostly, he worked as a roadie, but he also took photographs. 'Like I say, you'd get on,' Dan kept telling her.

So it wasn't until Dan's housewarming that they finally met. Dan was moving into a flat with a friend called Mandy and the infamous Finn. And then, after that party, it wasn't Finn and Dan any more, it was Finn and Georgie. And then, two years ago, it became just Georgie.

Now, as Kevin gets out of his rusty old truck, she wonders if calling him was such a good idea; this could be harder than she thought.

'Georgie,' he says, taking in her newly rounded shape. 'How you doing? It's been a while.'

'Yeah, it has.' She has a terrible feeling that the last time she saw Kevin was at the funeral. 'I'm fine, good, actually. I've moved out of London now. You might have heard?'

Kevin looks the same as ever, a wiry figure that never seems to stand still. Bouncing on the soles of his feet, he nods at her stomach. 'Looks like you'll be kept busy soon. Hey, I'm glad for you.'

'Thanks,' she smiles. 'It was kind of a surprise. But a good one.'

Georgie glances over at the motel, wondering if Dan is going to come over.

'Actually, I'm on a trip with Dan right now. Like I said on the phone, we've broken down.'

'How's he doing?' Kevin asks, as he starts to fiddle inside the car's engine.

'Dan? To be honest, it's hard to know. Not a great talker, my brother.'

'No, he was always a quiet one. Never got to know him that well. Shame.'

It doesn't take Kevin long to fix the car. 'All sorted. I'll be on my way, but it was good to see you, Georgie. And give Dan my regards. We were never big mates, but I know he was a good friend to Finn.' He rubs a cloth between two oily hands. 'And you – well, you were the best, Georgie. Brilliant for him.'

As he packs his tools away, Kevin carries on chatting. 'Man, he was so proud of you too. The way he talked about you – and that exhibition you were going to do together. It would have been so good. Did you ever think of putting the show on anyway? Like as a tribute?'

Georgie shakes her head and turns away. 'No. No, I didn't. The photos weren't ready, to be honest. It was still in the early stages and then, well . . .' She trails off. 'Thanks,' she says. 'For fixing the car. I really appreciate it. You saved my life.'

Too late, Georgie presses her hand to her mouth. 'Sorry,' she says. 'Poor choice of words.'

Slowly, Kevin puts down his toolbox. 'Oh no.' He shakes his head. 'Don't go thinking like that. I loved Finn, we all did. But sometimes, being with him was like watching a crash in slow motion. You knew it was going to happen and nothing could stop it. Not even you, Georgie.'

Chapter Thirteen

Georgie, 2015

'Come and rescue me'

The first time Georgie sets eyes on Finn is on a muggy, too-warm Sunday in July. She didn't really want to go to Dan's housewarming party and she'd set off with a hangover and low expectations. For all his good points, she and her brother are very different, and she always feels out of place at his gatherings. But Dan's new flat is only two Tube stops from Georgie, so she really has no excuse. 'Come over,' Dan had said. 'It's just a few of us getting together. Come – bring a bottle.'

And that's how Georgie finds herself standing on the doorstep of a tatty house in Kilburn, clutching a bottle of cheap white wine from the corner shop that's already losing its chill. The front door is wide open and she walks up a set of dark stairs. She passes other flat doors that are firmly shut, catches wafts of someone's Sunday dinner.

And then she's at the top of the house, walking into Dan's new flat, and she recognises a few things – a lamp, a red patterned rug – from Dan's old house-share. This place is a step up; still a bit rough around the edges, but the rooms are light and airy. There are stripped floorboards and tall windows and once he's got rid of the smell of cat litter, it'll be nice.

She spots her brother in the corner, laughing with some people from his office, and there's a group of girls talking loudly on the sofa, well on their way to daytime drunk. One of them is Mandy; they've met before and Georgie has a hunch that Dan would like her to be more than a flatmate.

Arctic Monkeys are playing and no one looks up, so Georgie wanders into the kitchen in search of a corkscrew. Instead, she finds Finn. He's sitting in the open window, smoke from his roll-up curling lazily into the sunshine. She knows it's him even before he tells her. It's something about his short hair and the way he dresses differently from everyone else. A knackered T-shirt, faded jeans and bare feet, while Dan and his mates are all in weekend slacks and shirts from Next or Topman.

She already knows several things about Finn: that he dropped out of uni and has been working in a bar ever since. Sometimes he picks up extra work as a roadie. He also has a few sidelines: photography and a bit of dealing, for the right people. She knows he's been a good friend to Dan, seen him through some dark times when he was feeling low. What she wasn't expecting is quite how beautiful Finn is.

From his perch on the windowsill, Finn turns, looks at her and smiles. 'Ah, at last,' he says, flicking his roll-up out of the window. 'Someone interesting. Come and rescue me.'

And from that day onwards, that is what Georgie sets about doing. Because while Finn is cool, he's also troubled. He shows her silvery scars on his arms and tells her how he has no 'off' switch. He talks to her about his addictions, to drink and to drugs she's never heard of. 'You sure you're not scared off?' he asks.

Georgie has had boyfriends before, but none of them were like Finn. Looking back, those men felt interchangeable, hazy around

78

the edges. But everything about Finn is sharply defined. When he talks, he demands attention, but he's also that rare thing, a good listener. He's interested in people's stories – Dan's, hers, and everyone he meets.

Sometimes she wonders if it's another sort of addiction, this urge of his to collect the stories of no-hopers. Or perhaps Finn does it to make him feel better about himself.

Other times, Finn is less attentive. He goes on benders for days and Georgie twists herself into knots, chastises herself for not being more interesting. For being so easy to leave.

That's when she rings Dan: 'He's gone. I'm really worried this time. I think he might do something stupid.' But then Finn always breezes back in, with bruises and stories of white nights with a bunch of French musicians, or of a New York filmmaker who wanted to see London's best clubs. There are also times when he doesn't tell her any stories, just sleeps it off and leaves her wondering.

Each time Georgie makes these calls to Dan, he's a little less sympathetic. Because after Finn went home with Georgie the night of the housewarming party, he never really returned to Dan's flat. Pretty soon, Dan and Mandy became a couple, so they didn't mind paying the extra rent between them. But Georgie knows that Dan was sad that he and Finn never got to be proper flatmates.

The words are never spoken but Georgie knows she has stolen Finn away from him. Sometimes, at night, when she wraps herself around Finn's curved spine, she feels a shiver of satisfaction. Dan has always been the Best Boy, the one who won all the awards and praise. But now she has the best prize of all.

Chapter Fourteen

GEORGIE

Georgie watches Kevin drive away and she shakes her head, determined not to get dragged back in time. She starts to walk towards the motel, but she must have moved too quickly, or perhaps she's been out in the cold too long. Because the next thing she knows, Georgie is being assailed by another of her dizzy spells, a lurch that makes everything around her simultaneously very far away and jarringly close. She's over-tired, she tells herself. She should have eaten properly – had a yoghurt instead of all those croissants. She stops, lowers her head and waits for the dazzle behind her eyelids to fade.

When she straightens up again, Dan's there. He's brought out her bag and he's loading it into the car. Without saying a word, he gets in and starts revving the engine. She climbs in beside him, but he's busy studying the wiggly line on his phone that wends its impossibly long way north. 'Nine hours and forty-eight minutes – and we're about to hit rush hour,' he says. 'Let's go.'

As the car picks up speed, they both listen to the rumble of the engine, willing it to keep going. 'Seems OK?' Georgie says tentatively. Dan nods but doesn't reply.

'You were right – starter motor. He said it'll be OK for a bit but you need to get it serviced properly when you get home.'

'Keep in touch, do you? With Kevin?'

'No, of course not . . .' she starts.

'I always thought Kevin was a session musician,' Dan says with a laugh.

'Yes, he is,' Georgie replies. 'But he's also a mechanic. And he did us a big favour.'

Out of the car window, she watches as the long bulk of a lorry passes by in a tangle of pneumatic cables and she's grateful for the rumble that drowns out any chance of conversation. Of all the things Kevin said, one keeps circling around in her head: 'You were brilliant for him.' And then her own ill-chosen words: 'You saved my life.' Georgie feels her mouth go dry because she knows she wasn't brilliant for Finn. And, in the end, she couldn't save him.

As for that half-baked plan for her and Finn to do a joint photography exhibition, she'd known deep down that it was never going to happen. Georgie had been working on a series of portraits of young mothers with their babies, but she hadn't done anything with them. So Finn suggested a collaboration: they could hang Georgie's photos alongside Finn's. He'd take some of older people and it could say something poignant about life and key moments and the passing of time.

But Finn never got round to taking more than a few shots and then the gallery he'd had in mind closed down. So, no, after Finn died, it would have felt wrong to exhibit her photographs on their own. Kevin wasn't to know.

But that's all in the past – and Georgie has her own future to think of. Right on cue, a text from Wilf lights up her phone screen.

Hi how are you doing? Who's the old friend you're visiting?

Wilf has written a few more lines and she skims over them: one of the journalists on his trip is demanding hot showers in even the remotest villages and the politician isn't as fit as he'd made out, so they are falling behind schedule. Wilf sounds down, not his usual positive self. But Georgie can't think about that now.

A few days ago, she was keenly following every leg of Wilf's trip, imagining every Berber village he walked through, each glass of mint tea he drank and every lodge where he unrolled his sleeping mat. She'd gone to sleep wishing she was by his side and woken wondering what mountaintop view he was waking up to. But now, Wilf and his adventures feel very far away; his fretting about hot showers, a little trivial.

'Any news?' asks Dan.

'Just Wilf, checking in.'

'Ah, the great Wilf.'

'What's that supposed to mean?' Georgie bristles.

'Hey, nothing. Just that Dad says he's nice.'

'Really, he said that?'

'Yes. Said he's a decent bloke.'

Georgie lets this thought settle. She and Wilf have visited Frank and Irena a few times, but her father has never said anything like this to her. 'Huh. Well, that's a first. Me finally doing something Dad approves of,' she says.

Dan clears his throat. 'So, what's he like? This Wilf.'

Georgie smiles. 'He's great. He's away right now, taking a group of journalists walking in the Atlas Mountains. If they give it a good write-up, bookings should start coming in.'

'Long way to go, when you're about to have his baby.'

'It couldn't be helped,' she says. 'I've still got two weeks to go and he's back on Friday, so it's all fine.'

'Dad says he runs his own company?'

'Yeah, he trained in sustainable tourism, and he's worked in lots of places – seen it succeed but also fail. Now he wants to show

how it can be done well: respecting the environment and the local people rather than ripping them off,' she says firmly.

'Uh-huh,' says Dan. She knows what he's thinking, that Wilf sounds nothing like her old boyfriends: the guitarist waiting for his big break, the scriptwriter with writer's block. The guy who'd invented an app that was going to change the world but was never heard of again, after she'd given him a loan. And then the one they are both taking great care not to mention – Finn.

'He's great, he really is,' she repeats.

'So where did you meet someone like him?'

'At a wedding, actually.'

She smiles at the memory. Georgie was taking the photographs and Wilf was a cousin of the groom. Usually, after the main photographs, Georgie tries to fade into the background, but Wilf had noticed her. She was standing at the bar, ordering a mineral water, when she heard a voice next to her say, 'I'll have the same, please.'

All around them, guests in outfits that were slightly too tight or bright were carrying away drinks on trays already wet with spilt beer. It felt as if they were the only two people in the room who were stone-cold sober.

'I'm driving,' he said by way of explanation, picking up his glass. Georgie's excuse was that she was working. Her secret tally of days sober – two hundred and seven by that point – remained unspoken. She'd woken up after Finn's funeral and known it was non-negotiable, started going to AA meetings every Monday evening in her local community hall.

Then this man with his neatly trimmed hair and soft accent said, 'I was only invited out of politeness. And I only accepted out of politeness. So . . .' He gave an embarrassed smile. 'Here's to good manners.' Together, they raised their glasses of sparkling water and drank to sobriety and propriety.

The wedding reception was in the basement of a hotel and, later, Wilf helped carry her photography kit out to a waiting taxi. The lift up to the ground floor was lined with mirrors and as they got in, she saw the two of them reflected from all angles.

Even then, Georgie saw they were a pair you wouldn't automatically put together. Wilf was tall and dressed in what he'd already confessed was a borrowed suit. Georgie was in her unofficial work uniform: black jeans and a black T-shirt, her hair scraped back into a tight bun. In the mirror, her dark eyes stared out from a pale face and she had the look of a startled animal, one that might bolt. But beside her, Wilf looked far more wholesome and friendly.

He messaged her a week later, said he needed to buy a camera – could he pick Georgie's brains? 'Sure. But not if this is your way of asking for a date,' she replied. 'I'm not ready for that.'

'I'd just really appreciate your advice on cameras,' Wilf had said. She's pretty sure it's the only time he's ever been less than honest with her. On their third date, she said she was sorry but this couldn't work. She told him about losing Finn, how she was still grieving and confused and it didn't feel right. She'd get back in touch if she ever felt ready.

But then she kept thinking about Wilf and all the things she wanted to tell him. So she texted him anyway and on their fourth date, Wilf asked Georgie a question. He asked if she thought it was possible to honour the memory of someone, but also enjoy your own life again. He pointed out that Georgie would always remember Finn, but her life didn't need to stop with his death – that she deserved her own future.

Now, in the car, she tells Dan, 'I think you'll like him. Come and visit when he gets back – once all this is over and done with.'

But her brother is pulling away from her again. 'Weekends, I'm usually training,' he snaps. 'Improving my times. Or competing.'

'Still doing cross-country then?' she says to Dan. *Still trying to drown out the thoughts in your head*, she thinks to herself.

He softens. 'I'll see if there are any races coming up near you. I could come and stay. Meet Wilf. And the baby, of course.'

'That would be great,' she says, because even this vague promise is better than nothing. It's something to build on. 'You're going to be an uncle, after all.'

'And what does Wilf think of this trip – his girlfriend travelling the length of the British Isles when she's heavily pregnant?'

Georgie looks straight ahead.

'You have told him, haven't you? Where we're going?'

She shifts in her seat. 'Not exactly. Not yet. I mean, it's hardly worth it. I'll be back by tomorrow.'

'Uh-huh.'

'Plus, it's hard to know where to start.'

'OK. So does he even know about Nancy?'

'Not exactly.'

Georgie's head hurts. The tiredness is wrapping itself around her again, along with the grime she can feel on her skin and wedged under her fingernails, and she remembers she never did go back to their motel room and have a shower. She wants Dan to stop asking difficult questions. Because it's not like he's perfect – she's certain there's something up between him and Mandy.

'Relationships can be tricky,' he says eventually.

Georgie wonders if they are still talking about her and Wilf or about Dan and Mandy. Or even the relationship they can't yet broach: her and Finn. But she knows better than to press him. Instead, she reaches out and pats his arm. 'Well, we did learn from the best.'

Dan gives her the whisper of a smile.

The driving app says they will reach their destination, a tiny island off the west coast of Scotland, by early evening. In this small and unsuitable car, she and her brother are racing as fast as they can towards their mother and the shocks from the past that continue to reverberate down the years.

The moment she found out she was pregnant, Georgie yearned for this baby. It was a chance to start over with Wilf and do things differently. But her fear is that she'll never be able to outrun what she's inherited from her mother: a propensity to ruin things and damage the people closest to her.

Chapter Fifteen

NANCY

Nancy's old carpet bag is waiting by the bothy door. She throws the dregs of her tea on to the fire, hears it hiss, then takes a last look around the freshly swept room that's been her home for two years. A home so remote that it finally felt safe to stop running. More fool her.

It had been a bit of luck, finding this place. She'd been on the mainland, living in a run-down caravan on Morag's campsite, rent-free in return for labouring, gardening, that sort of thing. But summer was coming and Morag would need the pitch back.

Then, one night in the pub, she'd overheard the local estate manager moaning to the barman about the bothy out on the island, the hassle of its upkeep. Every time he visited, he thought they should just lock its door. It was a relic from a different, more trusting age. 'Now people use it as a free place to hold parties or stag weekends. Mess it up, leave behind bottles, graffiti – and worse,' he said.

She'd sat in the corner listening, waited until last orders before sliding on to the stool next to him. 'I can fix up your bothy,' she'd said to him. 'Mend the roof. Paint it, keep it clean.'

He'd turned to look at her, sizing her up. Thanks to her spell in the caravan, Nancy was looking pretty respectable.

She didn't want to overstep the mark. 'Only until you decide what to do with it. Morag at the campsite will vouch for me,' she added.

The man drained his pint, wiped the froth from his moustache and went back to talking about the good old days, when bothies were respected. 'Used by those in need, people working on the land, then walkers. There was a code: keep it clean, leave it as you find it,' he'd said.

Nancy gave the nod for another round. As estate manager, surely he could say it was closed for repairs, she suggested. Just a temporary measure. She'd stay there, smarten it up. See off any louts that pitched up. 'I'm tougher than I look,' she said. 'Been living on my wits a long time. Plus, I've got the dog.' She'd gestured at Bree, who gave a willing thump of her tail on the floor.

That was two years ago and ever since, waking up here has felt like a second chance at life. Opening the door to a haze of greens, then russet browns as the seasons changed. Learning to pick out the different birdsong as she carried her bucket down to the brook to scoop freezing water, Bree trotting by her side. She could tell the dog was happy here too.

She doesn't mix with the villagers, just goes down to the shops when she has to with her carefully meted-out savings. She can guess what they say about her, though, because people will always talk. Last summer, the big gossip was how she'd single-handedly seen off a group of lads. They were students, boys with soft cheeks and wavy hair, used to getting their own way, who turned up to play music and drink in the bothy. First, she'd set Bree on them, then she'd bared her own broken and yellowed teeth, and growled at them herself. At first they laughed at her – 'Jesus, she's a witch!' 'A mad hag!' – but they soon hightailed it back to wait for the morning ferry.

She suspects that after that she was known as 'Nan the witch' – and she can live with that. Better than some of her previous incarnations. Nancy the drinker. Nancy the drudge. Crazy Nancy.

Yes, this bothy has been good for her. The peace turned down the volume inside her head for a while. Out here, she can't hurt anyone else. It's just her and the dog. Of course, the shame never leaves her side, but it's less insistent out here. A hum rather than a deafening howl.

In her old life, she hadn't realised what shame could do to a person. How it bleeds into everything you do. Rather like that other emotion that has been her constant companion for the past twenty years. Fear.

Chapter Sixteen

Nancy, 1988

'A prodigious talent'

Gerry Mac's summer party has swiftly become a thing of legend. Everyone has heard what happened last year, when a lecturer's wife got so drunk she was sick all over a visiting novelist of note. Then there was his Christmas do, when a chemistry student spiked the punch and the head of department took his clothes off and danced in the rain.

So when Nancy finds an invitation to Gerry Mac's annual summer party in her pigeonhole, she assumes it's a joke – another student playing a trick on her. She hasn't even been taught by Gerry Mac yet. He sat in on the auditions for *A Doll's House*, but it's unlikely he'd remember her.

She turns the purple card over, sees a typed message, a florid border around the edges:

DO JOIN ME FOR A SUMMER GATHERING, WITH GOOD COMPANY AND EXCELLENT CONVERSATION. 9 P.M. UNTIL LATE

Looking left, then right, she sees another student – Laurence, who edits the student magazine – pull an identical square of purple card from his pigeonhole. *So, the invitation is genuine*, she thinks.

She's not sure if she can bring a plus-one, but she asks Frank to come too. They arrive unfashionably early – apparently 9 p.m. really means 10.30 p.m. – so Nancy has a cup of rum punch to calm her nerves. The first one goes down so well, she has a second and then a third. 'Steady on,' Frank says, but she ignores him – free booze, what's not to like? In fact, she's beginning to think bringing Frank wasn't such a good idea.

She'd quite like to talk to that Laurence from the student magazine, but he's wandered out into the garden and Frank doesn't want to go outside. He suffers from hay fever and the pollen count is high tonight. So they stay in their corner and by the time Gerry Mac wanders over, Nancy has drunk so much rum punch she can barely see straight.

Gerry dips a ladle into the punch bowl, passes them each a fresh plastic cup. Nancy looks down at hers, sees slices of apple bobbing and wonders if she might be the one who disgraces herself by being sick this year. 'So, you've brought a friend,' says Gerry, looking Frank up and down. Frank stands a little taller and holds out a hand, like the well-mannered grammar schoolboy that he is. 'Frank Brown, second-year Computer Science,' he says.

Nancy feels embarrassed for him: Computer Science – how silly it must sound to a cerebral man like Gerry Mac. She fishes a slice of orange out from her cup, nibbles on it in a way she hopes may look alluring.

'Computing – hmm. Isn't that just glorified typing?' Gerry says. Frank gives a polite chuckle, starts to clear his throat so he can explain, but Gerry isn't listening. 'I suppose we creatives will always need secretaries,' he says expansively, looking around for an audience. But everyone else is chatting in small groups, so he turns back to Nancy and Frank. 'We creatives,' he repeats, his eyes now looking only at Nancy.

There is a long silence, not dissimilar to the one Nancy remembers from that freshers' week lecture almost two years ago. Except now, she can't think of a single thing to say.

'Nancy Jebb. Emilia in *Othello* last year?' Gerry asks, and all she can do is nod. 'And you tried out for Nora.' He nods slowly. 'A shame, I was overruled. You would have been perfect.'

Still she can't think of an answer, but Gerry doesn't seem to expect one. Instead, he reaches out, brushes a strand of Nancy's crimped fringe out of her eyes. 'A prodigious talent, this one,' Gerry says, directing his comment to Frank. 'She'll go far.'

'Is that so?' Frank says, but Gerry Mac barely acknowledges him. 'Couple more productions coming up soon,' he continues. 'One in particular might be just right for you.' He gives his beard a swift stroke. 'I always invite a few people from the old days. Directors, producers, you know . . .' He turns and steps out into the garden.

Nancy squeezes her plastic cup between tense fingers, hears a loud crack. Orange liquid spatters over the bib of her white dungarees.

'Oh,' says Frank, looking down in horror. He gets out his handkerchief and dabs at her front ineffectually until she brushes him away.

They leave soon afterwards. 'What a pretentious twat,' Frank says as they walk home. 'The world is changing – soon, everything is going to be done with computers. Dinosaurs like him will be left behind.'

Nancy grits her teeth. She can smell the sticky rum punch on her clothes, in her hair. She shouldn't have taken Frank. He's sweet, but maybe he's not her type after all. A bit too safe. No wonder he can't appreciate Gerry's creative insight, his energy. She thinks of Gerry's little quip about typing. Then, how he said she had talent, and she smiles to herself.

'I think he's interesting,' she says lightly.

Chapter Seventeen

GEORGIE

The miles tick by, unbearably slowly. This little car doesn't seem to go above 60 mph and Georgie's impatience grows as she watches faster, more efficient cars flash their lights, then cruise past with ease. Still, at least the car is moving. If they can just keep going north, get to the port and then the island, she can confront the woman who abandoned them and get some answers. Some closure.

She checks her phone but there are barely any more posts under the hashtag #mysteryrescuewoman, just people recycling the same old picture. Georgie looks at the grainy image again, searching for some clue as to what her mother has been doing all this time; what sort of person she is now.

'What do you think Nancy will look like?' she asks, zooming in on the picture. 'I mean, this photo is kind of blurry.'

Dan lets out a whistle. 'Ohh, I dunno. Older? Greyer? More wrinkly? Depends if she's still a drinker, I suppose.' He turns to practicalities. 'Anyway, when we get there, we'll ask around. The island is only small, so it shouldn't be hard to track her down.'

Georgie tries to imagine this final stage of their journey, but she can't. She gets as far as seeing her hand knocking on a wooden door and the door opening, but after that the image fades away.

Will it take Nancy a moment to recognise her children or will it be instant? And, when she does, what emotion will show on her face?

As a child, Georgie's visions of how she and Dan would find their mother were part of more exotic daydreams. They involved walking across rope bridges and hacking through leafy jungles to reach her. In more hopeful moments, she'd imagined Nancy coming back to find them.

'I used to fantasise about her turning up on our doorstep,' Georgie says. 'That first of all, she'd go back to our old house in London, but that would be OK because a neighbour like Claudia would come out and tell her we'd moved. Then she'd find her way to our new house in Redhill, burst in and say, "Give me my children back!" and start smashing all Irena's little glass ornaments or something.'

'Ha. Yes, me too,' says Dan. 'Although without the broken glass. I kind of felt like we'd had enough of that already.'

'True.'

Georgie lets herself dip back, just for a moment, to those days so long ago. Funnily enough, it's not the shouting or the broken shards she remembers, it's the lull that used to come before those storms. It was always worse, the waiting, but she learned to spot the signs. Her mother would become vague, absent-minded. Georgie would find Nancy's purse in the fridge, or notice that her mother was wearing odd socks. Wine glasses would accumulate on surfaces around the house, sour with dry dregs.

On those occasions, Georgie would spend the day at primary school feeling a dread growing in her tummy. At home time, she'd stand in the playground and watch the mums arrive, knowing deep down she wouldn't see Nancy's face among them. Often, Claudia from down the road would step in and take Georgie and Dan home. When their dad found out, he'd shake his head. 'You've lost it, Nance, you're crazy,' he'd say, but those words only made her worse.

Georgie saw how the drink made her mum sleepy and forgetful and by the time she was thirteen she swore, in that self-righteous way of girls that age, never to drink. Dan did too, but the difference was that he stuck to his word. He was always training for some sports event or cross-country race, so at parties he'd nurse a single can of lager all night.

But Georgie's resolve had evaporated the first time she got drunk. She was fourteen and someone had sneaked a bottle of vodka into the school disco. She knocked back her first fiery cup, then grabbed the bottle and swigged straight from it. Everyone else was hanging back, too shy to dance, but not Georgie. In her head, she was Britney Spears, Christina Aguilera and Shakira rolled into one. Lord knows what she really looked like, but that was the first time people at her new school noticed Georgie Brown.

'We always thought you were a bit boring. Bit of a swot,' one of the Mean Girls said. 'But you're all right, you know. You're a laugh, Georgie.' So Georgie drank at the next party and the one after that. Then it was the summer holidays and she and the girls who used to be mean but were now her mates all hung out at the park.

There was always drink or weed to be had – the other kids brought it, almost like offerings to the now great Georgie Brown. When she'd had her fill, she'd lie back and watch the clouds scudding across the darkening sky. And in those moments, Georgie had never felt closer to her mother because, at last, she got it. She understood why her mother had drunk herself stupid on those long afternoons. It drowned out the tedium and the loneliness and it turned you into a different person and now Georgie was doing the same thing.

When she stumbled home, she'd put her head around the living-room door and stick to short, easy words, like 'OK, night'. Most evenings, Frank and Irena would barely glance up. Sometimes, it felt as if Georgie's father couldn't bear to look at her for too long. Perhaps now she was growing up, she reminded him of Nancy too much. Or perhaps he just didn't like what he saw: the new piercings, the love bites on her neck.

Georgie looks out of the window at the motorway's hard shoulder. She sees banks of drab trees clinging to the dull earth. She glimpses the arc of a blown-out tyre by the side of the road, then sees a flash of blood and realises that the black curve isn't a rubber tyre but the pelt of a dead badger. That poor animal, hardwired to follow the age-old trails set by its mother and the mother before her, ancient ways that have long since been tarmacked over.

Perhaps, she thinks, we humans don't stand a chance either. We can't help following the same well-trodden paths, even when we know it'll end in disaster.

She looks over at Dan. 'I worry, you know,' she says.

'What? If we'll get there tonight?'

'No. About turning out like her. If that's what flipped a switch in Nancy. Her becoming a mother.'

There's silence and she wonders if Dan agrees. But then he says, 'Don't. You won't be like that, Georgie. You'll be a great mother.'

Georgie rubs her eyes, gritty with tiredness, tries to swallow down the lump that has formed in her throat. 'Thanks,' she manages.

'And I haven't met him yet, but Wilf sounds like he'll be a good dad, too.'

'Yes,' she says. 'I think he will.'

'But you need to talk to him. Properly, I mean.'

Georgie knows what her brother means.

'Because we all need to keep some secrets to ourselves. That's normal. But the big ones – well, they can ruin a relationship. They show a fundamental lack of trust. And respect.'

He's right – but this is a side of Dan she's not seen before, one that is acquainted with counselling-speak. Then she wonders if it's couples counselling-speak because, as far as she knows, Dan still hasn't spoken to Mandy, who works as a surveyor and wears glossy tights that rasp when she crosses her legs. Who always asks Georgie how her hobby is going and hired a 'professional' photographer for their own wedding.

Come to that, she wonders if Dan has spoken to his work. He's high up at some insurance firm, a fact her father reminds her of on a regular basis. But surely even Dan would need to ask for time off for this wildest of goose chases?

There's a ping on her phone, but when Georgie checks, the screen is blank. The sound comes again and she realises it must be Dan's. But when she looks down at his phone, which is sitting in the cup-holder, there are no messages; just the wiggly blue line on the map and the worrying reminder that they still have nine hours and two minutes ahead of them.

She glances over at Dan, sees a blush creeping up from his collar. The ping comes again. And that's when Georgie realises Dan must have a second phone somewhere in this car.

'Where . . . ?' she says, looking under the seat, in the glove box, over at him.

'Nowhere. It doesn't matter,' he says abruptly.

'But it might be Mandy, or your work, or some news . . .'

'Leave it,' Dan warns.

Georgie looks out of the window, watches a coach sail past them, a row of bored faces peering down at their little car. What's going on in Dan's life? He's talking as if he's been in counselling. And there's usually only one reason why people carry a second phone – as an affair phone. She feels a hot anger taking shape inside her gut.

Hasn't Dan learned anything from the chaos of their family life? Doesn't he remember how a betrayal hurts? Georgie has made plenty of mistakes in her life, but she has never been unfaithful. She knows how it feels when someone you love leaves without warning and Dan does too. He should know better.

They drive on.

This trip was supposed to lay Georgie's past to rest, but instead it's shaking it back to life, sending chaotic memories flying into the air. As Georgie fixes her eyes on the endless motorway ahead, she's starting to wish she'd never called that taxi, rushed to get on that train and then rung her brother. But most of all, she wishes she'd never seen the picture of Nancy that set this whole journey in motion.

Georgie has already wasted too many years of her life trying to understand that woman. As a child, she had dreamed up excuses for her, then imagined rose-tinted reconciliation scenarios. She'd fabricated lies to tell neighbours, teachers and the mothers of school friends. But, finally, it could be time for Georgie to harden her heart. She wants answers from Nancy and then she wants to walk away from her, once and for all. Because some acts of betrayal are beyond forgiveness.

Chapter Eighteen

NANCY

She and Bree catch the first ferry, Nancy looping her scarf over her head to keep off the early-morning rain. 'You're all over the news,' says Joe, who sells the ferry tickets.

'The news?' Nancy hopes this is his idea of a joke.

'Well Twitter, anyway.' He bares a gappy smile. 'Aye, we all used to call you "Nan" or "Nan in the bothy". But now you're the "Mystery Rescue Woman". You've even got a hashtag!'

Nancy has no idea what this means, but it doesn't sound good. She pulls her scarf closer around her face, strokes Bree's soft head to calm the thumping in her chest. She was right to leave and now she'll have to keep moving, because a mystery is what Nancy needs to remain.

On the mainland, the railway station is a quaint building with its windows and door painted a cheery red, but she discovers the door is still firmly locked. It's 10 a.m. – surely it should be open by now? She rattles the door, steps back and gazes up at the brick building.

'No point. They're on strike. Where have you been hiding yourself?' a man calls out from across the road. He's holding his morning newspaper, slaps it against his palm as if to make his point. She doesn't answer – it would take too long to explain.

But the man with the newspaper is right because nobody comes to open up, and Nancy knows that she's already missed the one bus a day out of here. Bree leans into Nancy's leg, unsure why they are here or where they are going. 'I know, girl,' Nancy murmurs. 'I know.'

In the end, Nancy does what she's always done when there's no other option: she sticks out her thumb to hitch a ride. Do people still pick up hitchhikers these days – especially one with a dog? There's only one way to find out, so she positions herself just before the main roundabout out of town. She stands there for a long time, facing the biting wind.

When someone finally pulls over, Nancy has become so used to being ignored that she almost misses it. Then she hears the toot of a horn. She looks around, sees the bulky shape of a camper van and hesitates, almost doesn't respond, because it throws up a memory of another journey in a van a long time ago, one that did not end well.

But above, dark clouds are gathering: rain is on the way. They walk over and Nancy sees that the driver is a woman about her own age. Spry, a ruddy glow to her cheeks that has come from outdoorsy camping weekends rather than Nancy's sort of sleeping out. The woman winds down the window. 'Where are you headed?'

'Wherever you're going,' Nancy says.

'South?'

'South will do fine,' Nancy says and she and the dog climb in.

Chapter Nineteen

Nancy, 1989

'I'm not feeling it'

Nancy is looking at a poster on the Drama department notice-board. She knows it's only a uni production, but there's her name in big letters: top billing. She feels a warm glow of pride spreading outwards.

It's a production of *Brief Encounter* – a surprisingly old-fashioned choice, Nancy thinks, but Gerry insists it has modern relevance. 'We are all trapped inside conventional roles and expectations,' he says, and she nods because it's uncanny, this knack Gerry has of saying exactly the right thing at the right time.

Anyway, he's giving the script a different feel by setting the play in the 1960s – a more revolutionary era, he says. So Nancy's costume is an orange minidress and white boots, like something out of a Beatles film or *Blow-Up*. The boots pinch a little, but Nancy doesn't like to complain because Gerry has chosen her costume specially.

She gives it her all, but at the dress rehearsal, Gerry, who is sitting in the front row, looks disgruntled. He chews on his pen, purses his lips so that his moustache wriggles. 'Something is missing from your performance,' he says, drawing out the words. 'I'm not feeling it.' And all the excitement that has buoyed Nancy up for the past few months drops, plummets like a stone.

She needs to inhabit her character, he says. Maybe a haircut will help? 'I'm thinking, Twiggy. Or Mia Farrow in *Rosemary's Baby*.'

Gerry has a friend, Adrian, who can cut it for free, so she sits in a swivel chair in his salon after hours and *snip, snip* he goes. She can feel his breath on her cheek and then the back of her neck as her hair falls to the floor, and soon she's sitting in the centre of a circle of auburn feathers. When Nancy looks in the mirror, she's hoping for sleek and gamine. Instead, she looks butchered, shorn like an animal. She runs a shaky hand over her head, tries to pull down the few tendrils he's left at the sides, but there's barely anything there. Not even enough to tuck her hair behind her ear, the way she likes to.

'There we go,' says Gerry. 'Perfect.'

Nancy feels a thickness in her throat. She wants to cry, but she mustn't, that would be childish. 'Thank you,' she says in a whisper.

But the play is a huge success. As soon as she's on stage, Nancy loves how she becomes a different person, someone with a clear backstory and – everyone else seems to think – great hair. As she takes her bows on the last night, people clap and whoop and she feels amazing. *This*, she thinks, *is what I want. This is my destiny*.

◆ ◆ ◆

'No Frank tonight?' Gerry passes her a glass of wine. It's the after-party, but she's here on her own. Frank came to clap and cheer on the opening night, but he said he probably won't make this one. He's got a big exam next week and he needs to revise.

'Doesn't look like it,' says Nancy, and she gives her brightest smile. She's not going to let Frank spoil her night. Gerry refills

103

her glass, says he's going to invite a West End director to the next production. One of his old mates. 'I think he'll like what he sees,' he says. 'I know I do.'

Later, there's music and dancing, and by the end of the night Nancy finds she's being lifted in the air, until she's up on the table, and then she dances some more. Oh, but it feels incredible! Everyone is smiling and laughing and it's her – Nancy Jebb – at the centre of it all. But then something shifts, the room turns swimmy and she needs to get down, fast.

The next thing she knows, she's in the bathroom, Gerry's bathroom, and she can smell a musty flannel that's draped over the side of the bath and then she's bent over the toilet bowl. But this is all wrong, she can't miss the party, it was going so well, and she tries to get up but she can't, her legs don't work properly. So she lies down on the floor for a little rest, just for a minute.

When Nancy wakes, she can't hear any music. Gerry is leaning over her, saying something, but it's not making any sense. She needs to go home – or maybe she should walk over to Frank's place, see if he's still awake. But it turns out she still can't stand up. She puts her hand out to the wall to steady herself and it's a good job no one else is here to see this. Kind Gerry is helping her out of the bathroom and it's so embarrassing because he's her lecturer and she's disgraced herself and she must smell of sick.

As they pass the living room, it looks so different – just empty bottles and ashtrays under the dazzle of the overhead light. And she's apologising, saying sorry she's such a mess, but Gerry is saying it's OK, he's here to help, and he's guiding her along the corridor and then they are in a bedroom.

This is where she left her coat, she remembers now, and the bed is so soft and it's so much nicer than the bathroom floor, so she flops back. Then she laughs a little because her dress, the orange one for the play that she's still wearing, has got ruckled up. 'Unseemly,' she tries to say, because that's what her mother would call it. 'Un . . .' she says, but Gerry isn't listening, he's stroking her hair, which is nice, but weird too, and then, almost as if by accident, he's on top of her.

She wonders for a moment if he's slipped over, if he's drunk too, but then she feels his hand pull down her tights and her pants in one go and his head is pushing into her neck. He's a short man, so his forehead presses into her windpipe, quite hard, which makes it difficult to say anything at all.

Then, almost as if she's playing a role again, she imagines how she must have looked to Gerry tonight: a girl who danced on the table, knowing full well people would be able to see up her skirt, who fancies herself as a modern-day Mia Farrow. She thinks of her mother's advice about men and she knows that it's not really Gerry's fault – if anyone is to blame, it's Nancy.

And to be honest, it's over so quickly – a sigh, then a sense of slippage as he leaves her – that Nancy wonders if it even counts. Because now Gerry is sitting on the side of the bed, smoothing his hair back into its ponytail, straightening his shirt, acting like nothing has happened. So Nancy does the same. She swings her legs over the opposite side of the bed and she's about to make a feeble joke about his-and-her sides, but when she looks up, Gerry isn't in the room any more. He's stepped away, discreetly, so that Nancy can sort herself out.

She stands, realises that it hurts in all sorts of places. She must have fallen over in the bathroom, she supposes. There's a coat on the bed and it's hers, which feels like a stroke of luck. She remembers leaving it here earlier, a hundred years ago, when she was full of excitement and laughing.

She finds Gerry in the kitchen, washing up glasses at the sink. He's humming to himself and he barely looks up.

'I'll be off, then,' she says.

'Hmm? Oh, sure, yes. Good plan,' he says. He's wearing yellow Marigold gloves, lifts one hand and wiggles four sudsy fingers.

He doesn't see her out, but as she closes the flat door and walks out into the cold night air, Nancy thinks that's for the best. He was doing her a favour, not drawing attention to what just happened. Barely happened, really.

In the morning, she tells her housemates she drank so much that she blacked out – can't even remember how she got home. 'Literally, everything after I got to the party is a blank,' she says. 'What are you like, Nancy?' says Daisy. 'You are crazy!' says Polly.

She feels hungover, shaky and sick, but she has an idea forming. She will go to the Co-op and buy a pack of croissants, Frank's favourite, as a Sunday morning treat. Then she'll sprinkle them with water and warm them in the oven – an old trick they used at The Beaufort when the bread rolls had gone stale. She'll lay a red-and-white checked tea towel over the top and find a nice pot of jam and put it all in a basket and carry it round to Frank's place, to surprise him.

They will have breakfast in bed, like people in romantic films do, and everything will be all right again. Already, she can feel the Nancy of yesterday disappearing, like a bad dream that fades as the day progresses. She will make that bad dream go away for good, by showing Frank how much she loves him. Nice dependable Frank, who didn't do anything wrong except stay in and revise for his exams.

But when she gets to the Co-op, there are no croissants. It is a Sunday and no matter how long she looks at the shelves, there is nothing to see but sliced bread and Mr Kipling cakes, and for some reason this makes her cry – a silent stream of tears that seems to have no end. And when the young man stacking the shelves asks her what's wrong, she is at a loss to explain herself.

Instead, she buys a packet of biscuits, even though it's not the same thing at all, and she goes straight round to Frank's. No checked tea towel, no fancy jam, just this humble peace offering.

'Sorry I didn't make it last night,' Frank says, as she hands him a cup of tea. 'Not really my thing – all those drama types. But I got loads done. Feeling quietly confident. How did it go?'

'Oh, fine,' she says, getting into bed next to him. 'You didn't miss much.'

He runs his hand over her shorn head, gives a sad smile. She reaches up, takes his hand in hers. 'Don't worry, my hair grows fast,' she says. 'I'll be back to being the old Nancy before you know it.'

'Yes, my crazy little Nancy,' says Frank, and he leans in to kiss her.

'Here, I brought biscuits,' she says, laughing but not really knowing why, her fingers fumbling as she tries to open the packet.

'Aren't you good to me!' Frank takes two.

'No, I'm not. I'm really not,' Nancy says, turning her face away.

'Nance?' Frank touches her arm. 'What's wrong, are you crying?'

She shakes her head, snuggles down next to him so he can't see.

'I expect you're exhausted – all those rehearsals and then the shows. But you can relax now. Have a day off.'

She rubs her face dry. 'Yes, you're right. I'm glad it's all over, to be honest. All I want is a nice quiet day. Just me and you.'

Chapter Twenty

GEORGIE

At first, Georgie thinks she's imagining it, but no, the needle on the speedometer is definitely wavering, dipping to the left too often for her liking. She divides her attention between watching it and refreshing the news feed on her phone. Neither is very reassuring. Online, there are no updates on the Mystery Rescue Woman; in fact, the story seems to be fading. A missing girl who was found is already old news. She looks up.

'Dan – why does it feel like we're going slower?'

Her brother rubs his face. 'What? Sorry, yeah, I wasn't concentrating.' He puts his foot down and the needle creeps over, but Georgie can tell that something is not right with him. The invisible phone has stopped pinging, but now she's pretty sure there's a low buzzing reverberating somewhere inside this car. It's the sound of someone calling Dan and whoever it is, they aren't giving up easily.

'Dan,' Georgie says. 'For God's sake – do you want to take that call? In fact, I could do with the loo, so let's stop at the next place.'

A few miles on, there's a service station, and as Dan drives into the car park, Georgie realises she now needs the loo quite urgently, and she waddles as fast as she can into the building.

Coming out, she meets Dan going in. 'Here.' He tosses her the car keys. 'I'll get us some food. What do you want?'

'A salad, if they've got it,' she says.

Back in the car, the air smells of old coffee and unwashed hair and something sour that Georgie fears might be down to her. She looks over to the building, but there's no sign of Dan. He's taking forever. Georgie opens one of her cereal bars and takes a bite. Just as she suspected, sugary cardboard, and she chews it mechanically.

Then a sound fills the car: the rapid ping-ping-ping of several texts arriving. Georgie has already checked the glove box and knows the phone isn't in there. She twists around, moves her bag aside on the back seat to look for this hidden phone: nothing. Straining forward over her bump, she looks down into the footwell and the dark recesses under Dan's seat. Then she spots the side pocket of his door. Without the rumble of the engine, the pings sound even more insistent. She glances up at the service station; still no Dan.

She leans sideways over his seat, reaches down and feels the plastic case of a phone. It's a cheap pay-as-you-go thing, the sort criminals in TV shows use as a burner phone. But Dan is no master criminal because when she taps in the first numbers she can think of, the phone unlocks. Dan's passcode is his birthday.

And then Georgie finds herself looking at a stream of texts, all from the same person. There's no name, just a number, and their messages all say slightly different things but with one word repeated.

YOU HAVE DEFAULTED ON YOUR LOAN. WE KNOW WHERE YOU ARE

YOUR LOAN PAYMENTS ARE OVERDUE. WE WILL BE SENDING THIS NEWS OUT TO ALL YOUR CONTACTS AND FAMILY. ENJOY YOUR SHAME

The messages go on and as she spools through, Georgie feels sick, but she can't stop looking at this torrent of malice and threats. Then there's a rush of cold air as the door clunks open and there's no hiding what she's doing – she's caught, resting on Dan's seat with his phone in her hand, peering up at him.

'What the . . .' Dan snatches the phone out of her hand. 'Can't you mind your own business, for once in your life?'

'Sorry,' she says, and tries to push herself back up. But she's stuck, the weight of her bump acting as ballast. 'Don't suppose you could give me a hand? Just a good yank to get me up again?'

Dan holds the top of her arm and lifts Georgie upright. Without speaking, he gets in, passes her a plastic tub of salad. Anger radiates off him. Georgie busies herself opening her salad and a sharp, vinegary smell fills the car. She picks up the plastic spork, puts it down again.

'Dan, I'm sorry. I shouldn't have looked.'

'No, you shouldn't have. I meant to put it on mute, but I forgot. Lots on my mind.' Her brother starts to unwrap a noxious sandwich – egg is her guess – and takes several neat bites. 'Better get going – still got hours to go,' he says, his mouth full.

As they rejoin the motorway, Georgie knows she should feel worse than she does for looking at his phone. But what she feels most of all is relief. Dan isn't having an affair; he's in debt. Not that this is good news – far from it – but to Georgie it seems more fixable. It gives her hope.

She puts her limp salad to one side, clears her throat. 'I know it was wrong to look. But I was worried. I thought you'd done something stupid.'

'Well, then I expect you're very pleased with yourself.'

'What? No, of course not. I mean, if you've got money problems, surely that's not the end of the world? You can get a bank
loan or ask Mandy to help. Whatever possessed you to go to some
loan shark?'

Dan is shaking his head and laughing a fake laugh, the one he
always used when Georgie tried to join in with his father-son chats
about rugby or fishing or golf. The one that means *Oh, silly Georgie.*

'You have no idea,' he says. 'No idea.'

'So tell me. What's happened? Were you a bit short this month
or something?'

He does that laugh again.

'Dan, stop being so horrible. I'm trying to help.'

He's still laughing and he's being so infuriating that she tells
him to shut up. But then she looks more closely and realises he's
not laughing. Dan is crying.

'Oh, oh no, stop,' she says. 'I'm sorry.'

She looks around them, wondering if there's any way they can
pull over, but the traffic is relentless.

Dan wipes his nose with the back of his hand and Georgie
rummages in her bag for tissues that she knows she doesn't have.

'I think I've got myself into a bit of a mess,' he says at last.

She waits for him to gather himself.

'I suppose I've let things unravel. It's not just this month,
Georgie, it goes back far longer. The interest alone . . .' He trails off.

'Oh, Dan, how?' Then she checks herself: 'I mean, don't worry.
I'm sure it can be sorted. There are organisations that can help – get
repayments set up.'

'These aren't the kind of people who do repayment schemes.
It's not exactly above board.'

'But why did you need it? You earn loads – masses more than
I ever will.'

'Georgie. I don't. I'm not working any more, haven't been for a while. They let me go, you see. I wasn't performing. I could never get out of bed, so I was always late. And if I did make it in, I'd sit at my desk staring into space. Then one morning I got as far as the glass doors and I couldn't physically go any further.'

'But that's terrible – they should have helped you. Given you some sort of support. I mean, isn't that unfair dismissal or something?'

'Ah, it's all water under the bridge now. It was almost two years ago.'

Dan's words settle on her like a weight. She looks down at her abandoned salad, smells the cheap oil and acrid vinegar and feels the nausea rise. She cranks the window open and the wind rushes in, whips her hair. But it's never going to be enough to drown out her thoughts.

Two years ago was when Finn died. Of course, she and Dan haven't spoken since the funeral, but she'd heard bits of news from their dad or Irena. And she never got through a visit without one of them reminding her how sad Dan was. 'He's taking Finn's death hard, your brother,' their father would say. Or Irena might chip in, 'It's not just about you, Georgie. Finn and Dan were best friends, you know.'

But now Georgie's thoughts are sharpening, sliding into place. 'So that's why you don't have your company car,' she says slowly.

'Uh-huh.'

'And it's why you're using Mandy's. With no insurance.' She knows she should stop pressing him, but she can't, not yet. 'Dan, does Mandy know you've got her car?'

'She left it on the front drive – well, it's more my drive now. So I figured it was fair game.'

This is bad, worse than Georgie had imagined. 'Oh, Dan,' she says. 'When did all this happen?'

'Ah, she moved out about six months ago. Said it was temporary, while we worked things out. But we're not doing much of that.'

'And where's she living?'

'In a flat. Closer to her office. But there's no parking there. So . . .' Dan raises a hand, gestures at the car.

All this time, Georgie has been imagining Dan living his brilliant life. Going to work in his corner office with a view of the Thames. Playing golf with their dad at the weekend. Sad, of course, grieving Finn in his own way. But not broken like this.

Outside the car window, Georgie catches sight of a flicker of black railings as they cross an overpass and it's happening again, that dizzying lurch as her world starts to tilt. Her mouth is sucked dry and her ears are ringing as she holds on to the leather loop handle, hoping this will anchor her. She repeats to herself, *It's OK. It's low blood pressure. It's pregnancy vertigo. It won't last forever*, and she closes her eyes.

But that's a worse idea, because all she sees is snatches of Finn's face. The hard-but-soft brush of his stubble; the shadows under his eyes, soft as a blue bruise. Bone-fine fingers, a tracery of veins on the back of his hand.

More images race in, but they are ones she has imagined. The deafening roar of the train entering the tunnel, sparks flying. Finn turning, his eyes widening as he realised what was about to happen.

What went through his head in that last moment? Did he look round for Georgie, cry out for her? Because, whatever Wilf or Kevin might say, she should have been there. Saving Finn had been her mission, but in the end she failed. She wasn't enough.

Georgie dearly wishes she was back in her neat eco home in Orchard Drive, folding sleepsuits and drinking camomile tea. But she isn't. She's stuck in a stolen car with a brother who is broken in more ways than she imagined.

Ahead, a blue motorway sign tells them in huge letters they are on track for 'Scotland and Carlisle'. A fresh hatred of her mother rises up in Georgie, unbreachable as a wave.

Chapter Twenty-One

Nancy, May 1989

'Not so clever now, are we?'

After the drama production and the party, Nancy spends a lot more time round at Frank's place. On Sundays, she cooks huge saucepans of bolognaise or chilli, enough to keep him and his housemates going for a few days. 'She's a keeper, this one,' says Dougie, who has a broad forehead and a mop of tufty ginger hair like a Highland bull.

She smiles, stacks their plates. Being the good girlfriend is her latest role and she's going to play it to the hilt. It's the least she can do and with every dish she washes, every meal she cooks, she feels slightly less awful about herself.

There's a comfort in this new routine, a homeliness. In the evenings, they all sit in front of the TV together and watch football, then Nancy and Frank go up to his room and she tests him for whatever exam or presentation he has coming up. She reads out questions he's written on pieces of card, about operating systems and data analysis. She should be writing her own essay about The Gendering of Tragedy in Shakespeare, but it's hard to work up the enthusiasm. Her last essay was graded C. *Disappointing – you seem to have lost your focus*, the lecturer wrote in red pen.

She starts to skip seminars, in particular the one she has with Gerry Mac. She didn't know what to expect the first time they came face to face again but, on reflection, she thinks Gerry handled it just right. He looked out at the class, skimming past her face, like nothing had happened between them. He doesn't explain why he behaves like this, not in so many words, but Nancy understands. She knows any sign of favouritism would be unwise.

People would talk and it could get him in trouble with the university. They might misunderstand the situation, think he took advantage of her when really it's almost the other way around. She drank too much, she stayed on after everyone had gone home. As her mother, Theresa, always used to say, a man can only resist so much temptation.

So she understands why he ignores her, she really does. But it's hard to sit there while he jokes with everyone else and tells them his thoughts on Ibsen, which she doesn't actually agree with but knows it's best to keep her opinions to herself.

Shortly after a new girl joins the group, Nancy stops going to that seminar altogether. The girl's name is Belinda and she is on a year-long exchange programme from America. She is willowy, with long blonde hair, and Gerry says she's a prodigious talent.

Nancy continues to spend less time in her own student house and more round at Frank's. It would be nice to go out to the pub every now and then, she thinks. Or a club. But that's not really Frank's thing and, after a while, Nancy agrees that going out does seem like a lot of effort. She can barely keep her eyes open these days and she's often asleep by the time Frank comes up to bed. Besides, she can't face drinking right now, so there's not much point. Even the smell of wine turns her stomach.

She carries the paper bag home from the chemist's under her coat, like contraband, sits on the toilet and watches the second line appear on the pregnancy test. She's been practically living at Frank's and they have both got careless, so she's not totally surprised. But she is terrified.

'It'll be OK,' Frank says. 'I'll support you, whatever you decide to do.'

She goes to the doctor to be sure, comes back and cries for so long that she leaves a damp patch on the collar of his blue shirt, not dissimilar to the one she used to wear with a belt and fishnet tights. That all seems like a long time ago: these days, she prefers comfortable, less showy clothes. Leggings or tracksuit bottoms; baggy sweatshirts. A baseball cap, while her hair grows back.

The appointment is for 11 a.m. but they get there early. She has to fill out a form and sees the receptionist press her lips together as Nancy writes 'student' in the box marked 'Occupation'. Georgie knows what she's thinking. It's what Theresa would say: 'Not so clever now, are we?'

It's 10.55 a.m. and beside her, Frank's leg is jiggling – he can't stop it, he says. She looks at the clock, tries not to think about the 'procedure', as her doctor called it. Instead, she tries to think about eighteenth-century drama, because she has an essay due in two days' time that she hasn't even started. Every time she sits down to write, her brain feels vacant, wiped clean.

The clock says 10.58. Frank is making heavy weather of this, sighing and taking deep breaths, like he's the one who has to walk through that white door in two minutes' time. Then Frank stands up; he's wiping his sweaty palms on his trousers. 'Nance,' he says. 'Come outside, please.'

'I can't, it's nearly time,' she says. But he's holding out his hand, leading her to the door, and then they are outside, standing on the concrete steps. It's a busy road and there's grit in the air, but also the stickiness of cowslip from the cloudy white blooms that are growing on the verge, a smell that reminds her of summers when she was little. Frank takes both her hands and looks into her eyes.

'Let's not do this, Nance. Let's get married instead.'

He's breathing hard, she can feel the tremor in his hands, and it's touching that he's so nervous. She thinks of the stern receptionist back in the waiting room, who is probably calling out Nancy's name this very minute.

She thinks of her essay waiting back in her room and the shame she'd felt as Gerry's eyes glided past her as he announced the upcoming auditions. She looks into Frank's eager brown eyes, so like a puppy's. Frank. Her and Frank, married. Forever.

As if watching from a distance, she hears herself saying, 'Yes, let's do that.' And then they are running, and she thinks about how they might look to the people on the bus that whizzes past, to the car drivers on their way into town, the people off to do their shopping. They will look like a couple who are young and carefree in love.

Back at Frank's place, he treats her like something fragile and special, bringing her a cup of tea and her favourite biscuits on a plate. 'Are you feeling OK?' he asks. 'Not too sick?'

'No, I'm fine. I'm really fine,' she says. And she means it. In her heart of hearts, Nancy knows that her dream of becoming an actor was never going to happen – that play had been a fluke, a one-off. Nancy Jebb isn't cut out to do something like that. Actually, she's fallen so far behind, there's little point in her doing her finals. But being a mother, being Frank's wife – that's a role she can do. It'll be a role for life, one that no one can take from her.

When they tell Frank's housemates that evening, there is roaring and banging on the table. 'Nice one,' says Dougie, high-fiving them both. When Nancy rings her mum, Theresa doesn't say that. In fact, she doesn't say anything. 'Mum, did you hear me? I said I'm getting married,' Nancy repeats down the line, stretching out the curly telephone cord as far as it will go, watching it bounce back into a tight coil.

All her mother says is a single word: 'Why?'

'What a question!' Nancy tries to laugh. 'Well, because we love each other, of course.' She pauses, gathers herself. 'And actually, there's a second bit of news. We're having a baby.'

When Nancy hears the clunk of the receiver, followed by the dull dialling tone, it's a relief. She knows she's a disappointment to them. But she also wonders if Theresa Jebb is a little bit pleased. Because, despite all her big ideas and ambitions, Nancy has proved that she's not so special after all. In fact, she's no better than her own mother.

Chapter Twenty-Two

Nancy, August 1989

'There's only ever been you'

Nancy doesn't believe in superstition, so she's showing Frank the dress she's bought for their wedding day. She and Daisy went to Monsoon on Oxford Street, which was having an end-of-season sale. Daisy said lots of nice things in the changing room, but now Nancy isn't so sure.

The dress is dark-blue velvet, ruched around the neckline. The sort someone else would wear to a ball, but Nancy doesn't have a ball to go to, just her own wedding. It has puff sleeves and she's hoping that, along with the ruching, this will draw attention away from her stomach and comedy-sized breasts.

'What do you think?' she says, turning this way and that. The velvet feels hotter than it did in the changing room and now she thinks about it, she's not sure the ruching is a good idea after all.

'Yeah, nice. Lovely,' Frank says, barely looking. He's lying on the bed, half watching the golf on the portable black-and-white TV. She knows he can't help it. He's a bit hungover after going out with Dougie, who has landed a job in the City that comes with an expense account.

She and Frank are staying with his parents in the suburbs until they get their own place. Surrey is, as Frank keeps saying, an easy commute to London. He's a few weeks into a graduate training programme with a PR company, setting up their database and a computer network.

She kneels down next to the bed, looks up at him in a way that she hopes is coquettish. Frank's eyes don't move from the TV.

'What's wrong?' she asks.

'Nothing.'

'I can tell,' she says. 'Please talk to me.'

Frank gets up to turn off the TV and the room falls silent. 'Sorry,' he says, rubbing his hand over his face. 'Just Dougie being an arse. Last night. Saying stupid things.'

'What?'

'Just stuff. About the wedding, getting hitched so young.' Frank flops back down on to the bed.

'I expect he's a bit jealous,' says Nancy, who thinks that Dougie has a mean streak. 'Little Miss Marxist' he used to call her, back in the first year when Nancy painted messages on placards and went on marches.

'Yeah.' Frank is inspecting his fingernails now, still not looking at her. She waits, because she can tell there's more to come.

'Just that he said something about you and that bloke, Gerry Mac. The drama lecturer. Something about how he had a thing for you.'

A heat spreads out from Nancy's gut, a molten slide of fear. 'Oh, that's so stupid,' she says, and she stands, starts unzipping the dress, but the zip won't budge. Already, it's too tight – what's it going to be like in two weeks, at the register office? She tugs again, feels sweat prickling her armpits. There's a rasping sound, but it's not the zip, it's the seam.

'Yeah, that's what I told him. He said there was talk in the last term. About the after-party for the play. You were dancing, he was looking at you, I dunno . . .' Frank tails off.

Nancy breathes in, gives the zip a sharp tug and it slides down. She steps out of the dress, inspects the small rip that has opened up in the side seam.

'Honestly, I paid £60 for this,' she says. She feels exposed, standing here in Frank's childhood bedroom in her maternity bra and big knickers. Looking down, her stomach is as swollen as a beer gut, traced with blue veins.

Frank doesn't reply, turns away on to his side.

Nancy slides on to the bed next to him. Breathes into his nape, reaches over to hug his chest. She pulls him in tight. 'Frank, don't be silly. There's only ever been you.'

Still his body is stiff, unyielding.

'I love you,' she says. 'We're having a baby. This is all I could want.'

Gradually, his body relaxes and he grabs her hand. 'I know. I love you too.'

A few stitches should sort that seam, Nancy thinks. The dress will be good as new. On the day, nobody will know any different.

Chapter
Twenty-Three

NANCY, 1990

'THE BEST JOB IN THE WORLD'

The baby cries a lot. More, Nancy thinks, than can possibly be normal. The jagged sound lives inside her head day and night, even in the brief stretches when the baby gives up and falls into a jerky sleep.

They name the baby Georgina, after Frank's great-grandmother, but shortened to Georgie. Nancy could gaze at her baby for hours; she's transfixed, filled with love that feels both wonderful and like a punch in the gut. It's a love like none she's experienced before.

But between those moments of wonder, caring for the baby is relentless. Rather like the birth, no one ever warned Nancy about this. Can it be right, she worries, for a baby to cry this much – or is there something wrong with her? Nancy carries the baby everywhere, she rubs her back and she lays the baby over her knees, like she's been shown. 'Could be colic,' the health visitor says, already packing away her paperwork, checking the time on the little upside-down watch pinned to her tunic. 'They all grow out of it. In the end.'

Nancy would like to know when this end might come, because she's half mad with the crying, the nappies and the laundry. But most of all, the lack of sleep. It feels like a very precise form of torture, one that hurts every part of her body but coalesces into a tight band of pain around her head.

When Frank gets home from work, she can't form full sentences. But Frank is tired too. The job is demanding, no one in the PR company understands why he's trying to install a computer network. 'They want to stick to their typewriters, Nance – typewriters!'

Nancy couldn't care less what these young and thrusting PR types want. After walking up and down the hallway with the baby in the sling all afternoon, she is teary with fatigue and her front is a wet mess of the baby's tears and snot and milky spittle. 'Can you just . . .' She starts to undo the poppers of the baby's sling, desperate to pass over this hot, wriggling bundle of fury.

'Sure, just need to jump in the shower first.' Frank chucks the baby under her damp chin as he passes by, loosens his red tie.

Nancy would dearly love to wash her hair, which smells of sour milk and scalp grease. If she ever makes it into the shower, she has to put the baby in a rocker a few feet away. Outraged, the baby screams and Nancy rubs soap over her body as quickly as she can. 'Sorry, sorry, I'm coming!' she calls out, pulling on clothes that snag on her still-wet skin.

But she's being unfair, because Frank works hard too. At the office and then on the house. At the weekends, he sands the floors, peels away ragged strips of wallpaper. They have bought what Frank calls a 'doer-upper'. It's also called a 'repo house', which Nancy learns means repossession. Frank says it's a good opportunity. This neighbourhood is on the up – they might even make money on it, he says, dipping his paintbrush into a tin of Brilliant White.

One evening, the phone rings. Nancy leaps up to get it because, for once, the baby has fallen asleep early. It's Daisy – she and some of the old uni gang are in the area. They've seen a play at the Tricycle Theatre. Can they pop by?

They troop in clutching bottles of red wine, bringing a steely cold in on their coats. Nancy watches helplessly as they rummage around in the kitchen looking for glasses, talking and laughing loudly.

She hears the baby's cry before anyone else – it's real this time, not the echo that lives in her head – and runs up the stairs, taking them two at a time. She brings Georgie back down, but she won't settle, kicks and roars. When Daisy holds her, the baby's mouth opens wider still, an ugly red maw.

Frank leaves them to it – he has to be up early. Nancy tries to be the fun person she once was, the crazy, kooky one who would do anything for a laugh. But really, she just wants her friends to leave and, eventually, they do.

The baby is around six months old when Frank starts staying out late on Friday nights. 'It's all about making connections – reckon I could pick up some freelance work,' he says the first time, ringing her from the phone in a pub. When he slides into bed, the glowing hands of the clock radio tell Nancy it's almost 2 a.m. Frank's hair smells of smoke and beer and some scent from the outside world that she can't place.

On Sundays, they drive to Surrey for tea with Frank's parents.

'Aren't you lucky,' says Frank's mother, Lorna, when the menfolk go out to the shed to find a drill. 'Frank's doing so well at work – and working all the hours on the house too.'

Nancy can feel Lorna staring at her T-shirt, so she looks down and tries to scrape a flaky brown stain off her top with her fingernail. It's Weetabix. Georgie is barely seven months old, but Nancy is desperate to try and get some solids into her. Helplessly, Nancy feels a tear run down her cheek. She watches as it lands on her T-shirt, then another.

Her mother-in-law watches too, then pats her hand. 'There there,' she says. 'She still not sleeping?'

Nancy shakes her head, wipes her cheeks with her sleeves.

'It gets easier.'

But when? Nancy wants to ask. Because she's not sure she can cope with this much longer.

'Perhaps it's time to get out a bit more,' Lorna says. 'Try a mums and babies group?'

It's a struggle to get them both ready in time for the 11 a.m. Baby Singalong session in the local church hall, but Nancy does it, arriving with seconds to spare. She's panting a little as she joins the others sitting cross-legged in the circle on the floor, places Georgie on her lap, like all the other mums. The leader puts on a cassette tape and all the women 'help' their babies clap hands and of course they also sing the words because their babies can't speak yet, let alone sing. Afterwards, a tray of drinks is brought round: cups of tea or instant coffee and custard cream biscuits.

'Ah, finally. Our reward,' Nancy says to the woman next to her.

'Yes,' smiles the woman. She wears a lilac polo neck that has a slight sheen and an embroidered waistcoat. Her trousers are elasticated at the waist. But Nancy is in no position to be snobby about clothes: her uniform of T-shirt and tracksuit bottoms is long overdue an overhaul. Her hair has grown back to a tricky in-between length that she's always tucking behind her ears.

'But, really,' continues the woman, 'our babies are our reward.'

Nancy almost chokes on her custard cream as she lets out a laugh. Finally, she thinks, a friend. Someone with a sense of humour. Still laughing, she turns to the woman, but then she stops.

'Yes,' the woman continues gravely. 'We're very lucky. This is the best job in the world.'

On the walk home, Nancy talks to her baby, because she doesn't have anyone else to tell these things to. Georgie regards her with dark, all-seeing eyes. 'I'm sorry, I don't know how to do this,' Nancy says. 'I think I've made a terrible mistake.'

Chapter Twenty-Four

GEORGIE

The viral story of a woman who rescued someone's lost child has definitely gone cold. Georgie keeps refreshing her news feeds, but nothing has changed.

Her mouth is sour and her stomach is growling with hunger, but they can't afford to stop again. The sooner this trip is done and dusted, she thinks, the better.

Every now and then she steals a glance at Dan, his face immovable as stone. But of course this is what Dan does: he covers up, he keeps pretending everything is fine. It's what he did when they were little, even when their world had caved in.

The driving app says they are 238 miles away – still another six hours and thirty minutes to go and this car is unbelievably slow and uncomfortable. Georgie tries to arch her back to ease the stiffness that's taking hold, but this makes the seat belt cut in under her bump, which doesn't feel right. Then she tries angling herself to the side, but that's no better. She's like an old dog that can't settle in its bed. In the end, she goes back to sitting squarely in the seat and looking straight ahead.

When her phone lights up, she scrabbles to open it. The hashtag #mysteryrescuewoman is trending again, because a reporter from the *Daily Record* has struck out and gone to the island. He's posted footage of himself standing outside a small stone building with a green front door, shouting into his microphone. Georgie watches the video three times, holding the phone to her ear so she can hear his words above the roar of the car's engine.

'I caught the first ferry over, but I can report there's nothing to see on the island. Clearly, someone was living in this bothy, but it is empty. I spoke to the shopkeeper and the ferry master, but locals remain tight-lipped. It seems likely that the woman known only as Nan has left the island, but nobody has any idea where she has gone.'

Here they are, on a motorway in the middle of Cumbria, and Nancy has outwitted them again. She could be anywhere by now. Georgie gazes over at the stream of traffic on the other side of the motorway. Nancy could be whizzing past them at this very moment, travelling in the opposite direction.

She tries to keep her voice calm and even: 'Dan, when you see somewhere safe to stop, I think we should pull over.'

'You're joking – you need the loo, again?' Dan says, but his scowl melts away when he sees her face.

'No. It's Nancy. She's gone, Dan. We've lost her.'

It's another ten miles before Dan can stop and it's a desolate place, just a toilet block, a burger van and a few pale patches on the wet tarmac where cars have recently departed.

'This is pointless,' Georgie cries out in frustration. 'We've got no chance of finding her now. I'm sorry for dragging you into this. I should have just stayed at home.'

She's crying properly now, the sort where the jags take on their own rhythm and it's hard to stop.

'Well, she clearly doesn't want to be found. And don't apologise. She's my mother too. Besides, as you might have guessed, it wasn't like I was doing anything at home. Playing *Call of Duty* with other sad losers. Watching reruns of *Seinfeld*. Watering Mandy's plants.'

Georgie blows her nose. 'That does sound a bit sad.'

He rewards her with the slenderest smile.

She thinks back to when Dan went off to university – an A* student who was a whizz at maths. He studied Statistics because he was good at it and he liked the idea of certitude, the predictable relationships between numbers. But he'd talked about taking a year out before he decided what he wanted to do. 'Don't want to get stuck behind a desk for the rest of my life,' he'd joked.

Except as soon as he'd graduated, Dan had been headhunted by a big insurance firm who made him an offer he couldn't refuse. And he'd ended up sitting in that glass corner office, drawing up presentations and reports – all the things he'd sworn he'd never do.

Then, with shame, Georgie remembers how she and Finn would talk about Dan behind his back. 'He's gone full-on corporate. The complete sell-out,' Finn would say. 'He just wants to impress our dad,' she'd reply, and together they would sneer at Dan's suits, his nine-to-five lifestyle, his company car, all the while pretending they had it sorted – the creative couple who were going to amaze the world with their photography. They already had an exhibition lined up. One day, their work would be collectable – and finally her dad would realise who was the talented one.

But now Georgie is a wedding photographer with no clients and Dan is unemployed and spends his days playing *Call of Duty* and Georgie isn't sure either of them has won anything, or if there was ever a competition, except in her head.

She reaches for her water bottle. 'Have you told Dad what you've been going through – about losing your job? And about Mandy?'

'Nope,' Dan says. 'I have the family tradition to think of: never talk about things. Never say what you feel. Keep smiling and pretending everyone is having fun.'

Georgie thinks of those Sunday carvery lunches in Redhill, Dan jollying everyone along, exclaiming at how 'yummy' the food was. He played his role to the hilt, while Georgie scratched her arms and sulked and Irena sipped her Chardonnay and tried to make conversation. Then the four of them would return to that empty, bleached-clean house, where neither child felt able to say how they felt, let alone speak their real mother's name.

A fine mizzle has frosted the windscreen and Dan flicks a switch to make the stumpy wipers swish back and forth. Georgie thinks of that Scottish news reporter, shouting into the wind. He beat them to the island, but he still found nothing.

But then Georgie realises that she and Dan do have one important advantage over that reporter. They don't know *where* Nancy is, but they know *who* she is. And they have access to all the people she once knew.

'You don't suppose,' she starts, 'that now her cover's blown, Nancy might decide to come clean, go back to her old life? That while we're charging up the motorway, she could be heading south to find us?'

Dan looks sceptical. 'Sorry, Georgie, but if she wanted a reunion, she could have done that a long time ago.'

Georgie runs her hands over her stomach, feels her hope fade. 'Yes, I suppose so. And we looked, didn't we? Dad looked – he tried really hard to find her.'

She can remember their father sitting in the hallway of their old London house, making endless phone calls. First of all, he rang around all the neighbourhood mums, then Nancy's family. Grandma and Grandpa Jebb. Great-aunt Annette, their grandmother's sister. Then he tried her old university friends.

'Yeah, I guess.'

'What do you mean, you guess? I remember it, Dan. He called the police, rang Grandma, all the neighbours . . .'

'Well, of course. That was a week or so after she didn't come home. But then he tried again, a bit later . . .' Dan trails off.

'Later? Like when he applied for a dissolution of marriage?'

'Yes, I suppose it was.'

And then it clicks. After they moved to Redhill, Dan became Dad's wingman and Georgie – well, Georgie was busy being Georgie, the one who couldn't do anything right. Who was untidy and clumsy and late for school and failed exams. And when things got worse, when she'd been caught shoplifting or smoking, her dad would look at her and say, 'Oh Georgie, if only you weren't so like your mother.'

But Dad and Dan – his 'Danny Boy' – made quite the team. The police had soon given up looking for Nancy – there was no evidence of foul play and she'd taken her passport. Then she'd sent those two postcards, proof that she was alive in a country thousands of miles away. So Dan and their dad did a bit of investigating together: a boys' project, with all the files kept on Dad's new computer. There was even a spreadsheet, so Dan could mark off names as their dad rang people.

'I'm sure you two had it covered,' she says, her voice hardening. 'Did you tick him off your list, then?' She glares at Dan. 'He whose name must not be spoken?'

Of course, she's talking about Gerry, the man who barged into their lives and ruined everything. 'I mean, on the news, people are describing this "Nan" as a loner, but who's to say that she's not still with him? Her older man. He could have been living in that bothy too – whittling sticks, weaving wicker. Whatever losers like that do.'

'But that's the weird thing,' Dan says. 'Dad never managed to track Gerry down.'

Even now, hearing his name feels wrong, because it had been her guilty secret for so long. The first time Georgie dared say it out loud, she and Dan were sitting side by side on his bedroom floor, plotting their rescue mission to Thailand that they both knew, deep down, would never happen.

'I think I know who she's with,' she'd whispered. 'There was a man. He's called Gerry—' And Dan had swiftly reached out and squeezed her hand, a gesture that told her it was OK to stop there. That she didn't need to say any more because he knew this too.

Because while Georgie hadn't progressed beyond her fantasies of hacking through jungles to find their mother, Dan and their dad had teamed up for a far more grown-up search, one that involved spreadsheets and phone calls. It hadn't involved Georgie – but clearly it had covered Gerry.

'Yeah, Dad contacted their old university,' Dan continues. 'But it turned out Gerry Mac had been sacked years before. Dad reckoned there was some scandal that was hushed up. Something about an American exchange student. Then he tried various theatre groups and Mum's old drama friends, but he drew a complete blank – for Gerry as well as Nancy. There were no company details, no tax records, no property in his name – the man seemed to have disappeared off the face of the earth.'

'He was a crafty sort of person,' says Georgie. 'So that doesn't really surprise me.' Georgie had been excluded from those father-and-son investigations, but over the years she too had googled Gerry's name and her mother's – with zero results.

There's a band of pressure around her head tightening, because things aren't quite adding up. Georgie knows she needs to think harder. 'So, did you keep checking, with Grandma and Grandpa, with Great-aunt Annette, with Mum's old friends?'

'Yes, Dad would do his ring-round to see if anyone had heard from her and then I'd tick off their names on the spreadsheet,' Dan says wearily. 'As time went by, I suppose it tailed off a bit. It went from monthly to every few months, then once I was off at university it became far less regular.'

Their grandparents are both dead now, but Grandma Jebb's sister, Annette, is still alive. She used to send Georgie and Dan Christmas cards with the same anodyne message each year: *Happy Christmas, Best wishes from Great-aunt Annette.*

'Do you think it's worth trying anyone who was on the list now? Like Annette – just in case?'

Dan shrugs, gets out his phone – his normal one – and puts it on speaker. Annette picks up on the second ring and as soon as Georgie hears her voice, it takes her back in time because her great-aunt sounds exactly like Grandma Jebb: that careful enunciation that tries to be posh but can't disguise the regional lilt underneath. But as they explain what's happening, Great-aunt Annette's words speed up and her accent slips. 'Eh, what do you mean, she's back? Oh, my goodness, when? And where is she now?'

As Dan explains the little they know, Georgie feels her hope ebbing away because it's clear Annette hasn't heard from Nancy. She leans forward and chips in: 'So, just to be clear, you haven't heard anything in all these years – no change since our dad last checked in?'

'I'm afraid not. To be honest, I feared she was long since dead. So this is wonderful news that she's alive. Please, let me know how you get on.'

'Of course. We definitely will,' Georgie says. What a shame, she thinks – the distance that opened up between them all in the aftermath of Nancy leaving. It had been the same story with their grandparents – a few faltering visits, until their father explained Grandma and Grandpa Jebb couldn't do the long journey to Redhill any more. There was talk of her and Dan travelling to Stamford for a summer holiday, but the invitation never came.

'Goodbye then, and good luck,' says Annette. Dan is about to end the call when they hear Annette call out, almost as an afterthought.

'Oh – I don't know if I'm speaking out of turn, but you mentioned your dad calling me.'

'Yes, he checked in every few months,' says Dan. 'I helped him at first. He told me who he'd called and I ticked your name off a list.'

'I'm sorry,' Annette says, 'but it wasn't like that. Your father rang me once, shortly after Nancy left home. But that was it. I used to ring and leave messages, but Frank never called me back. After you moved, I carried on sending the odd letter, cards to you both at Christmas, but I never got a reply.'

'But he rang you, I ticked your name . . .' Dan repeats, doubt creeping into his voice.

'It was the same for Theresa, your grandmother.' Annette is getting into her stride now. 'Your father made it clear he didn't want to keep in contact. He told her he was sorry, but you two didn't want to visit any more. I know my sister was a difficult woman, but it broke her heart – losing her grandchildren as well as her daughter.'

After the call ends, Georgie and Dan sit staring ahead, neither saying a word. Outside, trucks come and go; the man in the burger van appears at his window now and again to hand customers teas in white polystyrene cups.

Their father lied to them. He didn't check in with Nancy's family. He told their grandparents that Georgie and Dan didn't want to visit.

'So, did you actually hear these phone calls?' Georgie says.

'Now you mention it, I suppose I didn't. He just gave me the dates and the outcomes – "No contact" – and I'd tick them off. But why would he do that? Lie to me, to both of us? I mean, Grandma and Grandpa Jebb weren't a barrel of laughs, but they were our family.'

'We didn't even go to their funerals,' Georgie says.

'So now I'm wondering, if he didn't make those calls to her family, how hard did he really look for Nancy?' Dan says. 'Did he assume she was dead, so it wasn't worth looking? Or did he know where she was hiding all along?'

The car isn't moving, but Georgie finds herself gripping the seat because another wave of vertigo is swooping back in. But this time her dizziness feels different; it feels a lot like fear. Georgie has sent them on this journey into the past, but now she has no idea where it will take them.

Chapter Twenty-Five

'Hello, you'

When baby Georgie is one year old, Nancy stops eating. Not entirely, of course, but she manages to whittle her diet down to the barest essentials. She allows herself a black coffee in the morning and an apple for lunch, a nice crisp green one that is so sharp it almost hurts to bite into it.

In the evening she cooks for Frank, but doesn't touch that food. Instead, she has two slices of crispbread, charred under the grill until they are black, topped with a thin smear of low-calorie margarine. Sometimes, she blanches slices of raw courgette in spitty boiling water, drains them and sprinkles them with salt. She can no longer stomach sweet things; nothing passes her lips unless it is bitter and frugal and hurts her.

At first, she gets compliments. The churchy mums at the baby group who usually ignore her exclaim and tell Nancy how well she's looking, how they wish they could lose the baby weight that easily. But Frank says nothing, even when she wears vests that show her bony arms and shorts that reveal the newly carved hollow between her thighs. Her milk begins to dwindle and Georgie cries even harder, bangs an angry fist on Nancy's chest.

Nancy develops toothache, on both sides. At first she thinks it's because her jaw is always tightly clenched, but then her molars start to wobble in their sockets. It's as if the baby is draining any remaining goodness out of her.

Her mother, Theresa, arrives for a rare visit. 'Really, you're taking this too far,' Theresa says on day two. 'You can be too thin, you know.' She puts baby Georgie in the buggy, bumps it down the steps and marches off down the road.

Nancy flops on to the sofa with relief because this is what she needs – help with the baby, so she might get a grip on this impossible yet tedious life of hers, which is spinning out of her control.

But thirty minutes later, Theresa reappears, in an officious rustle of plastic bags. She's been to the supermarket, bought cereal and milk and a sliced loaf of bread. A nice pork chop for Frank, that was in the reduced section. Finally, with a flourish, she produces a box of Milk Tray chocolates, which she lays down on the coffee table. 'There you go – a treat, while you feed,' she says, handing the bawling baby back to Nancy. 'She's hungry again.' Obediently, in a fever of tiredness, Nancy unbuttons her top.

'This one is going to be trouble, mark my words,' Theresa says. Then, as she walks out of the room, 'Still, you've made your bed – now you have to lie in it.'

As soon as her mother goes home, Nancy shoves the chocolates into the bin, still wrapped in their shiny cellophane.

The thinner she gets, the closer Nancy gets to her goal. She would like to be invisible, as light as air, so that no one will notice her. But this confuses her, because at the same time she longs to be seen. She wants to shout at Frank, *Look at me! This is how I feel inside*. She wants him to see the ugly tangled thoughts that live inside her, to understand that she can't do this, the mothering that everyone else seems to find so easy. So natural.

But all Frank says is, 'What more do you want from me?' He works hard, he tells her, he's keeping them afloat. At night, he turns away from her and she can't blame him. She is a jumble of bones that clash and clatter and don't fit into the spaces she has to inhabit: the playgroup, the brightly lit aisles of the supermarket, even their home.

One lunchtime, as she's mashing a banana for Georgie, the phone rings and when she picks it up, a voice says, 'Hello, you.'

He doesn't need to tell her his name, she would know his voice anywhere. The way he draws out his words, as if he's really thinking them through. Or maybe just thinking about her. She can hear the desire in his voice: it's as if someone is reaching into her gut, twisting it into a tight, hot knot of anticipation.

Gerry talks about how he's parted ways with the university because he couldn't tolerate their narrow-minded views. 'They are self-appointed gatekeepers, Nancy – who legitimises their decisions?'

'I don't know,' Nancy replies. The phone is fixed to the wall in the hall and, from here, she can see Georgie sitting in her high chair. She watches as the baby plunges her fist into the bowl of mashed banana, looks at it intently then rubs it into her hair. Nancy turns away, so she doesn't have to look.

Gerry is talking about an improv show he's directing, how he wants to take it on tour, but he fears it will be too avant-garde for most audiences. 'For the middle-class masses, the suburban house-wives. The office drones,' he says, with a light laugh. 'But I'm on the road anyway. Touring in my own way.'

Nancy is remembering the Gerry Mac who used to stand at the front of a lecture theatre, the man who directed her with such enthusiasm. Who called Nancy a prodigious talent and dressed her in an orange minidress to look like Mia Farrow. The way he used to look at her, how it made her feel seen.

And now, finally, Gerry is telling her what she needs to hear. 'You understood, didn't you – that I couldn't show my feelings for you back then, Nancy. It hurt me physically to stifle them. I didn't trust myself to look at you.' The relief is a warm rush that fills Nancy up. She knew this must have been the reason, but it's nice to have it confirmed – to know they are on the same wavelength. That they always were.

'The gossip – it would have been so damaging,' he says. 'For my reputation,' he clarifies.

Gerry got her phone number from Daisy – she's running a drama collective in east London – but now he has Nancy's address, he'll try and drop by next time he's in London. He has a few meetings lined up: 'Producers, casting directors, you know.'

'Sure, I mean, I'm usually in . . .' Nancy starts to say, but Gerry's ringing from a call box and the pips are going, telling them their time is up.

◆ ◆ ◆

Two weeks later, she's walking back from the supermarket with the buggy, shopping bags looped over each handle, the plastic rain cover pulled down over Georgie. She's been up most of the night teething, but now, finally, she's sound asleep. As Nancy turns into their road, she sees a hulking grey van parked on the corner. It's an unusual sight: rusted wheel arches, the writing on the side roughly painted over and the back windows covered with pieces of plywood. Her first thought is, *Frank won't like that being parked there, it brings down the tone of the neighbourhood.*

Then the back door swings open and he's standing right in front of her. Shorter than she remembers, a little rounder, but it's the same Gerry Mac. He has that same twinkle in his eye. This van, he explains, is his home now: houses are for the bourgeoisie. Nancy rolls the buggy back and forth on the pavement so Georgie will stay asleep, and resists the urge to glance up the road at their very own bourgeois semi.

Nancy is lucky to catch him, Gerry says, because he's off to see a casting director tomorrow, discussing the up-and-coming faces. 'Your look is very "now", you know.' He puts his head to one side, appraises her with his professional eye. 'The gaunt look.'

Inside Gerry's van, the air smells of unwashed sheets and the tinned soup that Gerry warms up on a camping stove for his meals. There's just enough room for the buggy in there, if Nancy sits on the fold-down bed, next to Gerry.

'All it takes is me putting in a good word. Right face, right time,' Gerry is saying, adjusting the dials on his new video camera. 'Let's start, shall we.'

Nancy feels unprepared, she hasn't even brushed her hair. 'All part of the look,' Gerry says, zooming in and out. Then, because the casting agent will expect it, he takes some footage of her in her bra. When he asks her to take it off, he's impeccably polite.

'Perfect. Very now. Very Kate Moss,' he whispers. Nancy isn't sure who he's talking about, so she keeps looking at the camera. The rest doesn't take long and she keeps watching the camera's unblinking red eye until he's done. Briefly, she feels the flicker of an old memory, as if she's desired. As if she is special.

Afterwards, Gerry opens the back door and helps her lift the buggy out. It's only then that he seems to notice its occupant.

'Ah, good sleeper, then?'

'Not particularly.'

Nancy knows what she's expected to do next, just as when older women stop her in the supermarket and ask if they can have a peek. But this feels different – wrong somehow, exposing her baby to this situation. It was better when Georgie was hidden by the rain cover, oblivious to Gerry and his dirty van and the red eye of his video camera.

But Gerry is waiting so she shyly unties the cover and draws back the hood to show Georgie's sleeping face. Her flushed cheek, a glimpse of pink dungarees.

'A girl then. And she has your hair.'

'Yes,' Nancy says, pulling the hood down again firmly. 'It's turned chilly, better get her home,' she says.

It's only when she's standing in her kitchen that Nancy realises she left the two bags of shopping in Gerry's van. She can't go back, not now, and she stands and howls with frustration. Then the baby wakes and then she's screaming too, red-faced, straining at her buggy straps to get out.

The next morning, when Nancy walks to the shops to buy yesterday's tins and packets and jars all over again, the van is gone, leaving only an oily stain on the road. Nancy never hears from the casting agent. She supposes the gaunt look didn't appeal after all.

'We need a holiday,' Frank announces and he finds a cheap package deal to Greece, a last-minute thing. Nancy isn't sure: she dreads the hassle of the airport, knows Georgie will be a nightmare on the flight. But she's wrong. Georgie is fine, then they spend a week lying on the beach, reading and sleeping. Georgie is passed around the taverna, like a smiley chubby doll, while they eat (yes, Nancy eats too, ravenous for the olives and feta and slices of bread because it feels as if normal rules are suspended here).

They drink retsina and they talk. Nancy even plucks up the courage to tell Frank that she's finding it hard, being a mum. She needs to do something beyond laundry and cooking and cleaning

141

and shaking maracas at Baby Singalong. She feels lost, she says, like she has no substance.

'Let's look at courses for you when we get back. You could even finish your degree. My mum can come into town and babysit a few times a week. We'll make this work,' says Frank.

Frank has caught the sun and when he smiles she sees what a handsome, good man he is.

Back in London, Nancy sends off for a drama school prospectus, but she gets no further. She's been throwing up her breakfast and her breasts are sore and she knows, without even taking a test, that she's pregnant.

This time, she and Frank watch together as the blue line appears and then Frank hugs her hard. 'Amazing,' he says. 'Brilliant.'

They both know this is the fresh start they need. There will be no talk of procedures, no rumours spread by Dougie or her mother's stony silences. They are married and they live in a three-bed semi in Kensal Rise with a kitchen that is painted sunshine yellow. This will make them a proper family.

Already, she can barely remember Gerry's visit, his squinting eye beside the glassy lens of his camera.

'I'm going to be a dad!' says Frank.

Nancy laughs. 'Well, you are already.' But she knows what he means. This time, it will be different.

Already, Frank is dialling his parents' number. 'Yes, a baby! We only just found out . . . I know – imagine, if it's a boy. How perfect would that be?'

Chapter
Twenty-Six

GEORGIE

It's Dan who breaks the silence. 'So, do we ring him – ask why he lied to us?'

'Who, Dad?'

'Of course, Dad.'

'Well, I can't face it. Not right now,' Georgie says. She imagines what their father might be doing on a Tuesday afternoon in February. He got a good payoff from his PR company a few years back. These days, he volunteers at a food bank on Fridays. On the weekend, he does long rides with his cycling club. But today, he'll probably be at home, reading the latest autobiography by a sports personality or disgraced politician. Later, he might watch a quiz on the TV or do a sudoku puzzle.

Finally, their father has all he ever wanted – a small, perfectly ordinary life. She pictures him picking up their call, how his face will change as they ask, *Dad, why did you pretend you were looking for Mum, when you were doing nothing of the sort?*

What, she wonders, lay behind Frank's subterfuge? Was it because finding Nancy would have spoiled the new life he'd made with Irena? Or did he know more than he was letting on?

She feels tears welling. 'He didn't want to forget her. He wanted to erase her.'

Dan looks at her for a long time. Then he says something strange: 'Sometimes, we make ourselves forget things. To protect ourselves.'

'So are you saying Dad was protecting us? Because I think that's a warped kind of parenting.'

'No,' Dan says carefully. 'I'm just saying that . . . it happens. Someone once explained to me that when things are too difficult to deal with, to "process",' – here he makes quote marks in the air – 'our brain shuts things away. This person described it as putting memories in a box, until we feel able to open it.' He pauses, checks Georgie is still listening. 'So maybe Dad did a version of that. He closed the box for us.'

'Wow,' Georgie says. 'You've been doing some serious work on yourself, Dan. How much does therapy like that cost per hour?'

Dan shakes his head. 'Georgie, come on. I'm just trying to understand why he might have done it.'

'Sorry.' She feels chastened. Dan is only trying to help – just as he always did, back when they were a team. 'I kind of wish I'd never started this journey,' she says, 'but, Dan . . .'

'Yeah?'

'I'm glad we're talking again. Really, I am.'

'Me too.'

Outside the car windows there is little to see except scrubby grass and wet road. Their map app is still plaintively telling them their destination is six hours and twenty minutes away. Dan swipes it off the phone screen. They are a few miles shy of Gretna; they didn't even make it into Scotland before Nancy brought their journey to an abrupt end.

'So,' he says. 'Shall I take you home?'

Georgie has no idea. All she can think about is how tired she is, how her limbs feel weighed down, waterlogged, and her mind is a jumble of confusing thoughts. Niggling snippets and scenes that make no sense. She shakes her head, trying to ward off the next swoop of dizziness, the ringing in her ears.

Then she sees her own phone screen light up – the hashtag #mysteryrescuewoman is back in business. She scrolls through, then lurches forward, points at the radio. 'Quick, how do you make this thing tune in to Chat Time FM?'

'I thought you hated the radio . . .'

'Just do it,' she snaps. Someone has had the bright idea of launching a radio appeal to find the mystery woman who carried a child down from certain death on a hillside, but then disappeared without a trace. The parents of the child have offered a reward for information that will help find her.

'There's a phone-in,' she says. 'It's not just us, Dan – people all over are looking for her.'

For the next twenty-five minutes, Georgie and Dan sit in the cramped car and listen to random people claiming to have seen 'Nan'. A man in Sunderland swears she's working in his local fish and chip shop: 'She gave me a wink, and an extra scoop of chips,' he says by way of proof. A woman with a Glaswegian accent swears Nancy used to sleep rough under the railway arches. A mother of two in Peckham, south London, is convinced that Nancy is the local lollipop woman. 'She always has a cheery smile,' she adds.

'Oh, come on, this is just nonsense. Filling airtime, giving nutters something to fixate on,' says Dan. 'I think the most sensible thing to do is head home, let all this settle. I know some things don't add up, but then we can talk to Dad – get his side of the story.' He leans forward to switch the radio off, but Georgie grabs his wrist.

'Wait,' she hisses.

A new caller has come on and Georgie freezes as his voice fills the car. 'Well, good afternoon,' he says, stretching out the words in a deliberately ponderous way. 'I think you'll find I have some useful information. The woman you're looking for is called Nancy Jebb. She was a promising student of mine many years ago. If she's listening, I'm keen to see her again – to talk over old times.'

Georgie spins the volume knob, but it's too late – he's rung off. The radio presenter cuts in: 'Well, that was Gerry from Hoyton Beck, who says he taught our mystery rescue woman and seems to have given us her full name – how extraordinary.'

'Gerry,' Georgie gasps. 'Gerry Mac. Who wants to talk over old times.'

Long before they stopped saying Nancy's name at home, this was the other name that Georgie and Dan didn't dare say out loud. The last clear memory she has of that man is bumping into him on their family holiday in Wales. And less than a week later, their mother disappeared.

But did their father ever go in search of Gerry Mac – surely the most promising lead to finding Nancy? And if not, why not? Is it possible that this Gerry had some malign hold over both her parents?

Georgie feels wide awake, a fresh urgency flooding through her, and she reaches for her phone. 'Dan, look, this Hoyton Beck – it's only a few hours away,' she says. 'It's practically on our route back down south.'

But Dan is shaking his head. 'Hold on. Let's not jump to conclusions.'

'What? It was definitely him.' She stares at Dan. 'He knew her name. The way he spoke . . .'

'Even if it was him, I'm not sure going to find him is such a good idea . . .' Dan says in an oddly detached voice. 'I don't recommend this, Georgie. Seeing him could bring back all sorts of . . . associations.'

This is infuriating – why is everyone so scared of Gerry Mac?

'Come on, Dan,' she says. 'I have a feeling that if anyone can find her, it's him. Or maybe Nancy heard him on the radio too and she's on her way to see him, right this minute.'

'I really don't think . . .'

But she can tell he's wavering. 'Dan, aren't you a little bit curious? Please. We've come this far – we can't give up now. He's our only hope.'

Her brother's mouth is a thin, tight line, but he does as she asks. He taps the name of the town into his phone, replaces the phone in the rubber cup-holder. The map app announces it's re-routing. Then, 'Your destination is two hours away. You are on the fastest route.'

Chapter Twenty-Seven

Nancy, 1992

'It's all working out beautifully'

Right from the start, Dan is a very different baby to Georgie. He cries, of course, but not the ear-splitting, never-ending sound that Nancy remembers from the first time around. Even his birth is different. With Georgie, Nancy's waters had broken all over the floor of the delivery suite, streaked with green and brown. 'Meconium,' the midwife said grimly, snapping on a pair of plastic gloves. Then there was prodding and poking and someone told her sternly to 'Push, right now' because her baby could be in distress.

With Dan, she could swear her waters smelt sweet, of country verges and wild roses, and although it was painful, he arrived not in a rush but in a measured, almost gentle way. 'What a darling,' the Australian midwife said. And while Georgie had been born bawling, with an angry sweep of brown hair, Dan had just the finest light down. He gazed up at Nancy calmly, as if working out how best to approach this thing called life.

Back at home, between feeds Dan is content to lie in his pram in the garden, looking up at the patterns made by the dancing leaves of their apple tree. There is none of the pacing back and forth and snot and screaming she had with Georgie. 'You're wonderful. You're doing so well,' Frank tells her.

Her mother, Theresa, also seems begrudgingly impressed when they come to visit. 'He's a good lad,' she says. 'A fine boy,' her father adds, holding the swaddled baby in his arms. 'With a fine name.' She watches as Georgie goes over and strokes the baby's head, before turning away, already bored at all this fuss about her baby brother.

But, generally, it's all wonderful. She takes them both to Toddler Time, where Georgie can play with water and sand and Nancy can chat with the other mums. But something is niggling Nancy.

That visceral pull she felt with Georgie, the way Nancy used to sit bolt upright when she heard her cry, it's missing. This baby does all the right things at the right times: at six weeks, he lifts his chubby fist in the air and studies it with wonder. At eight weeks, he starts trying to raise his own head. Nancy notes these things with relief – her baby is normal. But they do not move her.

When he gives her his first proper smile, Nancy feels barely a flicker of emotion. She writes it in her diary anyway, so she can share the news with Frank when he gets home.

She knows it can't be true, because she never lost sight of him in the hospital, but it's almost as if her new baby is a changeling. Or perhaps he was born sensing that it would be best all round if he doesn't make a fuss about things. Either way, it feels as if the volume on life has been turned down and although Nancy craved a placid baby, it feels eerie. It's not what she's used to.

On the other hand, Georgie, aged two, continues to create chaos. She upends a tray of building blocks on to the wooden floor with a crash, just as the baby is falling asleep. She refuses to use the potty, demanding to go back into nappies, and she has tantrums – in the supermarket, at the park and every time they go past an ice-cream van.

One afternoon, while Nancy is feeding the baby, Georgie finds a set of crayons and draws shapes all over the living-room walls. The jagged lines leave thick, waxy ridges that no amount of scrubbing can get off.

Frank says Nancy should be firmer. 'She's got to learn, it's not all about her any more,' he says, dandling the baby. But while Frank is free and easy with advice, he's rarely there to help. His company is pitching for a big contract and he has to work late more often. 'I'm doing it for us,' he insists, when Nancy says she needs a break. 'How about your mum comes to stay?' But Nancy isn't going to fall for that one again. She'd prefer to deal with her problems in private.

Because underneath, Nancy knows there's nothing wrong with this gorgeous, happy baby. Even Georgie, her feisty, rumbunctious two-year-old, is just doing what toddlers do. It's Nancy who's the problem. From one day to the next, she feels as if she's wading through deep water, unreachable. Words are muffled and colours seem more muted. It's as if she's slowly drowning.

In the end, Nancy does what she's always done when life becomes troubling – she pretends. She smiles and nods when people say what lovely children she has. She agrees when they say it must be hard work now, but her children will always have each other as playmates. And because she had them young, Nancy can always go back to her studies once they are at school. 'Yes,' she says. 'It's all working out beautifully.'

Chapter
Twenty-Eight

Nancy, 1996

'It can be our little secret'

When Dan is four, Nancy finally finds a friend who understands her. They get together most afternoons, but sometimes in the mornings too. Or, to be more accurate, she goes back to an old friend. Drink has got her into trouble in the past – it made her act like an idiot at university – but now all is forgiven and she welcomes the bottle back into her life.

Because a tipple here and there helps her get through each day. It softens everything and makes the drudgery easier to deal with. It makes Georgie in particular easier to deal with. Aged six, she calls Nancy names, she kicks and screams when it's time to go to school. The teachers talk about star charts and time out and having a naughty step, and Nancy agrees these all sound like very good ideas. But she does none of them.

Georgie still likes to throw things on the floor – a bag of rice, books, a basket of clean laundry – so the house is always in a bit of a state. But after Nancy's first drink of the day, that doesn't matter so much. She leaves the washing-up and the muddle of clothes for later and she sits in a deckchair in the garden and she smokes her way through a packet of Silk Cut cigarettes. It's nicer out there, watching the clouds.

She usually manages to pick Dan up from nursery at lunchtime, but things can get a little hazy by the time Georgie's school run comes around. Sometimes a woman called Claudia, a school mum who lives nearby, brings Georgie home, appearing from nowhere and peering down with a worried expression. Nancy smiles up and scrabbles for her sunglasses to hide her face.

On those afternoons, after Claudia has brought Georgie home, Nancy tends to stay in her deckchair, lets her hand hang over the side and brushes her fingers back and forth against the tufty grass. After a while, she'll hear the suck of the fridge door – Georgie opening it to look for something for tea – then the clunk of it closing. Georgie is a good girl, really. She can fix herself and her brother cereal, or toast if she's careful. Nancy stays out in the garden until her skin prickles in the cold evening air but inside her head, all is pleasantly numb.

When Frank gets home, it's as if the children know to put on a performance. He'll find the washing-up done and Georgie and Dan sitting at the kitchen table, doing drawings or colouring in. Frank always goes straight over to Dan, ruffles his hair. 'What's this, Danny Boy?' he says. This is what Frank calls him. Or 'Best Boy' or just 'Son'.

Georgie will look up, smoothing out her picture of a horse or a cat. Or she'll have traced letters of the alphabet, smudged grey where she's rubbed some out and tried so hard to get them right. But Frank never looks her way.

Wordlessly, Nancy rummages in the freezer for something for Frank's tea. Sways slightly, as she tips oven chips on to a tray, kicks the oven door shut.

It's around this time that they go to a parents' evening at Georgie's primary school. Nancy makes an effort, wears a flowery dress she got from the charity shop, a pair of kitten heels that she hopes make her look respectable. She hadn't even drunk that much, but she'd forgotten to eat again and that, she supposes, was the problem. It wasn't a big deal, just a stumble on the slippery school hall floor. Oh, but Georgie's face, when she saw her mother on her knees, laughing, looking around for someone to help her up. And Frank's face, like thunder.

'Oops, I'm in trouble now!' she said to the teacher who had come to her aid – a young guy with kind eyes, wearing a sweater with leather patches on the elbows. She wants to say, *Why are you wearing old man clothes? Don't wish away your life!* but it comes out wrong – all those Ws are so hard to say.

Frank is frosty with her for ages after that. One night, emboldened by a few extra vodkas, she stumbles into the living room where he's stretched out on the sofa, watching the news. 'You're so boring,' she says. 'Why don't we have any fun?'

'You seem to be having fun on your own,' he says coldly.

She eyes him carefully. He's recently bought a new set of shirts in shades of pink and wears jazzy socks from Paul Smith that cost more than the weekly housekeeping. Actually, now she looks more closely, Frank doesn't look boring, he looks like a man who takes good care of himself. He goes to the gym these days, treats himself to a trim, wet shave and hot towel treatment at a fancy barber each month, and Nancy wonders who he's making all this effort for.

'And how about you, Frank? Do you make your own fun?' She lowers her face to his, says the words slowly. 'At all those after-work drinks. Networking.'

Frank recoils. 'Your breath reeks of alcohol.' He flicks the TV off. 'You're crazy, Nancy. And not in a good way. Sort yourself out.'

It's soon afterwards, with an uncanny sense of timing, that the van reappears. It's the school holidays and Frank has taken Dan to his parents for the day. Nancy has just picked Georgie up from holiday club. All the children got to paint hard-boiled eggs as an Easter activity and Georgie asks Nancy to carry hers, to keep it safe. It's wrapped in tissue and Nancy holds the egg in both hands, enjoying its simple, pleasing shape.

Georgie is skipping ahead, two untidy plaits bouncing on her shoulders, so for a moment Nancy loses sight of her. Then, when she turns the corner, she scarcely has time to take in the vehicle, to realise it's him. All she sees is the van door swinging open and that familiar, impish figure stepping down and blocking her daughter's path.

Nancy barely feels the egg slip from her hand, but she hears the dull crack on the pavement. She sees Georgie look back and her face crumple into hot, angry tears.

'Oh dear, oh dear,' Gerry says, crouching down to look at the cracked egg on the ground.

But he's not talking to Nancy, he's looking at Georgie. He reaches out, picks off the hair bobble that has come loose on one of her daughter's plaits and hands it to her. 'Well,' he says. 'You must be Georgie. I'm Gerry, Mummy's old friend.'

Only then does he look up at Nancy. 'I never noticed before,' he says.

'What?' Her mouth goes dry.

'Her name. How it begins with the letter G. How nice.' Gerry Mac gives Nancy a wide smile.

Inside the van, Gerry shows them all the improvements he's made. He's been 'on the road', although he's vague about where. 'You know, just touring. A wandering soul, following my instinct,' he says. He points out the shelves he's fixed to the walls and the upgraded hotplate. He points out another new addition, a rocking

154

chair. It has a crocheted blanket thrown over the back and he gives it a nudge. It makes an uneven creaking noise. 'Want to sit in it?' he asks Georgie, but she doesn't. She hides behind it, peers through the holes in the blanket. 'I want to go home now,' she whispers to Nancy.

That night, Nancy doesn't touch a drop of drink. The guilt is like a fever in her bloodstream, rising until she's filled with its queasy heat. Still, she tries to smile for Georgie's sake. She brushes her daughter's hair and they play a complicated game with dolls for what feels like hours. Then she reads her two bedtime stories and then another, as a special treat. Nancy promises to hard-boil some eggs tomorrow. Then they can paint them, to make up for the one that she dropped – yes, what a silly mummy.

'Georgie,' she says, as she bends down to kiss her daughter goodnight. 'Let's not say anything to Daddy or Dan about my friend and his funny van. It can be our little secret, can't it?'

Then Nancy goes and checks on Dan, brushes his blond curls to one side and kisses his warm forehead.

She sickens herself. She is the worst mother in the world.

Chapter
Twenty-Nine

NANCY, MARCH 2002

'WHAT WE ALL NEED IS A GOOD HOLIDAY'

Nancy has a bad feeling about this Easter holiday in Wales, even before they set off. On the journey, Frank is jangly with nervous energy, gripping the steering wheel, revving the engine and tail-gating other cars. Things aren't going well at his work. There are rumours of redundancies. Things aren't great at home, either.

Georgie is twelve, sulky and sullen, always plugged into her headphones. As ever, it's up to Dan, now ten, to jolly them all along. 'We're off on our holidays!' he announces to the server when they stop at a McDonald's. 'We're going to Tenby in Wales!'

Frank picks up on this mood, starts acting like he's the Best Dad Ever. He's pretending to be the father in the Peter and Jane books Nancy read as a child: a sensible, affable chap who washes the car and mends things with his son while the girls do the washing-up, but something is off key. It's all too try-hard.

'This is going to be great,' he says, slapping a hand on the steering wheel. 'What we all need is a good holiday. Ready for some fishing, Danny Boy? Then we'll have picnics on the beach, long country walks. Fish and chip suppers.' He grins at Nancy.

Seven days, she reminds herself. Six nights. She can do this. In fact, going away for Easter will be a relief – she doesn't know why she didn't think of it years ago. Because Easter is the time of year when Gerry always comes sniffing around. Ever since he turned up and gave Nancy such a shock that she dropped Georgie's painted egg, he's kept coming back.

She never has any warning, but as Easter approaches, she'll turn a corner and see the familiar shape of his van and her stomach will tighten. Once, he parked opposite the café where she'd got herself a part-time job waiting tables. He thought it was hilarious, kept laughing his high-pitched laugh. 'Did I surprise you, Nancy? I can't believe you didn't spot me. Always have your head in the clouds, that's your problem.'

Nancy's beginning to think that Gerry is the bigger problem. She sees things differently now. She's not a gullible young student, or a worn-out young mother who was pitifully grateful for any scraps of attention and believed his bullshit stories.

She'd like to tell him where to go, but it's not that simple. Because Gerry never did delete those audition videos, even though she has asked him to. Many times. And then there is the other piece of information he holds.

'Still time for me to have a heart-to-heart with Frank,' Gerry said one year, when he felt Nancy was being less than welcoming. 'Your computer geek who thought he'd got lucky. Might just knock on the door one day, renew our acquaintance.' Then he'd laughed his wheezy little laugh.

So she lets him carry on visiting, tries to keep on the right side of him. Once a year, she listens to his tedious stories about productions that will never happen and directors he's never met. She sees through it all now, yet Nancy still lives in fear of Gerry and his big grey van. It's just that she doesn't know what to do about it.

So, yes, she's almost looking forward to this holiday. Even though Frank is behaving very oddly: all this forced jollity – it's as if he's trying to prove something. To her or himself? She's not sure. She knows their marriage is dying, dead on its feet already, and something has to change. But she doesn't know what.

When they arrive in Wales, the cottage doesn't look like it did in the brochure. Nancy finds mouse droppings in the kitchen cupboards and mould on the bedroom walls. Secretly, because Frank is already cross and talking about making a complaint, she cleans the bathroom. She picks clots of hair out of the sink, scrubs at the stains on the toilet seat. It's like The Beaufort all over again.

She's desperate for a drink, but she resists. Since January, she's cut back to having just one glass of wine in the evenings. Frank's making an effort this week, so she will too.

On the first morning, they wake to the steady sound of rain. It continues all day, and the next. They play Scrabble. Georgie cheats, tosses the board in the air when Frank calls her out. Dan tries to remember the words so he can remake the board, but by the time he's finished laying out the Scrabble tiles again, everyone has lost what little interest they had.

On the third day, the sun comes out. Frank and Dan go fishing, with much preparation involving special green rod bags and long waders.

Georgie is slumped on the sofa, watching children's TV because that's all that's on. 'Fancy a walk into town? See what we find?' Nancy says, trying to sound cheerful. Frank's fake bonhomie seems to be catching.

Tenby is full of ye olde tea shoppes and gift shops and ice-cream stands. Loops of plastic bunting flutter in the wind and the pavements are rammed with tourists, all looking for ways to spend

their money. Georgie pleads with Nancy to buy her a plaster figure of a fairy. It is purple and hideous and Nancy knows that her
daughter will decide it is babyish by the time they get home. She
buys it anyway.

They find a table in one of the tea rooms, where the waitresses
wear black-and-white outfits and expressions of boredom. It is hot
and fuggy and smells of warm mayonnaise. Nancy drinks a black
coffee with shaky hands (the one glass of wine a night isn't quite
cutting it) and nurses her constant headache. Georgie demolishes
a cream bun, without any sign of enjoyment.

They are walking back home when Nancy hears it: that dis-
tinctive rumble of an engine. It's coming from behind them and
although she knows it can't be him, the sound makes her breath
catch. Then the engine revs up, rises in its pitch, and the vehicle
overtakes them. It's a grey van just like Gerry's. And then it pulls
up and parks. Nancy stops walking, feels her mouth fill with saliva,
and she wonders if she's going to be sick because ahead of them,
Gerry is getting out of his van.

'Fancy seeing you here!' he says, as he walks towards them
swinging his arms, like he's enjoying this little jaunt, this outing to
Tenby in Wales.

'How? How?' Nancy mutters, and she reaches for Georgie's
hand. Her daughter won't want to hold hands – she's too old for
that now – but Nancy doesn't let go. 'Listen, Georgie, I need you
to walk ahead now and go back to the cottage,' she says. 'Let me
handle this.'

That evening, the family plays Monopoly, but even Dan can't
feign any enthusiasm. The boys didn't catch any fish and Frank is
cross because he lost his favourite fly or something. But Nancy is
in a good mood. She treats herself to a second glass of wine because
she's earned it. She's managed to avert a disaster – she got Gerry

to understand that surprising her like that on their holiday wasn't a good idea.

'How did you know we were here?' she said. 'Surely you didn't follow us from London?'

'I have my ways of finding out information,' was all Gerry would say. But he could tell he'd overstepped the mark, that she wasn't pleased to see him. 'I just wanted to swing by – wish you a happy Easter, as always.' Then he gave that silly high laugh of his, the one she used to think was so clever. But Nancy didn't laugh back.

Gerry agreed to leave Tenby. 'And I can't have you turning up like this again,' she'd said firmly. 'It has to stop.'

She sips her wine and closes her eyes. Gerry has left town. She hopes he's finally got the message. He can keep his sleazy video for all she cares – as long as he leaves her alone.

The last day of their holiday is sunny so they all go to the beach and it's a genuinely lovely day. One of the best. Georgie forgets she's meant to be a sulky pre-teen and splashes and plays in the sea with Dan. Frank helps them build a sandcastle: it's huge and it takes them all day and Nancy gets a passing holidaymaker to take a photograph of them all together. As they walk over the slip-sliding sand dunes at the end of the day, Frank even pulls her in for a hug.

Back at the cottage, Frank says he'll nip out to the petrol station, fill up for the long drive home tomorrow. Dan starts putting on his shoes – he's expecting to go along for the ride because that's the sort of thing Frank likes. But then Frank surprises them all and says, 'Georgie – fancy coming? See if we can't find you some sweets, hey?'

Georgie grins and she's out of the door and into the car before her dad can change his mind. As they drive off, Nancy thinks that perhaps Frank was right. All they needed was a good holiday.

A while later, when she hears the thump-thump of Georgie's feet running up the stairs, Nancy thinks it's odd that she didn't come into the kitchen first. She must be thirsty and hungry. Nancy has done a round of Welsh cakes, one for everyone and an extra one for Frank. But then Frank comes into the kitchen and he closes the door and Nancy knows something is wrong, badly wrong.

'Is everything OK? Is Georgie OK?' she says, drying her hands on the tea towel. A few moments ago, waiting for them to get back, she'd opened the back door and stood in the sunshine. She'd watched a thrush hopping from branch to branch, smelt blossom on a tree, thought that they were doing OK, all things considered. Maybe they can pull through, her and Frank.

'You slut. You absolute slut,' Frank says. And Nancy's stomach drops, her knees buckle and she puts out a hand to find the chair.

'How could you invite him here?' Frank is saying, shouting really, so hard that she can feel his spittle on her face. And Nancy knows that he knows.

'I didn't,' she says. 'He must have followed us.'

'I think you told him to come here, Nance. You couldn't stand the thought of a week with your own family, so you invited him along, to meet in secret. After all this time. That man. Who, I now discover, you see every Easter.'

'No.' Her words are useless, barely louder than a whisper. 'It's not like that.'

Frank takes two short strides and he's pressing his face up to hers, so close that she can see how the skin on his nose is pink from their day in the sun. She sees how his teeth, clenched tight, have become stained over the years. He swears, calls her the worst things, and she doesn't dare move.

He's got the front of her T-shirt balled up in his hand, and he pulls her towards him, but then changes his mind and pushes her away, as if he's done with her. And she knows then that there's no

161

going back and she starts to laugh. It's not a laugh she recognises, it sounds like it's made by a machine, not by her. But she can't stop. It's all so ridiculous – an hour ago they were sitting on the beach talking about having fish and chips for tea.

When he next speaks, Frank's voice has turned cold and calm. 'You are unstable, Nancy. You always were – but it's not charming or funny any more. It's damaging. For the children.'

He starts to tidy the kitchen, wiping the surfaces and putting the mugs on the shelf in a neat line. 'When we get home, you need to leave. We need some breathing space. I don't think I can forgive you for this transgression.'

'Transgression?' she repeats. Frank sounds like something out of a nineteenth-century novel. Once upon a time she loved his formality, his sensible, stable side. But really, 'Transgression?' There's an ache in her side, like a stitch, but still she can't stop laughing.

But then Frank turns and he speaks in far plainer, simpler words. 'Nancy, I'm not talking about this holiday. I'm talking about a fundamental breach of trust. I believe you had sex with another man. You had his child and you pretended it was mine.'

And then Nancy isn't laughing any more. Her head feels very far away, as if it is floating, quite separate from Frank and his unkind words. In fact, all of her feels as light as air, insubstantial. And she wishes she could drift away and leave this place, these words that he's finally said out loud.

She thinks of her children upstairs. She looks at Frank, the man she never should have said yes to, all those years ago.

The fight has gone out of Frank, too; he looks broken, undone. 'Tell me I'm wrong, Nancy. Tell me.'

And, in all honesty, Nancy can't do that.

Chapter Thirty

Nancy, April 2002

'This was never the life for you'

They get back from the disastrous trip to Wales on a Friday and over the weekend, Frank and Nancy barely speak. Nancy explains to the children that she's sleeping on the sofa 'because I have a cough'. Then, on the Sunday evening, Nancy comes into the bathroom, where Frank is brushing his teeth. She stands behind him, looks at his face reflected in the mirror. 'I'll do it,' she says. 'I'll leave. Give us this breathing space or whatever you want to call it. But we need to work out what to tell the children.'

Frank barely looks at her. He's flossing now, seesawing the white thread between his incisors. 'I'll think of something,' he says. 'Say you've gone on a trip. To help endangered animals or something. Make you sound like a better person than you really are.'

Frank drops the piece of floss in the bin, bares his teeth to the mirror to inspect them. 'All you need to do, Nancy, is leave. Go to your parents. Go to him – I really don't care at this stage. My priority is the children.'

He turns, walks past her. 'Yes, both children. I'm not a monster – they are still brother and sister. They need each other. But at the moment, none of us needs you.'

Nancy does not sleep that night. She lies on the sofa, tears running into her ears and down her neck, and she thinks of all the moments in her life when she could have said or done things differently. And by the time the milky morning light creeps around the curtains she feels empty, hollow of any feelings except shame. She gets up, pours cereal into bowls for the children.

Dan leaves the house first – he's started walking to school with a boy down the road. She hugs him hard, but he pulls away, in a hurry to be off. She watches him go, already gangly and tall for his age.

Georgie is running late, as always. She's shouting because she can't find her school shoes and she needs money for lunch. With shaking hands, Nancy fishes around inside her purse. She can't find any coins, so she holds out a £5 note. Her last one. 'Here you go,' she says. 'I trust you not to spend it all.'

'Ooh, thanks,' says Georgie, her face spreading into a rare smile. 'See you later.'

Nancy is about to say how she might not be here tonight, she needs to go away for a few days, but Georgie is already heading out the door. Anyway, Frank said not to, that he'd handle it this evening.

This is a temporary measure, she tells herself. Once Frank has calmed down, she'll come back. They can behave like adults, talk about custody.

She rushes to the door to catch a glimpse of Georgie. She's wearing a checked school pinafore dress that had to be fished out of the laundry basket and she walks slowly, looking down at the ground, buried in thought. As she reaches the corner, Georgie pauses and looks back at her mother, as if she knows something is wrong. Nancy just has time to wave before Georgie turns the corner and is gone.

Nancy considers ringing her mother, but she can't face it: the questions she'd have to answer. As Theresa has often said, Nancy has made her bed, now she has to lie in it. There's Claudia, the neighbour who has been kind to her. But her daughter is at school with Georgie, it's too close and complicated and it'll be all round the school by tomorrow if she goes there.

Upstairs, she puts a few clothes in a bag; takes her passport, just in case. She might need it as some sort of ID, further down the line. She leaves her key on the hall table. And then she walks, that light-as-air feeling in her head carrying her along, past the post box, the corner shop where Georgie and Dan got to choose sweets when they were little. Past the bus stop and the gates to the park.

She doesn't know where she's going. She has no money; her only bank card is for a 'housekeeping' account that Frank tops up each Monday. She has a feeling there won't be any money deposited in that account today. She realises she has nowhere to go, no one to turn to.

There's a horrible inevitability to it when she hears the deep rumble of the engine behind her. Nancy's shoulders drop in despair, and she stops and waits for Gerry's van to draw alongside.

'Need a lift somewhere?' he asks.

She doesn't look at him as she says, 'He's kicked me out.' Gerry seems to know her every movement, so he might as well know this too. 'Somehow, he found out you came to Tenby and we had a huge row and now he knows. So he's kicked me out.'

Then Gerry talks to her in his smooth voice, says things that should make her feel better but drag her deeper into despair. He tells her he will take care of her. How they can be together now – and that soon she'll see that this is all for the best. 'It could be a blessing in disguise. It could be a whole new future, Nancy! This was never the life for you,' he says. 'This is where your real life starts.'

Nancy lets out a hollow laugh, remembering thinking that exact thing when she was eighteen, in the week she met Frank and Gerry and had no idea what lay ahead.

'Come on, Nancy, let me help.' Gerry is looking serious now, like he might even be sorry. 'There's a place I know. It's in the countryside – perfect for a break. Get you back on your feet.'

'Back on my feet,' she repeats, talking more to herself than to Gerry. 'A break. Just for a while.'

The journey in his rumbling van takes all day and at some point, Nancy sleeps. When she wakes, they are bumping along a rough track into some woods until they reach a point where the van can go no further. It is dark and they have to walk the last half mile, tripping over roots, low leaves brushing her face.

It takes Gerry an age to find the key – he says it's hidden under a flowerpot and he pats his pockets for a light. She hears the metallic rasp of his lighter, sees his lined face in the flame. Standing alone in the darkness, she breathes in the loamy air and looks up at the dazzle of stars, the enormity of what she's done beginning to sink in.

Gerry says the cottage is called The Hideaway. It's not really his, but his grandmother's. 'She's in a care home,' he says, making a sad face. 'I'm helping out, looking after the place for her.' He says Nancy can stay as long as she likes. Nobody will disturb them, this deep in the woods.

When she wakes the next morning, she's horrified to see where Gerry has brought her. It's like a house from a play: oil paintings on the walls looped in cobwebs, a mouldy loaf of bread in the pantry;

holes in the roof big enough to show blue sky. The wallpaper is mottled with water stains and paint flakes are scattered over a faded red sofa and the floor, like a dusting of snow.

Over the next few weeks, however, the cottage starts to look different. At first, she thinks Gerry is cleaning it, because two paintings disappear from the wall, leaving behind dark rectangles. Then the glass-fronted cabinet that was crammed with china and silver ornaments starts to look sparser. Next, Gerry goes through his grandmother's jewellery, picks out gold chains, brooches that gleam with red and green stones. 'Poor thing, it's to pay for her care,' he says with a sigh.

He drives Nancy to a town several miles away, to help sell it. 'They know me already at the local antique shops – never give me a good price,' he explains. 'You'll do better. Especially if you smile.' She tells the dealer a story about a great-aunt who left her everything. She thinks of her children and the tears come, quite easily. Outside, she hands over the roll of notes to Gerry.

It's a month before she dares write to Frank. It's a short letter, asking when they can meet and discuss things. 'Please, I want to see my children,' she writes. She puts the cottage's address at the top of the letter, says she's staying with an old friend. She waits, patiently, for an answer.

Chapter Thirty-One

GEORGIE

The small town of Hoyton Beck is the kind of place people moved to in the 1980s in search of an alternative lifestyle, to bake their own bread and lay down their yoga mats. These days, life has moved on and alternative has gone mainstream. The town square has an artisan bakery, a delicatessen and a lifestyle emporium that sells scented candles, oversized planters and a plethora of tealight holders. Dan drives around the square twice, as they take all this in and wonder what to do next.

'I really don't think any good can come of this . . .' Dan is saying, but Georgie ignores him. A woman with a tangle of ringlets is moving a display of outdoor planters back inside her shop; it must be nearly closing time.

'Pull over. I think this is worth a try,' Georgie says. As she walks over to the shop, she pushes a fist into the ache that has taken hold in the small of her back and stretches; it feels good to be out of the car. The woman straightens up, brushes a ringlet out of her face. She wears a long cardigan over a skirt in some silky material that shimmers and gleams in the low afternoon light. Below, thick socks and brown Birkenstocks.

'Hello,' the woman smiles. Georgie is willing to bet that business on a Tuesday in February in Hoyton Beck has been slow and any customer, even one this late in the day, is worth chatting to. 'I was just shutting up, but were you after something in particular?'

'In a way, yes,' says Georgie, a story already forming in her head. 'I'm Georgie and this is my brother, Dan. I love your shop. I bet it's a real community hub.'

'Hi, I'm Tabby,' the woman says. 'Well, that's my aim. We have workshops here: macrame, life drawing, dyeing yarns. Oh, and a book club — are you new to the area? All are welcome.'

'Not exactly.' Then Georgie tells Tabby how she met someone from this village a while back, a man called Gerry Mac. 'I was younger then, but he made a strong impression on me,' she explains. She points at her rounded stomach: 'So now I want to tell him my good news.'

At this, Tabby clasps her hands together. 'How wonderful,' she exclaims.

'Yes,' Georgie replies, getting into her stride. 'I almost feel as if Gerry had a hand in shaping my life. The path I took.'

'Ah, true.' Tabby nods sagely. 'That is Gerry's gift. To take people under his wing.'

Georgie doesn't trust herself to say anything more, so she adopts what she hopes is a beatific expression and rubs her tummy using large, meaningful strokes.

'So,' she says eventually. 'Is he still at the same place?'

'His forest retreat? Of course. He rarely leaves.'

Georgie turns to go, then pauses, taps her fingers on her forehead. 'Oh, can you remind me of the way? My memory is rubbish these days. Baby brain!' She lets out a laugh.

'Ah, bless. Back out of town, left at the crossroads, then fork right and look for the red gate. Remember?'

'Red gate, got it.' Already, Georgie is backing away and then they are back in the car, two doors slamming in quick succession, leaving Tabby standing on the pavement.

Already, dusk is falling, but the gate is easy to spot: wooden, wonky and, although it is now peeling, it's clear it was once painted a bright shade of red. Georgie gets out of the car, lifts a loop of rope and watches the gate drift open. She doesn't close it behind them; Georgie isn't planning on staying long.

Dan drives down what is little more than a rutted track, with no end in sight. Bare branches scrape against the side of the car and the wheels bump over unseen lumps, bulky as bodies. Just as Georgie's mind is racing towards disaster scenarios – Tabby is in cahoots with Gerry and has set them up; the car is about to plunge into a hidden river – the unmade track widens out to a clearing and a ramshackle cottage emerges from the gloom.

The front door opens and a man steps out. He's silhouetted against a glow of yellow light and Georgie watches as, in an all-too-familiar motion, he lifts his hand and smooths his beard into a point.

As they get out of the car, Georgie is aware of the crunch of leaves under her feet, crisp in the cold air. She hears herself drawing breath, feels the drumming of her heart. The moment feels oddly elongated and every sound is heightened. So much, she realises, rests on its outcome.

Then time slips back to normal and they are at the front door; Gerry is holding out a hand to shake Dan's, then hers. It feels oddly soft, not the hand of someone who chops his own wood or plants vegetables in the beds marked out in front of this house, and Georgie wonders if someone else is waiting inside, watching them from afar.

'Well,' he's saying, 'Dan and Georgie Brown. What a surprise. And also no surprise at all.' He looks them up and down, raises his eyebrows when he spots Georgie's bump.

Georgie's heart thumps harder. How did he know they were coming? Does this mean she's guessed right and their mother is on her way? Or is it possible that she's already here, hiding upstairs and about to surprise them?

'Come in,' he says, a grin spreading. Georgie can't take her eyes off his pointy beard, more grey than black now. She sees his wet lips and a flash of too-white teeth, fights off the sickening slide of dizziness that's tugging her down, harder and faster than before. 'Come,' he repeats, beckoning them into a tiny hallway then a living room.

Gerry lifts an old ginger cat off the sofa, pats the seat of an old rocking chair. 'Sit down. Make yourself at home.' Georgie is scanning the place, looking around for signs of Nancy, but there's only a single jacket hanging on a hook in the hall; in here, an empty glass on the coffee table.

Then she sees a crocheted throw on the back of the sofa in a pattern of blue and yellow flowers and she knows without touching it how it will feel under her fingers – its knots surprisingly tight and hard. She knows, too, that you can almost poke your little fingers through the gaps between those crocheted flowers, but you mustn't because then you will spoil the pattern. Even the rocking chair feels like part of a lost memory, smooth spindles that she pressed her face up to in another lifetime, in a small space that wasn't a room but felt like one. A room that didn't feel safe and she'd wanted to leave, tugged at her mother's dress.

Georgie realises she's straining to hear the creak of floorboards from above, something that will let her know their mother is here. But all she hears is the crackle of the fire in the grate, white wood spitting like it was only recently laid.

'How did you know we were coming?' she manages.

'Oh, I have a feel for these things,' Gerry says breezily. 'A sixth sense, if you like.' Then he lets slip a giggle. 'Not really. Tabby, bless her, rang me. Said a woman called Georgie was on her way. Travelling with a brother called Dan, and I put two and two together. That, and the fact your mother is in the news.'

He waits for a reaction. 'I like to keep abreast of the news. I see it all from my computer.' His eyes dart towards the ceiling, to the spot where he must sit day and night, combing the internet for who knows what. Calling in to radio chat shows.

Georgie finds she is holding her arms around herself. 'Is she here?' she asks, but it must have come out as a whisper because Gerry doesn't reply. He's looking at Dan. 'And how are you – the boy wonder!' he says. 'Losing a bit of hair, but then aren't we all.' He turns to Georgie, runs his tongue over his lips. 'While you, my dear, are looking most fecund.'

He wanders over to a dark Welsh dresser stacked with bottles of drink, starts lifting them up to the light to see which ones are full, which are empty. 'Quite a journey you've had,' he says, and a ludicrous thought enters Georgie's head: in his impish way, has Gerry somehow been watching them from afar on this hapless trip, laughing at their faltering, too-slow journey that has failed to find Nancy? No, too ridiculous. Again, her over-tired brain is running away with itself.

'Yes, bit of a trip,' Dan answers, and Georgie feels a twitch of irritation. They don't need to waste time with polite chit-chat – all they want is information and then they can get out of here.

She finds her voice. 'Gerry, we're looking for our mum. For Nancy. Clearly, she's been living up on a Scottish island, but she's not there any more. So we wondered if she's been in touch? With you.'

But Gerry isn't going to be rushed. He's still inspecting his array of dusty bottles with ancient labels and shoved-in corks. Finally, he lifts out a dark-green one and waggles it in the air.

'Not for me,' Georgie says.

'Nor me,' says Dan.

He pours two glasses anyway; fills a third with water from a metal jug. Then he places them on the coffee table, beside a half-completed crossword and a tattered dictionary. She smells the plummy richness of the port, takes a sip from the glass of water that must be for her. It tastes dusty, carries a whiff of leaf mulch and decay.

The port glasses are fussy things, with a pattern cut into their shape and twiddly stems: the sort of thing an old lady might own. Gerry raises his glass.

'So, you heard the news too?' he says. 'At last, it seems she may return to us.' He puckers his lips, takes another sip. 'The lovely Nancy.'

Georgie leans forward, waits for Gerry to say more. Then she realises this isn't how it should be – it's supposed to be them grilling him and then getting out of here, but instead this man has the upper hand. He's toying with them, pouring port and taunting them.

Dan, who is sitting in the rocking chair, seems to come to the same conclusion. He plants his feet on the ground and brings the chair to a sharp stop.

'So, when did you last have any contact?' Dan asks. 'I mean, we assume you were together after she left. When we were children. But neither of you thought to get in touch?' Dan's question fills the room. 'Two postcards. In twenty years.' He shakes his head.

Gerry takes another dainty sip of his port and regards Dan with curiosity. When he finally speaks, it is in the high, reedy tone that is beginning to grate.

'But my dear boy – Nancy left me, too. Took off one night. It's her party trick, I suppose, to vanish – poof – into thin air.' Then Gerry slowly wraps his palm around his chin and smooths his beard down in a gesture that feels vaguely sexual, and Georgie has to look away.

None of this is making any sense. 'But we thought you went abroad together. She wanted to help the animals. The tiger cubs.' She trails off, hearing how infantile she sounds.

'Well, if she did, that was something your mother did under her own steam. The last time I saw Nancy was some nineteen years ago, in this very room. She lived here with me, rather happily I might add. But then, as I say, she vanished. More's the pity.'

Georgie feels something stirring inside her, a realisation of the wrongness of this man and what he's saying. 'What the hell are you talking about?' she shouts, because this man drinking port in his cottage in the woods has no idea what damage he did. 'You barged into all our lives. The last time I saw you, you ruined our family holiday. And then you ruined our lives. You stole her away and then you went abroad, to Thailand. She sent us postcards . . .' But she's getting muddled now, fragments of memories colliding with pictures she made up in her head: Nancy bottle-feeding a tiger cub. Saving the wildlife – that was the story their father had told them.

A smile creeps across Gerry's face. 'My dear, you seem to be confused on so many counts. The last time I saw you wasn't in Wales. And you seemed quite keen to spend time with me . . .'

At that, Dan stands up abruptly, starts to move towards the door. 'That's enough,' he says. 'Let's go, Georgie.' He snaps his car key fob against his palm. 'He doesn't know any more than us. He's wasting our time.'

But Gerry isn't listening, he's reaching his hand out towards Georgie. 'Such lovely hair,' he says. 'Just like your mother's.' His fingers brush against a strand that's come loose from her hair tie.

Beside her, the fire in the grate is crackling, but a chill prickles Georgie's scalp. She tries to stand but then stumbles, felled by dizziness. The room starts to tilt and Georgie sees a dazzle of patterns, those tiny crocheted flowers repeated over and over.

She registers Dan helping her sit back down on the sofa, feels his hand on her arm, a steady, friendly pressure. Her kind brother, who has always been there for her. She blinks and her vision starts to clear, the spinning eases.

Gerry is still sitting, observing them with his hands clasped over his belly. He is wearing a leather waistcoat, an outfit that puts Georgie in mind of an animal character from a children's book. A badger, perhaps, or a stoat. One that might turn nasty.

With a cold certainty, Georgie knows they need to leave and now. This man was never a friend to her mother, he meant her harm and he still does. Whatever had gone on between Gerry and Nancy all those years ago was deeply wrong.

Gerry smiles and she sees how his lips are tinged purple from the port yet his teeth remain perfectly white, and she realises this is because they are false, every one of them. And she knows that if she got any closer, his beard would be prickly but soft too and that, up close, he would smell like clothes that have been left wet for too long, a sour, lingering smell that has always turned her stomach, and then she's standing, she's walking towards the front door and she's out in the cold evening air, bent double, holding on to her knees until she can breathe again.

Chapter
Thirty-Two

GEORGIE

She never thought she would be glad to be back inside this stupid car with its fug of old sandwiches and its carpet of scrunched-up sweet wrappers, but right now, it feels like a refuge. And, more importantly, it is their only means of escape. Dan turns the key in the ignition and she waits to hear the car's engine roar into life. But that sound doesn't come. Instead, the engine lets out a low, mechanical groan.

He turns the key again. The engine turns over; fails. Georgie can't bear to watch. A tremor starts in her legs, a shaking that's not from the cold, and she doesn't dare speak. She holds her breath, hears the engine splutter – and then it takes. They glance at each other, share a look of relief.

Dan eases off the handbrake and starts to drive back along the bumpy track. Branches scrape along the sides of the car and Georgie chances a look in the rear-view mirror. A gnomic figure stands in the doorway and he's moving his hand from side to side in a parody of someone waving goodbye. Georgie shivers, looks away.

She has no idea what her mother ever saw in that man or what hold he had over Nancy, but something is telling her to get as far away from Gerry Mac as she can. Georgie runs her hands over her bump, feels a shifting inside, a sinking down, as if her baby, too, wants to hide and leave him far behind.

It's only when they come to a halt at the end of the bumpy track that Georgie notices two rather worrying things. One is that the car headlights are not working properly, sending out the feeblest beams. And the second is that the map on Dan's phone looks different from usual.

They are a blue blob in the middle of a green area, but when she zooms out, there's nothing more to see on the screen. And in the top left-hand corner of his phone, instead of a line of bars, it says 'No service'. She waves it in the air. Dan grabs it off her and does the same. They look at each other, then at the crossroads.

'Not good,' says Georgie.

'Not good at all.'

'We should turn left,' she says.

'Why?'

'That's the way we came, from the town.'

'But what do we do when we get there?' Dan asks.

'I have no idea. All I know is we need to get away from this place, as quickly as possible.'

Dan turns left and puts his foot down. He's chatting away, talking about how he'll keep driving this car for as long as it holds out and, all things being equal, they should make it back to London by about midnight. But Georgie barely hears him. She's trying to make sense of the tangle of memories that are competing in her head.

Some have the unreal feel of scenes from a film, but it's one she can't quite recall. There's a flash of railings, a dark road below, and she realises that images from the past two days are meshing with ones she barely recognises.

'The last time I saw you,' Gerry had said. She remembers that grin of his, those plastic teeth that don't quite hug the gum.

His teeth that make her think of eating a big bag of lemon sherbets, one after the other, and biting down hard. Already, her tongue is thick with sugar but she can't stop. She's sitting in the bedroom of a holiday cottage, there's flowery wallpaper that goes into the alcove around a window seat, and outside she can see triangles of green and white plastic bunting that snap and crack as the wind tosses them this way and that.

They are on holiday in Wales, where people have a different language but can switch back to English when they want to, and Georgie knows how that feels, to have two lives going on at the same time. To behave differently, depending on who you're talking to. But she's just made a terrible mistake. She told a secret from one life – their mum's – to their dad, who belongs in a different life. Her dad kept asking her, over and over. He took her along for the ride to the petrol station and he bought her those fizzy sweets and he said, 'Come on, Georgie, you can tell me.'

He was being so nice to her, so friendly, that Georgie gave in – she told him who she and Nancy had bumped into in town, how she hadn't even been that surprised because he always seemed to visit around now. At Easter. Ever since she was little and Nancy dropped Georgie's pretty painted egg on the ground.

And when they got back to the cottage, there was shouting and doors slamming and horrible words and she stayed upstairs, eating those sweets until the insides of her cheeks hurt and she wished she hadn't said a thing. Because she seemed to have unleashed something terrible and she knew, even then, that it was not going to blow over. And three days later, her mother was gone.

Georgie blinks hard, concentrates on the steady rhythm of the wipers, then the way that the rain adds more of a snare drum swish between their beats. A feeling a bit like hunger is brewing inside her, yet she also feels quite sick.

'Dan,' she starts to say, but her next words don't come, they get swallowed back down her throat, because there's a hot pain burrowing into her back and spreading outwards. Georgie gasps. Then, just as suddenly as it came, the pain relents, lets her go, and she can draw breath again.

Braxton Hicks, she reminds herself. *My body limbering up; all perfectly normal.* Reassuring, in fact.

She lets her mind drift, but the beat of the wipers acts as a reminder that time is passing. And then she realises another wave of pain is gathering, stealthily but firmly. She arches her back as it seems to pick her up, toy with her and then dash her down.

Beside her, Dan doesn't notice a thing; he's hunched over the wheel and peering out into the gloom. Georgie waits, wonders what will happen next. Should she be timing these practice contractions? She can't remember. She gets out her phone, just in case. She waits for the next one . . . but then nothing happens. She's left with only the dull echo of a pain, as if she might have imagined it. Gradually, Georgie feels her body relax.

On Dan's phone, a blue blob floats aimlessly on an empty screen because they still don't have any signal. But at least they are leaving Gerry behind. They will drive home and, tomorrow, she and Dan will go back to their separate lives and probably never speak again of the time they drove Mandy's car hundreds of miles north, all for nothing.

They will never find Nancy, not now. She's outwitted them yet again. But in some strange way, Nancy has helped them. She has brought Georgie and Dan back together. And suddenly Georgie feels an intense, calm clarity and she knows what she must do. There is a way, she realises, for some good to come out of this journey and all this pain that's been stirred up.

Before they return home and her life takes another sharp turn, Georgie must tell her brother the truth. Because coming face to face with Gerry is a reminder of how secrets are a burden and their weight only increases over the years, rather than lessening.

She needs to tell Dan how his best friend died and how it wasn't drink or drugs or bad luck that killed him. The truth is, Georgie could have saved him and she didn't. First she stole Finn from her brother and then she failed him.

'Dan,' she says. 'I have something to tell you. It's about Finn and the night he died.'

Chapter
Thirty-Three

GEORGIE, 2020

'DON'T DO ANYTHING SILLY'

It's hard to pinpoint the exact moment that things start to go wrong between her and Finn. There are signs, of course. Those weekends when he disappears with obscure bands or the guys from the bar; the increasing frequency with which Finn asks her for money, then pouts like a spoilt child when she says, 'What about your wages?' Then there is the way he shuts her out when she asks him if something is wrong. She soon discovers that Finn has an iron will and can sulk for days, barely saying a word.

Georgie reads some self-help books and she realises that to make this relationship work, she needs to listen to Finn. After all, he's been a good listener to her – and to Dan. So she encourages him to talk about his mother who sent him away to boarding school and never loved him enough and his father who remarried and has a whole new family. She mentions how this is something they have in common, that she too had a troubled upbringing, but Finn sighs and says, 'It's not the same. You're more resilient, Georgie. Dan, too. I feel the hurt here, like a punch.' And he thumps himself on the chest.

She can help him in other ways, though, like paying the rent and the bills and buying the food. Sometimes Finn brings half-finished bottles of wine back from his bar job, but that's about it for his contribution. She lets his friends crash on their sofa for weeks on end, making everyone big casseroles or soups that, oddly, remind her of her mother's cooking. The smell of frying garlic and onions makes her feel lonelier than ever, while all around her Finn's friends laugh and drink and Finn holds an empty bottle in the air to signal that they need another.

They've been together for five years now and Georgie still hasn't made it as a creative photographer. She pitches for work with commercial agencies, but it's tough out there, so she keeps up the wedding photography. Finn is dismissive. He doesn't call her work 'reportage' any more, he calls it 'banal and unoriginal' – but Georgie carries on. Partly because they need the money, but she also secretly likes her days out when she gets to see families come together to celebrate a day that's all about love. It gives her hope.

At first, she admits, she took a greedy satisfaction in stealing Finn away from Dan, but now she thinks it would be nice to reconnect – to do things together. But Finn isn't keen. He says Dan has gone too mainstream; bought into the corporate world. Still, Georgie arranges for the three of them to go out for a meal together.

She thinks it goes well: Dan and Finn reminisce about their early student days, and at the end of the night the three of them stand out on the wet pavement and it feels sad to say goodbye. Her brother hugs her, then Finn, and he says, 'Let's do this again, soon.' Finn is busy flagging down a black cab, so it's only her who sees Dan's face fall when Finn calls out, 'Yeah, can't see it happening for a while, to be honest. Busy times.'

◆ ◆ ◆

Finn dies late on a Friday night. Georgie has been working in Dulwich, south London, all day, doing a shoot for a lovely couple, Dermot and Spike. As she packs up her kit, she wonders what she'll find when she gets home – an empty flat or one that's full of Finn's mates? She pictures them sprawled over the sofa, beer cans and takeaway cartons all over the place. No, not tonight, she decides, and she cancels her cab.

Instead, she calls up her old friend Lisa, who lives nearby, asks if she's free. Lisa meets her at a gastro pub and they have a great evening, just like old times. When Georgie sees a screen full of missed calls from Finn, she puts her phone back in her pocket. She's having a good time – and Lisa knows someone who works as a wedding planner, so it could be good for her business too.

He keeps ringing, though, so Georgie calls him back from the loo. He's talking a mile a minute but also slurring, repeating his words. With a cold certainty, she knows it's not just drink, he'll have taken something. He keeps saying his mates have gone on somewhere. 'I've lost them,' he wails. 'I'm on my own. How can I get home from Soho? I've got no money.'

Georgie swallows down her frustration. Finn doesn't do phone banking – he says it's the government's way to keep tabs on people – so she can't send him any money. Not that she wants to anyway.

'I'm out too, Finn. I'm miles away in south London so I can't come and get you. Sorry,' she says tightly. 'Maybe you can crash with someone. Or walk home?' She's half hoping this might sober him up.

'But you said,' Finn keeps repeating. 'I need you, Georgie. Don't abandon me.'

'I'm not,' she says, trying to stay calm. 'I'm just having one night out. With my friend.' Right now, Finn sounds like a demanding child, not a boyfriend. 'Don't do anything silly,' she says.

Afterwards, she wonders if that's what made him do it. His sheer cussedness, a desire to show Georgie that he can and will do silly things, unless she's there with him every minute of every day.

As soon as she wakes up alone on Saturday morning, Georgie has a bad feeling. Somehow, she senses it's not like the other times he's stayed out. Already, the air inside the flat feels different. It's thinner, emptier, and she knows that he's not coming back. It reminds her of pushing open the door to St Luke's Road, feeling the absence wrap around her like a fog.

She rings round all the hospitals, eventually hears how they couldn't get in touch any earlier because Finn's phone had been smashed into tiny pieces, lost among the debris. That's what they call it: 'debris'.

It makes the front page of Monday's *Evening Standard*: 'Tragedy of Tube station death'. There is talk, for a while, about installing more security cameras and the paucity of Underground staffing levels, but none of that is any help to Finn. It was at Oxford Circus station, so Georgie imagines that Finn took her advice and started walking back to north-west London from Soho. But then he must have got sick of walking and decided to jump the barrier and catch the last Tube home.

An eyewitness, a retired solicitor on her way home from the theatre, said he was beside her on the platform one minute, then gone. The next thing she saw was him walking down the middle of the shiny tracks and into the tunnel. He was ranting about how he might as well walk anyway, because this train was never coming. She ran to find an alarm, to tell someone, but it was too late.

Finn hadn't even been walking in the right direction. He was halfway to Piccadilly Circus when the train hit him.

At the funeral, Georgie looks at Finn's fair-weather friends, who have turned up in borrowed or ill-fitting suits, and she knows that she won't see any of them again. One woman with a sharp black bob and red lipstick cries more than is strictly necessary, reaching out to stroke the coffin, and Georgie wonders if she's being melodramatic or if she, too, was in the business of trying to save Finn.

His parents are civil but cool and she is not introduced to other members of his family. But it's Dan who cuts her to the quick. She saw him arrive at the chapel at the last moment possible, sliding on to the bench at the back. And when she plucks up the courage to go over to him at the wake, holding her glass of wine so tightly, he doesn't say a word. His eyes glide past her, as if the two of them are barely acquainted, and then he turns and walks away.

Chapter Thirty-Four

GEORGIE

'Dan, did you hear me, I need to tell you what happened, the night Finn died. I need to be honest with you.'

But her brother is looking distracted. He puts the windscreen wipers on because it has started to rain hard, squalls hitting the window in short, vicious bursts. 'Really, Georgie? Now – when we've lost track of Nancy, we've only just got out of that freak's house and I can't see the road in front of me because the lights on this car aren't working – you want to talk about this right now?'

But Georgie knows that if she doesn't, she might never tell him. Because that's what happens – you get a small window of opportunity to tell the truth and then it's gone. Life moves on; people build their lives around half-truths and misunderstandings and it becomes too hard to untangle.

'Yes, I'm sorry, but I do.' She takes a deep breath. 'When Finn died, I know it wasn't just my loss, it was yours too. And I get it, I understand why you didn't want to speak to me at the funeral. I stole Finn away and then I let him down in the worst possible way.'

'Come on, Georgie, that's not true.'

She knows what Dan's trying to do – smooth things over, pretend there's nothing to be sorry for. But she's not going to let him, not this time.

'I'm afraid it is,' she says, and then she tells him how things were already rocky between her and Finn. Which was why, on that Friday night, she'd made a conscious decision to stay out with her friend. And how Finn had called her – so many times.

'He asked me to go to him and I refused. That's the bottom line – he asked for my help and I didn't give it. And I will never forgive myself for that, Dan. But I want to own up to you. Because lies and secrets are no good . . .' Her words are starting to sound ragged.

She feels the car slowing down, hears the tick-tick of the indicator. Dan is pulling over and stopping the car and she realises he's going to kick her out, here in the middle of nowhere. She should have picked a better moment, she supposes, to come clean.

She waits for Dan to tell her to get out, but instead she hears him say, 'But Georgie, Finn wasn't your responsibility. Not that night.'

There's a long silence. 'But he was. I think I might have given him the idea.'

'What do you mean?'

'It was my suggestion, in a way. I said to him, "Oh, can't you walk?" and so he did. In his drug-addled brain, he took me at my word and he jumped down and started walking along the tracks.'

She watches the wipers, which are still going, scraping back and forth. 'So there it is. I was the last person who talked to Finn. And I failed him.'

Finally, she looks at her brother, to face up to what she did. But Dan is rubbing his head, hard. Then he starts to murmur things. 'Oh, no, this is so wrong,' he's saying, and she thinks he's having some kind of breakdown – the reminder of Finn's accident on top of everything else is too much.

He looks straight at her. 'You're wrong, Georgie,' he says. 'You weren't the last person to speak to him. I was.'

This makes no sense – all she can think is that Dan is making things up, trying to protect her all over again.

'But he rang me. He was so drunk, he wanted me to come and get him . . .' Georgie's words feel heavy, like clods in her mouth.

'I'm sure he did,' Dan replies. 'And he must have been really desperate, because then he rang me. He said, "Come out, Dan, come on, don't be boring. Come out. For old times' sake." And I'd missed him so much that I came running. I got a cab straight over to Soho.'

'You went there?'

'Yes. It was gone eleven when I found him and, to be honest, I don't think he even remembered ringing me. He was very drunk – even by Finn's standards – but manic too. Talking rubbish, saying he was invincible.

'I told him it was time to go home, but he was all over the place. I flagged down a cab, but the cabbie refused to take him. Another one drove straight past us. I managed to keep him walking and we made it up to Oxford Street.

'My plan was to get some food or coffee or water, anything, into him to sober him up, then try and get another cab. But he was impossible to handle: one minute he was slumped on the pavement, then he'd be up, running across the road to talk to someone. But I managed to get him into a burger bar. I went up to the counter to order – and when I looked round, he'd gone.

'I raced out, ran up and down the pavement. Then I saw the Tube station entrance. The rest you know: he jumped the barrier and there was CCTV footage of him pacing up and down the platform. Then he looked one way then the other, jumped down and he was gone, into the mouth of the tunnel. I didn't see it happen, Georgie, but as I came down the escalator, I heard the shouting. Someone screaming.'

'You were there,' is all she can say.

'At his funeral, I couldn't even look at you, or his parents. I'd as good as let him die – it was my fault.'

Georgie shakes her head – she can't take in what he's saying. 'But Dan, why didn't you tell me?'

'Georgie, I didn't tell anyone. I didn't even wait for the emergency services. The station was evacuated and, to my shame, I let myself be carried along with the crowd. I came out of the station and I walked home alone. Mandy was asleep the whole time – she didn't even know I'd left.

'I got your phone call on Saturday, after you'd rung round the hospitals, and when I put down the phone, I carried on watching the football. The next day, I visited Dad and Irena for lunch and on Monday morning I went to work, as usual.'

'I didn't know,' she manages.

'I should have told you,' Dan says. 'But I pretended it hadn't happened. Except I wasn't functioning at work. And then there was a restructuring and, surprise, surprise, my job was no longer necessary.

'As for Mandy – well, I don't think she signed up to be with this miserable git with no job. She liked the old Dan, the cheerful, smiley one who kept everyone entertained.'

Georgie's heart aches, for Finn's wasted life and for what Dan has been through. And, yes, for herself. 'I thought you hated me,' she says.

'I hated myself,' Dan says. 'For failing Finn. And taking him away from you forever.'

Suddenly, Georgie feels unutterably saddened by this never-ending cycle of guilt.

'I can't think straight any more,' she says. 'All I know is that Finn dying was a tragedy and a waste of life. But neither of us can take the blame. It doesn't help us and it won't bring Finn back.'

Eventually, Dan says, 'I'm glad we've talked. That you rang me.'

'And I'm glad you came,' she replies.

Dan starts the car again and despite the dodgy headlights and the loud engine and the smell inside this car, a feeling of calm descends. Georgie's brother is taking her home. They will never find their mother, not now. Their journey is over, but it hasn't been completely wasted because she and Dan are back together as brother and sister. And for that, Georgie is thankful. Oh, but now she's so very tired. She closes her eyes and lets the fatigue wash over her.

Chapter Thirty-Five

Nancy

The woman who picked up Nancy and Bree from the side of the road introduces herself as Veronica. 'And my camper van is called Molly.'

'Your camper van has a name?' Nancy asks.

'Yes, she's my trusty companion. You have a dog, I have my wheels. Both useful in different ways.'

Bree has curled herself into a ball in the footwell and Nancy holds her old-fashioned carpet bag on her knees. It smells of the bothy's wet stone and of earth, but she can't be getting sentimental now. She needs to put some distance between herself and the island.

She supposes he might not have seen the news story. In fact, he might be dead by now for all she knows, but moving on is what keeps Nancy safe. It stops her getting close to people or having to explain herself and it keeps her focused on the present. Because the past feels like another country, another lifetime, that Nancy can never return to.

Luckily, Veronica isn't the sort to ask questions; she's happy chattering away about herself. She tells Nancy how she was widowed two years ago and bought herself this camper van – 'My Molly' – to give herself a fresh start. 'I head off every few months or so. Always try and visit somewhere new,' she says. 'There's so much beauty to see, once you get away from the cities, don't you think?' Nancy couldn't agree more, but right now she feels the pull of a city, because it'll be easier to disappear there.

After a while, Veronica points to a Tupperware box that sits in a special cubbyhole behind the gear stick. 'Sandwiches,' she says smartly. 'Happy to share.' As Nancy pops open the plastic lid, she smells wholesome, yeasty bread, sees chunks of crumbly cheese – ingredients more exotic than her usual rations from the island shop's Super Savers range.

Veronica used to work as an accountant, but had to give it up when her husband got ill. 'I was his carer for three years,' she says. 'Then, after he died, I decided it was time for me to enjoy myself.' Nancy nods, thinks that this woman with her rosy cheeks and her hearty sandwiches deserves all the adventures she can find.

By dusk, they are on the outskirts of a town called Skipley, and with a jolt Nancy realises she recognises where they are. It's a place she was driven through many years ago, on trips to find distant antique shops and gold dealers. But it's still a good distance from Hoyton Beck – she's being silly. It turns out Veronica has pre-booked a pitch on a caravan site a few miles away, so she drops Nancy on the outskirts. 'Thank you,' Nancy says. 'For taking a chance on me.'

Already, it's icy underfoot. Nancy is tempted to keep hitching, to put as many miles between herself and Yorkshire as she can. But she's tired and the dog must be hungry. She'll find somewhere to shelter, then take stock. She sets off into the town. She has a bit of money, but she knows from experience that things can and will get worse, so she won't squander it yet.

Bree's claws tip-tap on the pavement, an alien sound after so long with grass and moss underfoot. Ahead, Nancy sees a car park and, more importantly, a squat building on one side. It's a toilet block and in a pretty, well-cared-for town like this, it might do them for the night. But as they get closer, she sees a hefty padlock on the door. 'Well, girl, where does that leave us?'

Bree gives a feeble wag of her tail, looks up with her brown eyes. It's cold and it's past her teatime.

'How about a nice tin of sardines, as a treat?'

Nancy carries on until she reaches a fork: to the left she can see a row of flat-fronted terraced houses, but to the right lies a brightly lit mini-market. It's tricky, this junction, but there's no traffic so she steps out into the road. She's just wondering if she can ask the shop for some water for the dog when everything changes.

She hears the angry roar of a motorbike coming from her left. He's not going that fast, there's still plenty of time for her to get across, so she gives Bree's lead a tiny tug. Then, in a split second, the motorbike stops behaving as it should. All at once, she sees the slick of black ice, the glint of the rider's helmet and then the bike spins out from underneath him and shoots off at an angle, still roaring.

There's the thwack of flesh on tarmac and she glimpses a man's face, eyes wide in shock, but then it's her who is being pulled, moving too fast because Bree is bolting in the other direction. There's a sharp pull and the dog is away and Nancy is toppling over as if in slow motion, until she feels the slam of the road on her cheek. Grit under her palms, a crack of pain in her ankle. Blood in her mouth, maybe teeth too.

She hears her own wet breathing, then feels the rise of panic as she realises she is lying in the middle of a road, on a corner. She needs to get up and get the motorcyclist out of the road too. She looks across, sees he's flat on his back. Beside him, the front wheel of his bike is still turning.

'Are you OK?' she calls out.

He doesn't answer, at least not in words. She hears a groan and wonders which of them made it.

Then, from nowhere, car headlights are coming straight towards her, but she can't move, she knows something is broken and she needs help. She raises a hand, tries to wave and stop the dazzle of lights. And then it's OK – the car is slowing down, someone has got out, and people have come running out of the shop.

She sees a muddle of legs and hears someone say, 'He's knocked over that old lady.' For a second, she wonders who the old lady is, then almost laughs as she realises they are talking about her, and she wants to explain that it didn't happen that way.

Someone is standing over her, telling her not to move. They are wearing Dr. Martens boots and she can see the yellow stitching around the edges and it puts her in mind of freshers' week at university and her big boots that took an age to lace up and her skinny legs in black tights and her own leather jacket, maybe not so different in style from the one the man on the motorbike is wearing.

Someone is talking about a homeless person and asking her name and she can't remember if she's Nan or Nancy or one of the other names she's used over the years, always beginning with N because that made it simpler. And then, talking of making up names, she remembers Bree and she keeps asking the same thing but nobody's listening to her.

Even when the ambulance finally comes and she asks again, 'Where's my dog? Where's my girl?', nobody replies. As she's strapped on to a gurney, Nancy raises her hand to her face. There's a red groove on her skin, a rope burn where the lead must have pulled.

Poor Bree, spooked by the man and the roar of an engine and the primal knowledge that her life was in danger. She obeyed her instinct and took off. Nancy doesn't blame her. She'd do the same in that situation – run and keep running.

Chapter Thirty-Six

GEORGIE

In her dream, Georgie is surfing. She's never actually been surfing, but in this dream she is a natural. She has complete control – her body and the water are as one. She can feel herself smiling as she stands up on the board and rides the cresting wave, sees the roiling, foaming water beneath her. She trusts her body, feels her core muscles take control and her legs and torso working in perfect balance. Below, the water is transparent but solid at the same time. It's supporting her but she knows she needs to be careful because it could turn and dash her down at any moment.

And as soon as she becomes aware of the danger of this moment, the magic is broken. The dream starts to fade and a different sensation takes over. She's not surfing any more, she is awake and she hurts.

It's like the worst backache and a low, dragging feeling in her pelvis and her bowels all at once, combining into one endless moment. It's not exactly pain, though, more a force that seems to be taking over her body, subsuming all other functions so they seem petty and pointless. Who cares if she hasn't washed her hair, that her ankles are swollen and her knees ache from sitting in this car for so long? The rest of her body is insignificant, subservient to this more important force.

And then, like a wave that's raced up to the top of the beach, it recedes, dwindles away almost to nothing. Georgie rubs her face, looks around her.

When the next Braxton Hicks contraction comes, Georgie is wide awake and ready. She breathes through it, like she's been taught to do, a silent whistle through her pursed lips. She gets out her phone and opens the stopwatch, watches the numbers flick by. This will be good practice, she thinks, for the real thing in two weeks' time, when Wilf will be timing them. She starts to type out a message to him:

> *Hi lovely, heading home now. I have lots to tell you. I miss you. Hope everything worked out . . .*

But she doesn't get to finish her message, because bang on four minutes, another band of tightness wraps itself around her middle. She breathes, waits and resets the stopwatch. As the numbers tick up to 3:48, another wave comes. Impressive, she thinks, the way that the body has its own inner clock.

The next time it happens, a groan slips out of her mouth. She can't help it, it emerges from somewhere deep inside and she registers that it helps: it makes her feel like the different parts of her body are joining up, working together.

She closes her eyes as she rides the next wave and the sound comes out of her again, a higher note this time, like the start of a song. When she opens her eyes, Dan is looking at her. His eyes flick back to the road, then to her.

'You OK? Everything OK?' He sounds breathless, a little panicked.

'Yes, all good. Just my uterus limbering up. Braxton Hicks contractions,' she says, trying to laugh, but then she can't because the wave is rising up again and she's riding it, almost getting to the top, but then it's too much, she's not skimming over its surface any more she's under it, she can't breathe, she's gasping and making a noise that she has no control over. She needs to stand up, to move around, and she can't, this tiny car is a trap. The seat belt is digging in her belly and she needs to turn to her side, to kick away the pain and stretch out.

'Oh, God, no, don't, not now,' Dan is saying, and she wants to reassure him, to tell him it's fine, it's just a practice run, show him the stopwatch on her phone, but she's dropped her phone, it's slipped somewhere she can't reach and it feels as if she's only just got her breath from the last wave when the next one hits and she's under, she's flailing and panicking.

She holds on to the seat belt, feels its shiny surface, and turns her head so she's grinding her face into the headrest. Her mouth is open, her dry lips snag on the man-made fibres. *Oh, no, not in Mandy's car*, she thinks. *Think of the upholstery.*

'Oh shit, oh no.' Dan is signalling to pull over and she can feel the car jerking as he changes down gears too fast. Then they are on a slip road, a smaller road, and finally he pulls to a stop.

'Georgie, is this still Braxton Hicks, or . . .'

She still has her face turned away, breathing into the headrest, which feels like her new friend, something she has to stay close to because it's going to help her through this.

'I don't know,' she wails. 'But it's too early, it's not time. It's not . . .' Again, the force is gathering, burning into her back, and she wants to press her fists into the small of her back to ease the pain but she can't, and it feels very important that she holds tight to this headrest. She's groaning, she's too hot and she knows that she has to move.

'Open the door, I need to get out,' she gasps.

She catches a glimpse of Dan running around the front of the car, and he's so speedy he looks like a cartoon character and she wants to laugh, but then he opens her door and it lets in a rush of cold air that feels so good. She smells the wet night, grass and claggy mud, a hint of manure from cattle that must be somewhere nearby. She thinks of how cows do this, standing in a field or kneeling on a bed of straw, lowing and swaying until they calve, because animals do this all the time, don't they?

She puts one foot then the other out of the car, realises too late that she'd taken off her boots to ease her swollen feet. Hoists herself out and leans against the car, feels the wet earth seep through her socks and the cold metal of Mandy's car against her hands. She feels an urge to sway her hips, so she does and this helps, and she notices that it's better out here in the open air where she can move.

Then there's a lull; the pain all but disappears, just a memory of it tingles in the small of her back, and she lets out a laugh. 'Oh my God,' she says. She lets go of the car, uses the heels of her hands to rub her back as best she can, but her sweater is too thick and the ground is soggy and this is all wrong. This is not how it's meant to happen.

Dan has gone very quiet and all Georgie can hear is the distant rush of cars. She sees her breath, white puffs in the cold air, thinks again of those nearby cows: wet muzzles, snorting breath. She notices the headlights on Mandy's car are still not working, faded to a weak beam that barely illuminates the scraggy verge Dan has parked up on.

Dan is swearing at his phone, lifting it up in the air. Swearing again.

'Jesus, Georgie. There's still no signal,' he says. 'Sorry, we need to keep driving. I can't even get through to 999.'

Georgie groans, turns back to the car and rests her forehead on her hands. She wants to stay standing but now her legs aren't working, they are shaking back and forth like they are made of some rubbery material, not even connected to her. She reaches one hand towards her brother, grabs his top. This is all wrong, she wants Wilf here and he's so far away. He doesn't even know. 'Dan, I can't do this,' she says, her voice rising in a shriek of panic.

'Yes you can,' says Dan firmly. 'Georgie, you're the strongest woman I know. You're going to be fine. We just need to get you to a hospital.'

He holds her hands in his and they take a step towards the open car door. Simultaneously, they look down at Georgie's mud-sodden socks. 'Oh,' Dan says.

'Do you want to get a plastic bag or something – for me to sit on?' Georgie asks. 'I mean, my waters might break in the car. Isn't that what happens?'

'No. Forget the upholstery.'

Dan holds her by the elbows as she eases herself back in. By the time he's shut the door, she's turned herself sideways and is holding on to the headrest again, her old friend, letting out a low bellow. She needs to vomit and go to the toilet, both at the same time, but she can't make the words to say this, so she just bangs on the headrest with one hand.

Dan seems to get the message because the car starts up. But it's not moving. There's the sickening sound of wheels spinning on wet grass, followed by a whining and a churning.

Dan lets out a whimper, tries again, more slowly, and the car starts to move. There's the smell of burnt rubber in the air and Dan is hunched over the wheel because the headlights are worse than ever. He's muttering to himself about staying off the motorway because who ever saw a hospital next to a motorway, and Georgie isn't sure this is a good idea because when she turns her head, the

199

road he's taking is dark and narrow and this feels wrong in every way possible.

As another shock of pain spreads across her back, she pushes her face into the soft fabric and curses herself and the bad decisions she's made. Georgie has notched up a fair few, but surely taking a road trip to find their mother two weeks before she's due to give birth has to be the worst yet.

◆　◆　◆

Dan's instinct was right because, at some point, Georgie becomes aware of street lights, then houses and traffic lights. And then Dan's pulling up, parking, and he's got a signal because he's talking into his phone. He's asking for an ambulance and then he's saying 'Yes, the patient is breathing. No, there's no blood.' Then there's a pause and he's shouting about her going into labour early. It's a first baby yes, but no, he's not the father, and is that really relevant? Then he's saying, 'Two hours? That's impossible . . . Fifteen minutes? OK, yes, I can do that.'

'They're coming?' she says.

'No, they can't get to us in time. Too stretched. But they say the hospital is only fifteen minutes away, so we'll go straight there. Hang on, Georgie.'

There's more driving and Georgie doesn't want this bit to end. She's almost used to the pain now, the reliability of how it forces itself through her, pushes her to a point where she can't bear it, then recedes. If she closes her eyes, she can dip back into her dream of surfing, riding this unstoppable wave, but then it all changes because they are somewhere with bright lights and people are opening the door and peering in and there's the clank of metal latches clicking into place.

'Hello Georgie, we're going to take care of you now, don't worry,' says a woman, and two people in uniforms are reaching in for her, telling her where to put her feet in their wet, muddy socks so she can sink down into the seat of a waiting wheelchair. Georgie wants to walk, she wants to know where Dan is, but the voice of the person pushing her through endless bright corridors tells her there's no time for that.

She's trying to breathe deeply, but the air here is hot and stale. It smells of sour breath and disease and disinfectant and she yearns to be outside again, standing under the stars with the cows and the air.

Georgie looks down at herself, suddenly conscious of what people are seeing. The top she's been wearing for the past two days is dotted with stains and her hands are grubby with mud. She thinks fondly of her overnight bag, so carefully packed by Wilf, sitting in Mandy's car. Her coat, too, is still lying on the back seat and her phone – actually, she has no idea where her phone is. Dan has to find it so he can ring Wilf. Because Wilf should be here, right now – it was all planned – but as always, Georgie has messed things up.

There's a swivel and a bump as the nurse puts the brakes on and Georgie realises she's been parked in a triage cubicle. The nurse says she won't be two ticks, she's going to make a call to the maternity ward, but Georgie doesn't hear the rest because the hotness is back and it's spreading, burning her back, and she moans, a sound that gathers volume with this contraction.

All she can see is blue curtains on all sides, and she can hear a different world going on behind them – trolley wheels turning, doors banging, the slap-slap of someone's shoes running. A phone is ringing and no one is picking it up. And then, from somewhere closer, perhaps it comes from inside her own head, she hears a different sound. It's a calm, low voice.

'Hush, there,' it says. 'You can do this.'

Georgie holds her breath, wonders if she imagined that voice. Then she feels the oddest sensation, a small 'pop' somewhere near her bladder, then a soft release that she supposes is her waters breaking. But there's no one here to tell. Dan must be parking the car and she's been left in this curtained cubicle and no one is coming.

She looks down at the lino floor, sees a small trickle of liquid, and she allows herself a sob of self-pity. It reminds her of the time she wet herself in a PE lesson, thinking she could hold it in but she couldn't. It made a far bigger puddle that time, on the parquet floor, and she'd had to wear spare pants from the lost property box all afternoon. They were bright green and meant for a boy. Her mum had been waiting for her at the school gates and when she told her what had happened, Nancy hadn't been cross like the PE teacher. She'd wrapped her in a huge hug that made it all right. 'You got some splendid green pants out of it though,' she said, and the two of them laughed about it all the way home.

Then she hears someone marching up the lino in shoes that squeak and the curtain beside her is suddenly whisked back. The hooks make a jangling noise and Georgie looks up with a start, feeling exposed.

Next to her, an older woman is lying on a gurney. The hospital orderly with the noisy shoes has come for this other woman, he's unlocking a brake and saying, 'Off we go then, time for your X-ray.'

But Georgie isn't looking at the man with the squeaky shoes. She's staring at the woman lying there, her head turned towards Georgie, and she knows this is the person who whispered 'Hush' through the curtain. Dark eyes, framed by wrinkles. Two ragged grey plaits and the pale scrape of a centre parting. A mole just above her top lip.

The woman's mouth opens as if to form words, but it's too late because the gurney is moving away – and then a wave of pain picks Georgie up and carries her off to an entirely different place. And when she returns to the hospital cubicle and she can think in sentences again, the woman on the gurney is nowhere to be seen.

Hospital sounds crowd back in: voices, the clatter of a metal tray. Far off, someone crying or laughing, it's hard to tell. Georgie shakes her head in astonishment.

Remarkable, she thinks, how the brain conjures things up, takes thoughts that are floating around inside your head and rearranges them into a story. Tricks you into believing it, just as it does with a vivid dream.

But an hour later, when Georgie is standing and holding on to the end of a bed base, swaying her hips and making a bovine lowing, the woman's face comes back to her: its kindness, its complete familiarity. And when she starts to cry out, 'Ma . . . Ma,' she's not picturing the Nancy she barely remembers from her childhood but the grey-haired woman she glimpsed when the curtain was drawn back and it's too much to bear, so she roars to banish that ridiculous thought.

Then the midwife is encouraging her, cheering her on like this is a sport and she's close to the finishing line and Georgie feels it too, a gathering of strength and she knows that, yes, she can do this. The midwife asks if she wants to feel her baby's head, so Georgie reaches down, touches a circle of damp hair, and she wonders if it is russet brown, like hers, or darker like its father's. There's the surreal knowledge that a small body exists inside her body and soon it will start its own life on the outside. Then there's a rush of emotion and a rip of pain and Georgie feels like she's standing on the edge of a precipice, dizzy with the realisation of what is happening.

With an impossible slither, her baby is out in the world. The midwife has a hold of it, someone else helps Georgie on to a birthing stool and then her baby is laid on her chest, bloodied and wet. Georgie dares to look down, sees two eyes trying to take in the world. She wants to magically dim the lights, whisper that same word, *Hush*, to these people around her who are talking too loudly about the baby's cord and how it's unusually short.

'Short cord – that means she'll stay close to you,' says the older midwife in a broad Yorkshire accent. Then she gently reaches under the towel that's wrapped around the baby and there's the sound of scissor blades slicing, cutting loose the purple-grey twist of flesh.

With a final drag of pain, Georgie delivers the placenta and it's carried off, like a trophy, in a silver tray to be inspected. 'Not going to take it home and fry it up with onions, are you?' the same midwife is asking.

'No, I'm vegetarian,' Georgie says faintly, aware she should be treasuring this moment with her new baby, not talking nonsense with strangers.

She's holding this bloodied bundle to her chest and it feels too new for this bright world. She doesn't dare shift position, but she must look. She glimpses its nose, a clasp of fingers, tiny nails fully formed. A mewling mouth, a whorl of brown hair.

'Did you say "she"?' Georgie asks.

'Yes. Lovely baby girl you have.'

Then they whisk the baby away because she's come a bit early and they need to check she's OK and Georgie nods. She looks down at the gown someone must have helped her into earlier, sees blood and gunk. She's given more towels and helped on to a bed. Her head is spinning, so she lies back. Already, she feels bereft. Her baby was right here, cleaving to her skin, and now she's gone and the sense of loss is so huge Georgie can barely breathe.

The midwife returns with the baby expertly swaddled, and Georgie holds out both arms for her with a raw hunger. Someone has wiped her baby's face clean, dressed her in something white, and she feels the bulky crunch of a nappy under the hospital blanket.

The midwife is talking to her about breastfeeding and colostrum and how the baby is a good weight – but Georgie isn't listening. All she's thinking is that she's holding her baby daughter and she never wants to let go of her. She can't imagine how any mother would.

Chapter Thirty-Seven

NANCY

If Nancy could get out of bed and run, she would. But every time she tries to move her left leg, a shaft of pain shoots up from her ankle. She supposes she should be grateful that she's even got a bed – she's been moved on to a ward because nobody can look at her X-rays until the morning. She's on nil by mouth, just in case they need to operate tomorrow, so there's not even the comfort of hot, sweet tea. Nearby, she can hear the nurses in their little office, talking about an 'RTA' and an 'NFA', an old woman who was knocked down by a motorbike.

They've got it all wrong and Nancy wants to shout out and correct them. Why do people see how something looks from the outside and decide that's the truth, without asking any questions? *It was black ice*, she wants to say – she saw its lethal sheen as she lay there on the hard road, listening to the soft moans of the motor-cyclist. But nobody has ever been interested in Nancy's side of the story.

If a nurse comes back, she won't waste her breath trying to tell them. What she'll do is talk about the pain in her hip and her ankle.

It's not as bad as it was, but Nancy isn't going to let on. She wants them to give her all the drugs going – something to knock her out so she doesn't have to think any more.

She can still hear the metallic jangle of the curtain rings, the swish of the wipe-clean curtain as the orderly pulled it back. Then the sight of her own daughter, who had been sitting not two metres from Nancy. The woman who had been making those desperate, lonely sounds had been her own flesh and blood.

Then the look on Georgie's face, a split second of recognition, her eyes widening in horror. And before Nancy could say a word, she was being whisked away, down a corridor and into a lift, barely believing it herself. Then she'd lain on the X-ray table, where her leg was turned this way and that and the pain was terrible, but she'd welcomed it as a distraction and a fitting punishment rolled into one.

Now she's been put to bed on this hot, sour-smelling ward and so many questions are flitting around inside Nancy's head. It was Georgie, without a doubt. But why is she here, of all places? Yesterday, when that man took her photograph, Nancy knew her cover had been blown and someone would come looking for her. She just hadn't expected it to be Georgie.

The old panic begins to gather in her chest, working its way up her throat. 'Nurse, I need something. For the pain,' she calls out.

She's had snippets of news about her children over the years, but she hadn't known that Georgie was pregnant. Maybe a letter went to Morag's campsite. Or maybe it was decided, on balance, that Nancy had no right to be told.

She can still hear that keening sound that came from the cubicle next to her. Even before she saw her face, Nancy felt the urge to soothe this woman, because it was clear that the person next to her wasn't making that noise because she had a broken bone or a grumbling appendix. It was the unmistakable sound of a woman getting ready to give birth.

It had taken Nancy back to her own first time, those dark hours of pushing into pain. Frank must have been there too, but all Nancy remembers is terror and thrashing and feeling utterly alone. Then, a baby handed to her, raw and helpless, in need of protection she felt unqualified to give. The midwife wiping the baby's face, saying, 'It's clear who she takes after.' Then, lying back and feeling hope draining away, like so much unstaunched blood, because on some level she already knew having this baby wasn't going to be the end of her troubles, but the start.

'Nurse!' she calls out again. 'I need something, for the pain.'

Chapter
Thirty-Eight

Nancy, 2002

'I'll be back before you know it'

She doesn't tell Gerry that she's seeing her children today, only that she is meeting Frank in London to talk things over. It felt safer, somehow, to keep her children out of the conversation. In fact, she tries to play down the whole event, because she knows Gerry doesn't want her to go. Bar the times when he waits for her outside antique shops, he hasn't let her out of his sight since they arrived in Yorkshire. 'I'm only meeting Frank so I can talk money,' she tells him. 'Surely I'm due something from him – I can't live on air, can I?'

Gerry raises an eyebrow and says, no, he supposes not. 'You can't rely on my largesse forever,' he adds. The walls of the cottage are looking barer than ever, but Nancy has no idea what Gerry intends to do with the money he squirrels away. She's long since realised it doesn't go towards any care home fees.

She gets a coach down to London because it's cheaper than the train, and all the way there, a nervousness flutters in her chest. It's partly the shock of being back in the outside world after so long, but it's mostly because she's excited. If she thinks too hard about what's happening today, she can barely breathe.

She's wearing the old T-shirt and jeans she left in three months ago, but as soon as she steps down from the coach, she realises how shabby she looks. Washing her clothes in the kitchen sink never gets them properly clean and she has no make-up. Not even a hairbrush – she has to make do with Gerry's greasy comb. Her plimsolls are crusted with dried mud, the soles worn thin.

She is due to meet Frank and the children outside the Royal Festival Hall at 2 p.m. Frank picked the spot – 'neutral ground', he called it. It took a lot of cajoling and reassurance to get him to agree.

I've told them you're abroad, helping animals. I really don't know if it's a good idea to disrupt their lives again. We're getting into a new rhythm, we're managing fine. I've even hired a cleaner, he wrote to Nancy.

As if cleaning is all a mother does, Nancy fumed, and she scrunched his letter up. Then she smoothed it out again and wrote a reply.

> *I think the break has done us all a lot of good. Please could you say I've come back and I'm really looking forward to seeing them again. Please, Frank, it would mean the world to me. I can't begin to tell you how sorry I am and I hope we can work something out, for the children's sakes.*

Finally, he agreed. So today, the plan is that he'll leave the kids with Nancy, then collect them at 4 p.m. *There's lots to see around there. Or take them for a late lunch?* he wrote. *If it goes well, we can all go for a walk along the river afterwards.* She hopes this will be when she and Frank discuss things – work out a rota, talk about the house.

Nancy gets to the pre-arranged spot early, sits on the edge of the bench checking her watch and looking this way and that. When she sees them coming, she can't help herself, she runs to meet them, hugs Dan first, then Georgie. Her daughter feels stiff in her arms and she's wearing a pink vest top and khaki cargo pants that Nancy doesn't recognise. At the side of her face hangs a long thin plait, twisted with blue thread and beads, and Nancy touches it.

'My friend did it for me,' Georgie says shyly, and Nancy can tell she's proud of it. 'It took ages.'

Frank doesn't come over, he watches from a distance, but as the three of them walk away it gives Nancy a small thrill when neither child looks back at him.

At first it's wonderful, like the best gift she could have, and her heart swells with hope. They watch some kids skateboarding up and down slopes and there's a jazz band playing in the foyer of the Festival Hall. It's not Nancy's thing and definitely not Georgie's, but it's nice, just standing and watching something together. It puts off the moment when she has to talk to them, explain why she went away.

They wander back outside. She felt too embarrassed to tell Frank she didn't have any money to treat them to lunch, but she does have enough to buy the children an overpriced ice cream each. They head back to their bench and Nancy dares to let herself think, *yes, this could work*.

She can imagine Frank and herself coming to some agreement, taking it in turns to have them at weekends. They'll have to sell the house, of course: buy two smaller places. Today, getting away from Gerry and his damp, depressing cottage is doing her the world of good too. She realises how her life has shrunk down to the walls of that claustrophobic little house and how it's not helping her, not at all.

The sun comes out and Nancy closes her eyes, feels it warm on her face. Once the children have finished their ice creams, she will explain everything to them. She will say that she's been unwell and that's why she had to go away, but now things feel clearer. She will tell them how much she misses them.

But then a shadow falls across Nancy's face. She opens her eyes, sees the gnarly buttons on his cardigan, his belt buckle, glinting.

'Gerry?' she manages to say, not quite believing it.

She gets to her feet, places herself between him and the children. But already Georgie is eyeing him warily, frowning at Nancy. Dan is still licking his ice cream.

'Thought I'd join you,' Gerry says. 'Moral support.'

Nancy looks around, sees happy families strolling by. She doesn't want to make a scene – already, her time with her children is running out. She looks at her watch: only twenty-five minutes left. She decides the best thing to do is play along, not make a big deal of it. It's a busy public place – people often bump into each other.

But inside, she feels fear gathering. This is her one chance to see her children and make things right and Gerry's done it again, he's followed her. Will she never be free of him? After today, she decides, things have to change.

She feels Dan's eyes on her. 'Mummy?' he says.

'It's all right, everything's fine,' she says tightly.

'No, Mummy, I need the loo.'

She looks at Dan, whose face has turned oddly pale; then at Georgie, who has stopped eating her ice cream. Long white dribbles have run down the sides of her cone and on to her hand.

'Oh, Dan,' she says. 'Can't you wait?'

'No, I can't. I need to go now. Please, Mummy.'

Nancy picks up her bag. 'Come on, Georgie, let's go.' There must be a toilet inside and she looks up at the concrete building, trying to remember where to go.

She feels Dan slip a sticky hand into hers, but Georgie isn't moving. Instead, she's looking at Nancy in an odd way.

'No,' Georgie says slowly. 'I think I'll wait here, thanks.' She stands, lobs her unfinished ice cream into a litter bin.

Dan is squeezing Nancy's hand, pulling her towards the building – now is not the time to argue with Georgie. Nancy is loath to acknowledge Gerry's presence, but she has to. 'Gerry, just keep an eye on her, will you?' Then to Georgie, 'I'll be back before you know it.'

Georgie doesn't answer, but Gerry does. 'Sure, sure,' he says, stroking his beard in that way that used to make her go weak at the knees but now makes her want to slap his ferrety face. 'We'll be right here, won't we, Georgie?'

It takes ages to find a loo – the first one is being cleaned and then they have to go up several flights of stairs and all the time Dan is saying he's desperate and they are walking as fast as they can, almost running. But then it's done, it's all OK, and as they go back down the stairs, Nancy feels calmer, more in control. And by the time they walk back out into the sunshine, she realises she can do this.

She will calmly explain to Gerry that she values this time with her children and she would prefer to be here on her own. Surely he'll understand, give her a bit of space? And if he doesn't, well, it's time for Gerry to start listening to her.

At first, she thinks nothing of the sirens; this is London, after all, there's always a siren going off somewhere. But then she sees the bench where Georgie should be and it's empty. And that man, he's nowhere to be seen. She starts to run out on to the concourse, looking left and right. Her tongue feels dry and too big and slow to work but she manages to shout. She doesn't care if people stare: she shouts her daughter's name over and over, cupping her hands around her mouth.

And then she feels Dan tugging at her and he's pointing up at the footbridge, the new one that spans the river, where pedestrians walk alongside the trains that go in and out of Charing Cross station and the brown river churns far below.

Then they are running, her and Dan, towards the bridge where a crowd has gathered around the base of the stairs, all looking up. The first thing she sees is a girl with long hair hanging down, as if she is reaching for something far below in the water. But she's at the wrong angle – everything about the scene is wrong. She's leaning out too far from the bridge and her top is short so you can see the naked curve of her back. It's a pink vest top, and in the girl's hair, Nancy sees the flash of blue beads.

They won't let her up on the bridge, even when she cries and shouts and tries to push through. There are two policemen with their arms crossed and they don't listen when she says she's the girl's mother. Then she hears the crackle of a walkie-talkie and there's a policewoman next to her, leading her away, asking if she has any proof of identity and asking for the girl's name. In a daze, Nancy feels herself and Dan being led to a bench and the funny thing is that it's the same bench as before, where they sat eating ice creams.

'I left her. How could I have left her?' That's all Nancy can say and she keeps saying it until she hears the whoop-whoop of an ambulance arriving. It drives up as close to the steps as it can get, and Nancy lets out a cry.

'It's all right, love,' the policewoman says. 'Sounds like she's fine. Just a precaution.'

Nancy is shaking and she squeezes Dan's hand tight. 'It's all right,' she whispers to him. 'The policewoman says Georgie's fine.'

She sees the crowd parting, people in uniform coming down the steps, and then there is Georgie. She looks different, older somehow, or maybe it's because, in this moment, Nancy realises a distance has opened up between her and her daughter, one that will be impossible to close. Nancy stands, tries to run to her, but the policewoman who'd seemed so kind a moment before has a tight grip, and all she can do is watch as Georgie reaches the bottom step and holds out her arms to the person waiting at the bottom. It's Frank, who has come back at the appointed time to find this scene of devastation.

She sees Frank with his smart haircut and his weekend shirt, the way the two police officers nod and listen. She sees Dan – who was here only a moment ago – being led over to join his father and his sister. And then she watches as one of the policemen talking to Frank turns, raises a finger and points at Nancy. And she knows all the things Frank will say: 'A breach of trust. Endangering a child. An unfit mother.'

All around her there is noise and movement, and Nancy fights and she screams. She wants her daughter, but she knows there is no coming back from this: no excuses or apologies can repair this damage. Frank is right – these children are not safe in her care. It's a long time before she has screamed herself quiet.

Chapter Thirty-Nine

NANCY, 2002

'WE CAN STAY HERE FOREVER'

For weeks, it feels as if something is broken inside Nancy. She lies in her bed and imagines that her heart has detached itself and is floating aimlessly around inside her, bumping against her bones before drifting off again, battered and bruised. At other times, the ache shifts to her stomach and she draws her knees to her chest, staying in that position for a long time.

Like all those years ago, food feels like an affront to her senses, a comfort when she deserves none. So, a hollowness returns to her cheeks. The bones in her arms look satisfyingly skeletal, a badge of her pain.

After that dreadful afternoon by the river, she'd been taken to the police station. An officer had locked her in a room and then come back to write some things down. But eventually, Nancy was told she could go. It was Saturday night in the West End and the police had the usual fights and vice and drunks to mop up. Most importantly, Georgie was OK.

'No thanks to you,' Frank had said. He was waiting for her out-side Charing Cross police station, with the sole purpose of telling Nancy she needn't think about seeing her children again for a long time. 'You put them in grave danger. They are safer without you – and that sick man who seems to follow you everywhere. There is no way any judge would give you custody now,' he said as his parting shot. 'Probably not even access.'

Gerry, of course, had vanished. The police said he'd greeted them on the bridge with relief, told them that he'd pulled this young girl back from leaning too far over the railings. It looked dangerous, he'd said – it was a good job he'd spotted her in time. As they moved forward with their walkie-talkies to take over, Gerry had stepped back. And when they looked around for the girl's res-cuer, he had gone, melted into the crowd.

Georgie had been taken to hospital, then home, where Frank's parents were looking after Dan. She hadn't said a single word since she'd been brought down from the bridge, Frank told Nancy. 'Is this what you want for your daughter – catatonic, terrified, heading for a breakdown before she's even a teenager?'

'No,' Nancy had whispered. Then she'd asked, 'And how is Dan?'

'They say he's fine. Showing my dad his Transformer collection. Acting like nothing happened.'

'Tell them I'm sorry,' she said. 'I'm so sorry. I'll never forgive myself.'

But Frank didn't make any promises. 'Just stay away. For their sakes,' he said.

Frank had left Nancy sitting on the pavement outside the police station. She has no idea how long she stayed there until, inevitably, she looked up and saw a pair of dusty brogues.

'What a pickle,' Gerry said, shaking his head. Then he told her how it had all been a big misunderstanding. He'd taken Georgie to see the boats and she'd leaned over a bit too far. But Nancy knew that wasn't the truth. She knew Gerry was sending a message to her: *Try and run away and I'll be right behind you. And if I don't find you, I'll always be able to find your children.* It was a message she understood, loud and clear.

'Yes,' Gerry said again, shaking his head. 'She's a live wire, that Georgie – wonder who she gets that from?'

Sitting on the damp pavement, Nancy made up her mind that she must never give Gerry a reason to go near either of her children again. She would do as Frank said and stay away from them. It will be her punishment – and their salvation.

Now Nancy and Gerry are back at his grandmother's cottage, which is looking even more bare than before. There are no paintings left on the walls and they are down to the last of the silverware. The episode in London has changed Gerry, too. He's more watchful. Makes her empty her pockets when she returns from the antique shops, the gold merchants and the auction houses they visit around Yorkshire. 'Can't trust you, can I?' he says. 'Sneaky Nancy might go scuttling off to London again. But I'll soon find you.' He takes to locking the cottage's front door at night.

One evening, Gerry gets drunk on his grandmother's port, sits down beside her on the sofa. Until now, he hasn't tried to sleep with her. But tonight, he lays a chubby hand on her leg. 'This is us, now,' he says. 'To think, I used to dream of moments like this. All I had was a few blurry videos to keep my fire burning. But now, here we are: Gerry Mac and his muse. And we can stay here forever.' Nancy shrinks from his touch and goes to her room. She wedges a chair under the doorknob, sits on her narrow bed and nurses her hatred. She will bide her time.

Six months after the incident on the bridge, Nancy creeps down the creaky wooden staircase, tiptoes across the kitchen floor to the cupboard where Gerry keeps a tin stuffed with money and takes the lot. She had already slipped her hand into Gerry's waistcoat pocket, found the front door key he secreted there, when she helped him up to bed. She closes the cottage door softly behind her.

Her first lift is from a lorry driver who takes her to Liverpool, the first of many cities, which she soon discovers are the best places to hide. Nancy knows Gerry will be furious that she's taken his cash, so she can't risk going near her children. He'll come in search of his money and his so-called muse. So, fear of Gerry keeps her away from her children, but most of all it is a sense of shame.

When she thinks of all the damage she's done, this shame is a weight that crushes her, confines her to the hostel where she lives, for weeks on end. And when she finally surfaces, she is sure her children are better off without her. She has to trust that Frank will have found a way of explaining things to them, just as he did when she first left London.

As Nancy lies in her hostel bed and listens to the slamming of fire doors, the roars of other humans in pain, she makes a decision. She cannot face asking anyone from her old life for help. Definitely not her parents, who would only make her feel more ashamed. And the thought of ringing her old friends, her neighbours, even distant relatives, would only drag her deeper down, as she has to explain how comprehensively she has ruined her life and her children's. So there is really only one solution. She will exile herself.

Chapter Forty

Nancy, 2003

'The creatures here have been through a lot'

Nancy takes a long time choosing the two postcards, rotating the creaky metal stand and touching each dusty card in turn. In the end, she buys two that are identical: she worries that if she sends different pictures, one of the children – most likely Georgie – will decide they got the inferior one. It's hard to keep her hand steady, so she writes each word carefully and slowly. She keeps the message simple too: *The creatures here have been through a lot. Thinking of you back in England. I miss you every day.* She adds, *Hope to see you soon*, knowing it's a wish rather than a promise.

Each postcard has a picture of a tiger cub on the front. She suspects they are already too childish for Georgie and Dan, now thirteen and eleven, but she doesn't know what else to pick. When she first left, Frank said he'd make up some story about her helping the wildlife, so this might make some sort of sense to them. It's the continuation of a lie, but it's better than the truth.

Nancy isn't looking after tiger cubs, but she is getting better at looking after herself. It was a woman she met in a hostel in Leeds who told her about this place. It's in the north of Thailand, a place where humans, addicts of all sorts, are sent to get healed. 'I know, right – you'd think it would be the worst place to go, but it works,' Luna had told her. Luna has a shaved head, tattoos and an attitude to match.

In the hostel, she often stayed in the room next to Nancy's and kept order along the corridor. Nancy pays for Luna's flight – she wonders if this was all part of the plan, but she doesn't mind, not really. And Luna was right: gradually, this place of wet heat, red dirt and mosquitoes does her good. At night, she sleeps alongside other women, in a long hut made from bamboo. In the day, she and the other walking wounded sit in a circle on woven mats and talk about all the ways they have been broken, and then all the ways they have broken other people.

There's a warped comfort in knowing she's not the worst sinner in this bunch, not by a long chalk. All are recovering addicts of one sort or another. In these sessions, Nancy learns that drink isn't her only issue. She's told she's also a co-dependent and she got herself locked into toxic relationships. She learns phrases like *coercive control* and *power imbalance. Breach of trust* is another one that chimes with her.

She's told that in order to move on, she must forgive others and accept her own faults, and Nancy agrees, up to a point, but she also thinks it's unfair because nobody is telling Gerry to do that, are they? Or Frank, for that matter.

She writes Frank long letters, where she tries to explain how it was for her in those early days with one baby, then two. Feeling her sense of self disappearing down the plughole with the dregs of Weetabix and rusks and pureed pear. She mentions Gerry, too, because she thinks she's worked out how he found them in Wales, on that holiday where everything spilled out, but it barely matters. Because if Gerry hadn't succeeded in finding her there, he would have come back another time and it would have happened in another place.

For months, Nancy doesn't receive a reply. And then, one morning, she sees the slender blue sheaf of an aerogramme waiting for her, laid next to her breakfast bowl of rice porridge. It's unexpected. It takes her a while to get her head around this letter, but it gives her a glimmer of hope.

From then on, she receives irregular snippets of news, missives sent to the places where she has an address that feels semi-permanent. There's never much news, but it's enough to know what her children are doing. In the years that follow, she hears how Georgie is off to college and then how Dan has a place at university in London. How her own mother has died from a stroke, her father not long afterwards.

Thousands of miles from their gravesides, Nancy sends up a small, agnostic prayer. She tries to remember the moments of love and she forgives Theresa and Mike their failings. With a shiver, she remembers the yellow cloud of resentment that emanated from her mother, her father's cold disinterest. How Nancy had never felt liked, let alone loved, in that bed and breakfast that was anything but homely.

Luna with the tattoos is long gone – she quit the programme and got a flight to India for the full-moon parties in Anjuna. For a while, Nancy misses her friend – not to mention the wad of cash that disappeared with her. It was never really Nancy's money, but the episode teaches her a lesson: don't get too close to people again.

Finally, Nancy has had enough of the circle discussions and the people in white robes with shiny faces and their endless talking. She flies back to the grey drizzle of England, picks up shifts in factories and warehouses, working alongside women who do this as a second or third job, needing the extra cash to buy their kids Christmas presents and food.

Under harsh strip lighting, she works nights, packaging up toys and electronic games that none of the women on the production line can afford. When she's asked if she has a family, Nancy gives a small shrug that people take as a no. She rents a room above a launderette, folds and irons people's service washes. As the weather gets warmer, she works in a beach café, but there are too many families there, visions of what she could have had, and that hurts too much so she leaves.

Mostly, she stays off the drink, but the guilt is harder to quit – it's always with her. It uses small, ordinary objects to sneak into the cracks in her mind. A toy car left on a café table. A boy carrying his school bag who has a particular long-legged gait. In a park, Nancy sees a girl jumping into a skipping rope, her plaits flying. It takes weeks to get that image out of her head and she falls off the wagon in her desperation to forget.

She has a rock-bottom year, scraping by, then she picks up night shifts cleaning offices. Her boss comments on how she doesn't shirk when she does the toilets and Nancy thinks how those years of scrubbing the pink porcelain at The Beaufort finally paid off after all.

In 2011, she moves on again, this time to Ireland, where she gets work mucking out and helping with milking on a dairy farm. As a sideline, the farmer takes in unwanted dogs, the ones that are too old, worn out from breeding or can't hunt to earn their keep. To save these no-hope hounds from the council's kill list, the farmer, Declan, keeps them in a set of ramshackle sheds. When Nancy feeds them, she remembers the made-up story from all those years ago about how she was going to work in an animal sanctuary, and wonders about coincidence and fate.

Counting up the years that have passed, she works out that Georgie will be twenty-one now, probably getting ready to leave college; Dan two years behind. She sends a short letter with an updated return address and, a few months later, she receives a photograph of Georgie in her graduation gown. Dan standing beside her, wearing a suit for the occasion.

She's grateful, but it knocks her for six. She tells Declan she has the flu and doesn't leave her room for a week. Her beautiful daughter is so grown-up and she wears her hair in a high ponytail. But Nancy would recognise her anywhere. Dan, of course, is giving the world his biggest grin and he's got his arm around his sister. Looking at the two of them together hurts, but it warms her heart as well. They will always have each other.

A new dog is dumped at the farm's gate. She's a collie-cross, so scared she can barely walk. Instead, she creeps around the edges of her pen, keeping low down and trying to make herself invisible. There is a red weal around her neck, a ghost of her brutish past. This dog howls day and night and nobody wants her.

Declan despairs: she won't even eat because the sound of food clattering in the metal bowl scares her. He admits defeat, says she's a lost cause. Every day, after her work is done, Nancy sits in the dog's pen, lays nuggets of food on a blanket so she can pick at them in silent safety. Slowly, the dog learns to trust her, and she names it Bree.

Years pass. Times get harder and Declan can't afford to keep Nancy on. But he knows someone who runs a caravan site over in Scotland. It's a place where a woman called Morag sometimes lets people stay in exchange for cleaning and gardening. He'll put in a good word. Nancy says OK, that'll do her fine. But only if she can bring the dog.

Chapter
Forty-One

NANCY

The nurse who wakes Nancy up is a cheery sort, all bustle and lipstick smiles. She still can't give her anything to eat or drink, in case Nancy needs surgery, but the consultant will be doing his rounds soon. As Nancy surfaces from sleep, the jumbled events of yesterday start to crowd in. She eases herself up, winces at the splintering pain, and starts with the easy questions.

'The man on the motorbike, is he all right?'

'The one who knocked you over? I can find out.'

Then Nancy tells the nurse that it wasn't like that, it was an accident. 'It was nobody's fault – his bike went over and then I did. I hope he's OK.'

The nurse is busy – Nancy can tell she's already thinking about all the jobs she has to do this morning – but she has to ask.

'I don't suppose the paramedics said anything about my dog?' she says. 'She was spooked, you see. Took off. I can't bear the thought of her out there. Still running. Or she might be hiding under a bush. Or on the roads . . .'

At that, the nurse pulls up a chair, nudges it closer to Nancy's bed. She is called Sandrine and Nancy is in luck because she's an animal lover. 'Cats, dogs, rabbits. I've had them all,' she says. 'I've got a friend who runs a shelter – let me ask her if your dog's been brought in. You should have said last night,' she chides. 'Is she microchipped? Or have you got a photo I can send her?'

Nancy says no to both. She doesn't even own a mobile phone. 'But I can describe her,' she says, and then she tells Sandrine about Bree's brown-and-white coat and the way her tail rises like a flag and the dot of black fur on the third toe of her left paw. 'She might still have a lead on her. Well, more of a rope, really.'

Sandrine nods, pauses, and looks at Nancy's chart at the end of her bed. 'Nancy Jebb,' she reads. Gives a wry look. 'Not "Nan", by any chance?'

Nancy cannot speak, shakes her head.

'Coincidence, then,' says Sandrine. 'Lots of people are looking for someone with a similar name. But of course, they should probably mind their own business.' She gives Nancy a wink as she walks off. Nancy pulls the covers around her, swallows down the pain and the other questions that she can't give voice to: she wants to ask about a pregnant woman who was brought in last night, about to give birth. She's desperate to know if she's OK, if the baby is well.

But Nancy realises she's the last person Georgie will want to see. Whatever the reason for Georgie being up in Yorkshire, she'll have her nearest and dearest around her. A husband, maybe proud grandparents. She won't want Nancy there, a ravaged ghost from the past, dragging bad memories in her wake.

Because Nancy is the evil fairy, the one whose presence could inadvertently put a curse on her daughter and grandchild. Nancy has been running for twenty years, but she has never really broken free of the man who ruined her life and her family's. She tried to outrun him, but three days ago she broke cover and now she's exposed, like a deer in a hunter's sights. As the nurse told her, 'people are looking'. And every minute she stays here, trapped in this hospital bed, she could be leading her hunter right to her daughter and that's a chance she can't take.

Nancy looks up, lets out a gasp, because already the figure of a man is standing at the foot of her bed. She feels the hair on her arms prickle, but then she blinks, sees him more clearly. It's a doctor with a lanyard around his neck and, even before he speaks, Nancy knows he means business because she's met his type before: policemen, council officials, warehouse bosses. She sees how his eyes dart from her face to the old carpet bag on the floor and her mud-crusted greatcoat that hangs on a hook beside her bed.

He clicks the end of his pen. 'Well, Ms Jebb, it looks like we'll be saying goodbye to you today.'

'Goodbye?' she echoes.

'Yes, indeed. The X-rays show no fractures,' he says. His pen makes a scratchy noise against the clipboard as he signs her off with a flourish. 'I'm afraid the National Health Service cannot extend its hospitality any further. We'll patch you up, bandage your ankle and you can be on your way.' He looks at her over half-moon glasses. 'Wherever that may be.'

'Not even the hip?' she says, just to be sure.

'Not the hip, nor the ankle. Some nasty bruising, certainly. Cartilage wear in the knees, but that's to be expected. Lifestyle choices and so on. But basically, Ms Jebb, you have what we used to call a twisted ankle.' He shoots her a final look of owlish disapproval.

The nurse is nicer, not Sandrine but another one, who eases a stretchy tubular bandage on to Nancy's ankle, then binds it up nice and tight. She slips Nancy a spare one to take with her. 'You got somewhere to go tonight?' she asks as she tidies away the scissors, drops the paper wrappers into a clanking pedal bin.

'Now there's a question,' says Nancy. 'I was on my way to a city. I was thinking of Liverpool, but I'm not sure where's best to go now. The game might be up.'

'The game?' says the nurse, a crease forming on her forehead.

'Yes. I was making myself scarce. But I've got a terrible feeling he's closer than ever.'

The nurse looks confused, then her face brightens. 'Oh, I forgot. Sandrine says to call in before you leave. Something about a dog.'

They give Nancy a crutch, an ugly grey thing with a rubber foot on the end and a curved cuff that cuts into her arm, and she hobbles to the nurses' station to find Sandrine.

'So, my friend at the shelter says she'll keep an eye out for your Bree.' She tilts her head to the side. 'Nothing yet – but they arrive at all hours, so you never know.'

Nancy clings to this information, a sliver of light in so much darkness. Sandrine is writing down a number and an address on a piece of paper. 'This is the place.'

'Thank you,' says Nancy, balancing on one foot and shoving the paper into her coat pocket. 'Just one more thing,' she says. 'Funny question, but the maternity ward, I won't pass it on my way out, will I?'

'Maternity? No, different wing altogether. Nice and new, not like this bit. Falling down around us. Visiting someone, are you?'

'Oh, I wish,' Nancy says. 'But unfortunately, I need to avoid it.'

Sandrine helps Nancy out of the double doors to the ward. 'Oh,' she calls out. 'You asked about the motorcyclist.'

Nancy tries to turn, but it's too tricky. 'Yes?' she calls back.

'Good news. His bike's a write-off, but he was lucky. Like you.'

Nancy starts making her lopsided way down the shiny corridor, presses the button for the lift. She hopes Sandrine is right and that her luck holds out a little longer. The idea that Georgie and her baby might be in a hospital room not far from here shimmers in her mind, but that scene has nothing to do with her. And the longer she stays in this hospital, the more likely she is to spoil that happy scene.

As Frank said all those years ago, 'They are safer without you – and that sick man who seems to follow you everywhere.' Twisted ankle or not, Nancy needs to get away from this hospital, as quickly as possible.

Chapter
Forty-Two

GEORGIE

Georgie is sitting up in bed and someone has brought her a breakfast tray. There is tea and toast, which is made from white bread and spread thickly with butter and marmalade, and Georgie thinks it is the most delicious thing she has ever tasted. It's as if she's been transported to a heavenly place where the air is sweet and sheets are clean and crisp and people bring her manna in the form of hot, buttered toast.

But then it turns claggy, sticks in her throat, because she should be sharing this moment with Wilf. He should be here and he should have been part of the birth, in all its messy, raw beauty. It wasn't his fault, she reminds herself. But still, it hurts and her body hurts. When will people stop leaving her when she most needs them? She puts the plate of toast to one side, swallows hard.

Beside her, the baby lies in a transparent plastic crib and she takes in the wonder of her all over again. She knows she's high on endorphins or oxytocin or both – and that at some point she will come crashing down. But for now, Georgie is elated: in love with her baby and amazed at herself. Because the only upside of Wilf not being here is the knowing she did it all by herself.

Of course, the midwives were there, but in the end it felt like it was just her and the baby and the physicality of their two bodies working together, that endless sequence of pressure and release and a process they had to see through. Until a few hours ago, that task had seemed impossible, but Georgie did it. And her baby is beyond beautiful.

The awful thing is, she can't even call Wilf because somewhere in the confusion of the past twelve hours, she lost her phone. She imagines it must have slipped under the car seat, so Dan has gone back out to the car to look for it. She's never been good with numbers and she can't remember Wilf's number off the top of her head – all she knows is that it has several sevens and a nine. But her need for him is an ache, just one of the many all over her body. She hurts all over, feels pummelled and spent.

When she closes her eyes, Georgie's head spins, replaying scenes from the past two days: white road markings whizzing by, orange traffic cones. An endless blur of headlights, the glimpse of a badger's carcass beside the road, wet with blood.

More blood, this time her own, and the twisted blue of her baby's too-short cord. The liver-like jiggle of the placenta, carried off in a silver dish. And the face of a stranger that is also a face she knows better than her own. The echo of her mother's voice from behind a blue curtain: 'Hush, there. You can do this.'

Her eyes snap open. No, she refuses to believe that bit happened. There was a jangle of curtain rings from the next cubicle, that bit was true, but then her confused brain conjured up some vision, splicing together her childhood yearnings with a photograph she'd seen on the news. It was a fever dream – the product of tiredness and old needs and wants.

This sort of thing used to happen after Finn died too: she'd see his face in the crowd or glimpse his silhouette walking past the window of a coffee bar. Several times she was fooled, rushed out after a stranger only to realise he looked nothing like Finn. Eventually, her brain got the message: Finn was never coming back. She should have learned years ago – when people leave Georgie, they never return. No matter how much you love them.

Georgie was moved on to this ward in the small hours, but now it's the morning proper and the woman in the bed opposite is feeding her baby, stroking its soft head in an absent-minded way as if she's done all this before.

Georgie needs the loo. As she manoeuvres herself to the side of the bed, she feels the ominous slide of the maternity pad that should be wedged safely between her legs. She stands, making sure to hold on to the bedside cabinet, because she's been told to expect some mild dizziness.

But when it swoops in, it's not mild at all, it's the same violent lurch of vertigo she's had through pregnancy, and she lets out a whimper because all this was supposed to stop after the birth. She'd been promised it would end. But the ringing in her ears is back and all Georgie can do is blink into the blackness behind her eyes and wait for it to pass.

When she comes to, the woman opposite is peering at her with a worried expression. 'You OK, love – shall I pull the cord for some help?'

'No, I'm fine,' Georgie replies. 'I've been sitting in a car for far too long, that's all. Hours and hours. Days, really.'

'In a car – for days?' The woman's tone makes Georgie realise how bizarre this must sound.

'Yes. It was a mistake, really. A bad idea,' Georgie says as she takes slow, steady steps towards the bathroom.

When Georgie returns, her head feels lighter, cleansed. She has made a decision not to waste any more time thinking about that fever dream and the face she saw. The two grey plaits, that mole . . . No, Georgie will only think about her baby daughter, still sleeping blissfully in the cot. She climbs back into bed, runs her hand over the sheets, trying to smooth out the creases.

Dan appears, looking ragged and tired – and empty-handed.

'Did you find my phone?' she asks.

'Georgie, I looked everywhere, practically pulled the car apart, but I can't find it. All I can think is that it fell out on the ground when I pulled over. You know, by the field, where I couldn't get a signal and you got your socks wet.'

Ah, yes, that muddy verge. Georgie imagines her phone lying there ringing out, while Wilf wonders why she isn't picking up.

'Dan, please can you look again? Or find his friend Mehdi, Mehdi Alaoui. Or Wilf's parents – they are called Ruth and John and they live near Taunton in Devon. They'll have his number.' The door swings shut as Dan rushes off again. Poor Dan. Just as well she didn't tell him about her fevered imaginings of last night, how she thought she saw Nancy's face. He's got plenty to deal with.

She looks down at her baby, with her dark eyelashes and her perfectly formed nose and lips, and all over again, Georgie is in awe. She has a daughter, who she will stay close to forever. As she watches, her baby starts to stir, making small pouty shapes with her lips. Then comes the jagged beginnings of a cry, a sound that sets off a tingling in Georgie's chest. It's a feeling that reminds her of the breathless excitement of Christmas Day mornings, so long ago. She pulls the red cord, so a midwife can come and help her with feeding.

The crying is getting louder and Georgie pulls the red cord again, but nobody comes – in fact, outside the corridor she can hear footsteps and doors banging; they must all be busy. Georgie lifts her baby out of the cot. But something has changed, the baby is crying in a different way now, a frantic, breathy scream that scares Georgie. She's no longer a placid bundle, she's gone rigid and seems impossible to hold. Georgie's face, her hands, her whole body is sweating, and the baby is slipping from her grasp. A stray finger pokes Georgie in the eye and she feels the sting of her own tears.

The woman in the bed opposite is saying something, but Georgie can't hear her, the crying is everywhere, all around her. She sees her baby's mouth open wide, a tongue vibrating in fury, and she tries to jam that mouth on to her breast, the way she was shown at some hazy hour this morning.

There's a brief nip of pain and Georgie thinks it's worked, but then the baby slides off. Georgie tries again, but it's impossible – this baby is an open-mouthed hungry bird that can't find its food. She tries to nuzzle, but then seems to rear back in fury or pain. Georgie looks down at her swollen hot breast and has the sudden, sure thought that she's poisoning her baby, that her milk is bad and she's passing on some foulness that's always been lurking inside her and was inside her mother before her.

All Georgie can hear is the screams of her baby and everything is a blur because Georgie is crying too. She can't do this. How foolish she has been. Three days ago, she thought she wanted answers, so she could purge her past and start her new life. But there's no way she can escape it.

Her head is woozy, as if an emptiness is opening up beneath her, and she feels a desolate fear. More than ever, Georgie wishes she wasn't here, alone in a hospital far from home, that she'd never seen that news story and gone in search of the past. Because now more memories are clamouring to be let back in and she's not ready for them, not ready at all.

Chapter
Forty-Three

GEORGIE, MARCH 2002

'BEST YOU DON'T BOTHER MY MUM RIGHT NOW'

It's the last day of term before the Easter holidays and Georgie is walking home. All afternoon, she has been working on an art project, a gigantic painting of a red London bus. She'd wanted it to be spectacular – so it would win the admiration of her teachers and classmates. Except it hasn't ended up looking like she'd imagined. She's way behind schedule and today, because she was running low on red paint, she had the not-so-bright idea of diluting it. But she'd watched in horror as the watered-down colour seeped into the paper and left soggy, ragged holes.

She knows this painting is a disaster – like several other things in her life right now. The way that her mother veers from being tightly wound to worryingly relaxed, floppy from the drinks that make her kisses sticky. Then there's the way her dad smiles too hard and talks to Dan like a character from an old-fashioned film, all Danny Boy this, Danny Boy that, doing high fives and laughing at odd moments. Her dad doesn't have a pet name for Georgie and sometimes she catches him looking at her in a weird way. Like he's just smelt a bad smell, but is too polite to say anything.

For the past few weeks, their dad has been talking about going on holiday to Wales. He uses his fake-happy voice and tells Dan about fishing trips and football. He doesn't mention doing anything with Georgie.

So as she walks home, Georgie is dragging her feet a little. Back at St Luke's Road, all she'll find will be the same plates strewn with crumbs, the bowls with caked-on cereal left from breakfast, so she's in no particular hurry.

All this means she almost bumps into the blocky figure that's standing on the pavement in front of her. She stops just in time, is about to apologise, but then she looks up and sees his glistening teeth, springy hairs all around his mouth, and she finds she can't say a word.

'Hello there, remember me?' he says.

And Georgie does, so she takes a step back.

'Good day at school?' he says, and she hates this, the way that grown-ups can never think of anything else to ask, so she finds her voice and says, 'No, not really.'

She knows this Gerry bloke is an old friend of her mum's, the one who pops up each year. In fact, she realises that's probably why her mum is all jumpy and sharp edges right now, because it's nearly the holidays and she wonders if Nancy knows he's parked here, on this quiet side street on Georgie's route home from school.

Then the man says, 'Looking forward to Easter?', and he strokes his beard like it's a small pet. Watching him do this makes Georgie feel a little sick, but she can't explain why.

Georgie blows her fringe out of her face. It's a sunny day, unseasonably hot for March, and her bag is heavy and she realises she would quite like this man to go away – he's the last thing her mum needs right now. Like her dad keeps saying, they all need a good holiday. Georgie decides it's up to her to get rid of this Gerry.

'Yeah, I am. Because we're going away to Wales,' she says, jutting out her chin. Then, to make sure he gets the message, she says, 'We're going in the car, pretty soon actually. So best you don't bother my mum right now. She's got loads of packing to do.'

'Ah, OK,' says Gerry, holding up two hands. 'No problem. Good to know.' He turns, as if he's about to walk away, and then he says, 'Well, have a great time. I suppose it must be Llandudno you're going to?'

This place name is unfamiliar to Georgie and he says it in a way that suggests going there is laughable and beneath people like Gerry and in that moment she hates this man, who she only remembers in a hazy way but still makes her stomach tighten. He's a know-it-all and he reminds Georgie of her strict maths teacher and her dad when he's cross and the girls in her class who pretend there's no room for Georgie on their lunch table.

So Georgie puts her hands on her hips and she says, 'No, actually. You're wrong. We're going to a place called Tenby.' She thinks, *that'll shut him up*, and she tosses her head and walks away, much faster than she was going before.

It's only when she gets to her front door and turns her key in the wobbly lock that she pauses. And as she steps into the quiet cool of the house, she wonders whether what she just said was so clever after all.

Chapter
Forty-Four

NANCY

It takes an age for Nancy to walk from the lift to the exit – her ankle is a mass of hot pain if she tries to put any weight on it. When the automatic doors open, it's a relief to be back out in the real world and she takes in big breaths of fresh air.

She's making her slow way to the bus stop when she sees a familiar gangly figure striding towards the hospital entrance. Her first impulse is to call out and wave because she'd know that walk anywhere, the way he dips his head down and bends his knees. The last time she saw him do it, he was ten years old and starting to be embarrassed by how tall he was for his age, and it tore at Nancy's heart because she wanted her son to walk tall and be proud.

But then she freezes and realises that she mustn't call out. She can't be here and she can't go near either of her children. Definitely not Georgie, but she must also stay away from Dan, who must be visiting his sister. But it's too late, because her body hasn't caught up with her mind and she's already raised her arm to wave. Except it's the arm that is using the crutch and the ugly thing falls to the ground with a loud clatter and she can't even bend down to get it because then she'll lose her balance completely.

Damn it, now people have seen her, a stupid old woman who has dropped her stick like the embarrassment that she is, that she always was. A young woman is first over and Nancy notices how she has eyelashes that look like two spiders stuck in place. She's asking if Nancy is OK and Nancy just wants to run away but of course she can't do that, she can barely walk. She's trapped, standing here telling the girl with the spider eyelashes it's fine, she's fine, and the girl is backing away now. Perhaps she's seen the mud on Nancy's coat, the way it's tied in the middle with orange twine, and that, up close, Nancy is not the nice old lady she had imagined.

The girl is turning away, but behind her there is another person and Nancy can't speak because it's him, the tall man. Her beautiful son.

There's an unreality to this moment, as if it's being played by actors, not her and Dan, and she wonders what lines they will say next. She's aware of her heart thumping, the hard muscularity of it, and the way her mouth has gone dry, and she wonders if it feels the same for Dan.

She forces herself to look into his face. Of course, he's older than the boy she keeps safe in her memory, but his eyes, that sharp nose, are unmistakable. And so is the expression on his face. Her son looks at her with anger and, yes, she sees loathing. His lips are pale, drained of blood.

'What the . . .' he says. 'What the hell are you doing here?'

Her crutch is still lying on the ground and Dan reaches down, picks it up with ease. For one horrible moment, she wonders if he's going to throw it far away to punish her, just as she deserves. Instead, he hands it to her and waits for Nancy to right herself.

He starts rubbing his face and backing away. 'No, this is too much. It wasn't supposed to happen like this,' he says.

'What wasn't?' she asks.

His voice hardens. 'We had questions,' he says. 'Georgie did. A lot of questions. We were coming to find you. And now you do this – you appear, from nowhere. With . . .' He gestures to her foot. 'Bandages.'

'I'm sorry,' she starts to say. 'I had a little accident.'

But Dan isn't listening. He's running his hands through his hair, looking every which way except directly at Nancy. 'It's not up to you, you don't get to do this. You stay away. I knew it was a bad idea. I knew we shouldn't have come looking for you. It was too much for Georgie, I'm sure that's why it came early . . .'

Then Dan stops speaking and puts a hand over his mouth.

Nancy seizes her chance. 'Has she had the baby then – is everything OK?'

'What? How did you know?'

Nancy feels so sorry for her boy, trying to make sense of this. 'I heard,' Nancy says, which is sort of true.

Dan frowns, still not understanding. 'Actually, she has. Early this morning. A little girl.'

A warmth spreads inside her. 'A granddaughter,' she whispers.

'Yes, but not yours,' Dan says swiftly. 'You forfeited that right twenty years ago.'

His words are a body blow and Nancy needs to sit down. There's a bench not far away, so she hobbles towards it and eases herself down. Looking back, she half expects Dan to be gone, but he's still standing there.

'You,' he says finally, 'you, wait there. I've got phone calls to make. To Georgie's partner. Her family.' And he walks to the far side of the car park.

For the next twenty minutes, she watches Dan stride up and down, talking to people more worthy than Nancy. But every now and then he glances over, checking she's still there, and this gives her the smallest glimmer of hope. That, and what he said. If she heard right, Dan said they had come looking for her.

◆ ◆ ◆

When Dan pockets his phone and starts heading towards the hospital, Nancy fears he'll walk straight past her, but at the last minute he swerves and comes over.

'Please, Dan, will you sit down?' she asks. 'Just for a minute.'

She can almost feel his internal struggle, the angry urge to leave fighting a desire to stay. And then he gives in, sits at the other end of the bench. She knows he won't stay long – Georgie needs him – but she wants these seconds to last forever. She chances a look at his face, sees dark shadows and worry lines. 'You came looking for me?' she asks.

'It was Georgie's idea,' he says finally. 'She saw you on the news. Although it seems the story has spread. Now everyone wants to know who you are – total strangers are looking for the mystery woman who saved a little girl.'

'Ah,' she says.

'Oh, yes, the hero who saved someone else's child. Except they don't know that she left two of her own, without a second thought.'

'Oh, Dan,' Nancy says, because where does she start trying to explain? 'That's not true. I thought about you both. Day and night. Always.'

'But not enough to come back.'

'It wasn't like that, it wasn't that simple. I thought that you were better off without me. Safer.'

He looks at her then, a hard look. 'Safer,' he repeats. There's a pause. 'She still doesn't remember, you know.'

'Remember?'

'The bridge. What happened that day. She blanked it out afterwards, but they thought it would come back to her. The school gave her therapy sessions, because her behaviour got really bad. But it never did. She'd shut it away for good.'

Nancy draws breath. 'But you do.'

'Yes,' he says quietly. 'I remember it all. So coming to look for you was one thing. But when she said she wanted to go and see Gerry, I knew it was a terrible idea, but she'd made up her mind. She said if anyone knew how to find you, it would be Gerry. And that made me curious as well, I suppose. I secretly hoped we'd find you there. I think we both did. At Gerry's.'

Hearing his name brings Nancy back to her senses. She looks left and right, feels her heart thumping, trying to escape. 'You what? You saw Gerry?' she manages.

'Yeah. Went to some creepy cottage in the woods. Listened to him drone on, but he knew nothing. He was full of crap.'

'He didn't hurt you?' she gasps. 'Or Georgie?'

'Hurt? No, he's a pathetic old man. A loser. A fantasist who lives on his own. Sits there stroking his beard or looking at his computer, having sick thoughts. Creepy as hell, but harmless.'

Nancy grips the strap of her bag. Dan doesn't know what he's capable of. 'He might have followed you,' she says. 'He could be watching . . .' She struggles to her feet, tries to slot her arm into the cuff of the crutch, but in her rush her sleeve gets caught.

'What are you doing? Stop.' Dan is looking at her as if she's mad. 'He doesn't even have a car. He had no way of following us. He's a sad old man in the woods, nothing more.'

She pauses, tries to imagine a world where this might be true. 'Did he say anything to you?'

'Just a load of rubbish about how you'd run out on him as well. Stared at Georgie. Wanted to stroke her hair.'

A chill runs through Nancy.

'I don't know what happened between the two of you back then. I can only guess that he had some hold over you that we didn't understand. And maybe you didn't either. But now . . . now he's a nobody. A sad old man.' Dan rubs his arms. 'Anyway. Soon after we saw Gerry, Georgie went into labour. She's a couple of weeks early.' Then he seems to come to his senses and remember why he's here. 'So, I need to go back up there.'

Nancy nods.

She sees a softening in Dan's face. 'She's OK, the baby's OK. But Georgie's a bit spaced out. I don't know, kind of distant. Tired, of course. Possibly in shock.'

Nancy does not dare say a thing, she barely breathes, because this is almost her son telling her about her daughter and her grandchild, and in a moment Dan will remember Nancy has no right to know.

'Anyway.' He waves his phone in the air. 'She needs this. To ring her partner. I've just got hold of his number.'

Nancy nods, mutely.

'I already rang Dad first thing. He's on his way with Irena. She's our stepmum.'

Again, all Nancy can do is nod.

He checks the time on his phone. 'Listen, none of this is right. It's all so fucked up. But I suppose we did want to find you, to talk and get things straight. Because, to be honest, Georgie and I have gone through some rough times, back then and more recently. It does things to a person, being left like that as a kid. And something happened a couple of years ago that shook us both up. We lost someone we both loved.

'For me, it brought it all back. Being abandoned. Not being enough. Not doing enough to stop it happening.' He gives a sharp cough. 'I think that's one reason we both leapt into action when we saw your picture. Because we still need answers.'

242

Nancy feels the guilt wash back in.

'Will you tell her you saw me?' she asks, as Dan gets up to go. 'If only to give her a message?'

'Right now, I don't know if that's a good idea,' he says. He checks his phone again. 'Can I take your number, let you know?'

She shakes her head. 'No phone.'

Dan presses his lips together tightly. She remembers this face – it's the one that means Dan has made up his mind. He reaches into his trouser pocket, pulls out a car key.

'Look, I can't think straight now,' he says. 'It's cold out here, why don't you sit in my car and wait? Until I've decided what to do.'

She holds out her palm and Dan drops the key, without touching her hand.

'It's the old VW Beetle up there, sky blue.' He points towards the car park. 'To be honest, I can barely look at you right now. But I know if I let you walk away again, I'll regret it. Or Georgie will make me regret it.'

Nancy makes a fist around the key, scared he might change his mind.

'What would it be, though?' Dan calls back. 'Your message?'

'Tell her I'm sorry and I love her. And you, Dan.'

He turns and almost runs into the building. She waits until he's out of sight before she lets her head drop. She's never stopped thinking about her children, but she'd kidded herself that they were doing OK. She'd imagined them living a happier life in a nice suburban cul-de-sac with a father and a stepmother who took good care of them. She thought she was keeping them safe, but now it sounds as if her walking away wasn't the end of the damage. It was only the beginning.

Dan's car isn't what Nancy is expecting. It's an old one, a shape she remembers from her own childhood, and it is spectacularly dirty, with scratch marks along the sides. Inside, there's a mess of sandwich wrappers, crumpled takeaway cups and sweet wrappers. There's an odd smell as well, a mixture of vinegar, coffee dregs and something sour, like spilt milk. Gingerly, Nancy lowers herself into the passenger seat.

For the first hour that she sits there, she barely moves. There's too much to take in – coming face to face with Dan, the thought of Georgie and her newborn baby somewhere inside the building she can see from here. Then she turns her thoughts to Georgie and Dan coming in search of her – and how they ended up finding Gerry instead.

Dan had called Gerry 'a pathetic old man' and 'a loser'. But is Dan being naive? After all, it took Nancy a long time to see him for what he was.

But it wasn't just the things Gerry did that kept Nancy hostage all those years ago – it was what he knew. Each spring, as Easter came around, she was a bundle of taut nerves. She lived in fear of him popping up – in the street or, even worse, in her home. Every time she left the house, she feared she might come home to find him waiting for her, sipping tea with Frank, about to tell the secret that would destroy her family forever. And if Frank didn't believe him, Gerry could always play his trump card – those videos he'd taken.

Without the engine on, this car is barely warmer than sitting outside and Nancy is wrapping her coat tighter around herself when a glint of light catches her eye. Someone in a parking bay opposite is opening their hatchback and the winter sun is catching on the glass.

Waiting to one side is a woman, wearing neat court shoes and a navy coat with buttons down the front. She carries a handbag looped over one arm, and Nancy thinks, *how old-fashioned, how quaint.*

The old-fashioned woman is waiting for her companion, who is getting something out of the boot. Nancy sees him pull out a bunch of flowers. They are quite ugly ones, yellow chrysanthemums, and Nancy wonders who would bring those to a hospital, flowers of death. The man straightens up, pushes the flowers into the woman's arms and slams the boot.

As he turns, Nancy feels her stomach drop. He's older, but there's no mistaking him as he strides towards the hospital entrance. He's setting quite a pace and the woman in the court shoes has to hurry to keep up, holding the flowers to her chest like a big yellow baby. Nancy watches as Frank and Irena Brown walk into the building, ready to meet their first grandchild.

She thinks of the last time she saw Frank, outside a police station in central London. His fury as he told her how she'd put her children in grave danger and she stood no chance of seeing them again. He hadn't even asked for her side of the story.

If he had, she could have told him how she was effectively being kept captive. But the Frank she'd married, a man she'd loved for his fairness and his belief in doing the right thing, was nowhere to be seen that day.

Watching as he marches towards the hospital, she mourns the loss of that man and what they both lost. What, she wonders, is Frank like now? Has he mellowed – or become more set in his ways? Does he have any fond memories of the Nancy he once knew, or did he erase her entirely from his life?

Nancy wonders what Frank told their children in the aftermath. Did they ever receive her postcards, see her long letters? Of course, she got her intermittent updates in return and she's grateful for those snippets of news. But now she feels the injustice of all she's missed out on – the times when her children might have needed their real mother, even one as useless as Nancy. The fact that they came looking for her must mean something and this gives Nancy the strength she needs.

Barely registering what she's doing, Nancy steps out of the car and hobbles back towards the hospital. Frank isn't a monster in the way Gerry was, but he, too, has questions to answer. There is a roaring gathering inside her head and Nancy won't run away from it, not this time.

Chapter
Forty-Five

GEORGIE

As long as Georgie makes no sudden movements and keeps the baby pressed against her chest, it seems to sleep. The two of them have been stuck in this position since Dan left to get hold of Wilf. It feels like hours, but Georgie can't be sure – she's lost all track of time.

All she knows is that she needs to talk to Wilf, feel his reassuring presence in this mad world she's been dropped into, where nothing makes sense. She's reeling from the birth, the endless journey and their very bad decision to visit Gerry. She can still feel that urgent need to escape, a sudden knowledge that she would do anything – unpeel her skin, sacrifice herself – to get away from him and protect her baby.

Now, with a creeping unease, she wonders if, all those years ago, Nancy felt the same visceral fear. Is this a missing piece in the puzzle – did something happen between Nancy and Gerry in that cottage that made her run and keep running?

Dan strides back in. He's got a number from Wilf's mum and is tapping it into his phone. He passes it to her and the two of them listen, willing the call to connect. There's a distant clunk, but then, instead of Wilf's voice, she hears his voicemail message. He must be out of range or out of charge.

'Wilf,' she says. 'It's me. I'm fine, the baby's fine, but she came early, Wilf. We have a little girl. Ring me as soon as you can. I'm here, on this number.'

'Don't worry, he'll call you straight back,' says Dan. 'Wilf's mum sounded lovely – concerned for you and then excited. And I called Dad and Irena earlier. They are on their way. In fact, Dad almost sounded excited too.'

Could this be a turning point, a thawing in her relationship with her father, she wonders. She's about to ask Dan when she realises something isn't right with him. He's pacing back and forth, raking his hair, shaking his head.

'Dan,' she says. 'Sit down – what's the matter with you?'

But when he stops and pulls the grey plastic chair closer to her bed, Georgie suddenly wishes she hadn't asked. She wants to cover her ears and close her eyes because she knows, deep down, what her brother is about to say.

'I've got some strange news,' he begins. 'A bit of a shock. I saw Nancy outside. Yes, outside this very hospital. She had a small accident, nothing bad. She was about to leave – can you believe it?' He rubs his head again. 'But we talked, Georgie. And I still don't know what I think, but our journey is done. She's here – waiting downstairs in the car. I said I'd tell you. And that we'd decide what we want to do next.'

Georgie strokes her baby's back in small circles. The motion is keeping her body grounded while her head seems to be floating away, untethered, unable to grasp this shift in reality.

'She sends her love. For what it's worth. Says she's sorry,' Dan adds.

Georgie feels the perfect smoothness of the baby's sleepsuit, the warmth radiating off its tiny body. Two fragile shoulder blades. She can smell the buttery sweetness of her baby's hair and she knows that if she raises her fingers to the top of her daughter's head, she will feel the soft gape of her fontanelle. The thought of it, so vulnerable, makes Georgie shiver.

Three days ago, Georgie was full of hard, sharp questions. She wanted to know how a mother could be so heartless as to leave her children. She wanted to ask about the sickness that raged inside her mother – when it started and what kind of things it made Nancy do, because Georgie was terrified of following in her wild, drunken slipstream. And now, Dan says Nancy is here. That soft voice Georgie heard from the cubicle next to her was real.

She feels panic rising, because this is all so wrong – today should be about her and the baby and Wilf. Soon he'll ring and then get a flight back and when he arrives, she wants it to be just the three of them. This new start can't be tainted by her past – she can't have her two lives colliding.

'No, this can't happen – that woman can't be here,' she says. 'I mean, we don't even know her. She could be dangerous. Unhinged. God, Dan, this is too much. I mean, what did she look like? Is she like before?'

'No. Not like I remembered.' He motions to his own head. 'Two long plaits, grey hair. Calmer than before. Twenty years older.'

Georgie nods. 'OK, right. But still . . .'

'I mean, she's obviously had a hard life, she looks a bit rough around the edges. But she seems like a decent person. I think she's ready to talk.'

But Georgie can feel her once urgent need for answers evaporating into the air. That was then – but everything has changed. Now she has her baby, Georgie has no desire to drag up the past. She wants to stay safe in this sleepy, milky bubble, where nurses shoosh in and out, bring her cups of tea and top up her water glass and smile in a comforting way. If only Wilf was here – then her safe new world would be complete.

'No, I'm sorry. I can't think about that now. I need to sleep,' she says firmly. 'Sleep when your baby does – that's what they tell you. But if Wilf rings, wake me.'

'What about her – Nancy?'

'I have no idea. I mean, we've waited twenty years for answers. I don't see why I have to respond in a matter of minutes. When I've just given birth.' Georgie closes her eyes, waits to hear Dan's footsteps recede. But he stays right there, waiting beside her.

She's woken by the sound of doors opening and footsteps and chatter. It must be visiting time. She opens her eyes and sees a man and a toddler heading for the woman in the bed opposite. Then an older couple arrive for the woman in the bed beside Georgie's, but they duck out of sight because the curtain is drawn.

And then Georgie's heart starts to thump because she can see Irena and her father standing in the doorway. Irena is carrying a bunch of spiky yellow flowers, and her father's mouth is turned up at the edges in his version of a smile.

They come over in a flurry of hellos and taking off of coats, then there is clattering and scraping as extra chairs are found and arranged. Dan sits on one side of the bed and Frank and Irena sit on the other.

'Well, congratulations,' says Frank. 'You gave us all a surprise! An early arrival.' He peers forward and Georgie draws back the tip of the white blanket that covers her still-sleeping baby. 'Mind you, shouldn't be surprised. You were both early too.'

Georgie hadn't known this – and she wonders why it was never mentioned. It would have been useful information for Frank to pass on in the absence of her own mother, who is probably still sitting in the car park downstairs, but who neither she nor Dan dare mention. Just like they weren't allowed to talk about her after the move to Redhill, where Irena kept house and everyone else kept their feelings in check.

Irena leans over to look too. 'Sweet,' she decides, and sits back down. But Georgie notices that Irena's eyes have taken on a glassy look, and she wonders if there were certain compromises that Irena made all those years ago in return for Frank's offer of marriage.

The bunch of flowers has been placed at the end of the bed and Georgie can see that the stems, tied with a criss-cross of blue elastic bands, are leaking water through the paper and on to the bedcover. She's about to say something about getting them in a vase when she becomes aware that another person has appeared. She's standing at the end of the bed, a dark figure in a coat that's caked with dry mud, and she's placed one hand on the bed frame for support.

'I've come to join the family celebration,' the woman says. She is the only one standing and, to Georgie, she looks statuesque, monumental, as if hewn from stone. Her hair is dark grey, twisted into two plaits, and her hand is a weathered brown.

There is silence, then the shriek of a chair being pushed back as Dan stands, all flustered, and offers their mother his seat. As Nancy drops into it, Georgie breathes in the smell of her mother's coat: old, wet wool and cold air. It's the smell of mountains and bracken, a wilder place than this. She can't bear to look her mother full in the face yet, so she looks down at the baby in her arms. Georgie is about to tilt the baby towards Nancy, just as she did with Frank and Irena, and then she stops. A coldness runs through her.

'No,' she hears herself say. 'No, you don't get to do this.'

Nancy seems to shrink in her chair.

The air hums with expectation – the whole ward seems to have fallen silent, as if there is a spotlight on this muddle of people clustered around Georgie's bed.

'Twenty years ago,' Georgie continues, 'you walked out on your own children. So, no, you don't get to waltz back in and play grandmother. Forget it.'

She can feel her baby stirring, hears a mewl that means she'll have to feed her again in a minute, so she doesn't have much time. 'How did it feel, holding that little girl you saved? You must have felt very special and worthy, everyone calling you the hero of the hour. But they don't know the real you, do they?'

Dan is saying something calming, trying to smooth things over, because that's Dan's role – the peacemaker, the happy-go-lucky one who jollies them all along. She glances at her father, whose face has turned an ashen grey. In fact, Irena seems to be the only one who is retaining any composure and she sits neatly, her handbag on her knees, looking quizzically at this newest arrival – Nancy.

'I'm sorry, Georgie. I'll leave,' says Nancy, getting to her feet, but it's not an easy manoeuvre because she seems to be using a hospital crutch and carrying a battered bag. 'I was wrong to come here. I'll wait until you're ready – and if that time never comes, that's fine too. That's your decision.'

As Nancy starts to move away, Frank seems to wake up and seizes his chance. 'Yes, off you go,' he calls out. 'Leave, like you did before.'

Very slowly, Nancy turns. She fixes a steely eye on him and speaks in a low, steady voice. 'Frank, you know that wasn't the whole story. It was more complicated. I did as I was asked. And if you'd wanted to, you could have found me. I wrote so many times, but you never wrote back.'

Georgie hears the words, pictures the single postcard she received. A tiger cub on the front, the same as Dan's. A message written in a wobbly hand, three kisses at the end and a promise to see them soon. But now Nancy says she wrote other letters.

Frank's jaw is making an odd juddering motion as he tries to form words, but Nancy isn't waiting for his reply. In fact, she's not looking at Frank any more but at Irena, of all people.

'Thank you,' she says with feeling. 'For all you did. Letting me know how they were. Their graduations, bits of news. I appreciated it.'

Georgie and Dan look at each other, trying to make sense of this. Then they look at Irena with her bouffant hair, her A-line skirt and her boxy jacket. Quiet Irena, who came into their lives as a cleaner and, just as quietly, became Frank's wife. But now it seems this meek woman saw and knew far more than she let on.

Irena shrugs, fiddles with the clasp of her handbag, looks up at Nancy. 'You're welcome.' Then she faces Frank, her chin set at a tilt. 'She had a right to know those things, Frank. You received those letters and I knew you wouldn't write back, so I did. They were always her children.'

'I've had enough of this – of both of you twisting things.' Frank is up, trying to get past Irena's chair, but he's backed himself into the blue curtain and it's twisted around him. He turns one way then the other, breaks free with a cry of frustration. 'I'm calling security. Someone needs to get this homeless woman out of here.'

Georgie goes back to making small, firm circles on her baby's back. It's time for a feed. She looks down at the whorl of hair on her baby's head as she speaks. 'Actually, can you all leave now? Take this drama somewhere else. I want to be left alone with my baby.

'Dan, can you keep ringing Wilf? It's him I want to see. Nancy, Dad, and yes, you too, Irena – you all did a pretty good job of messing up our childhoods. You don't get to do it again for my baby. Just go – go now.'

A nurse appears – she's not pleased at this disturbance – and she holds the door open to usher Georgie's rag-tag family out. Then she draws the curtain so that it wraps around Georgie's bed and comes over to check how the feeding is going. In her blue-curtained space, Georgie swallows down the pain as her baby latches on. She breathes deeply and this helps it subside. But she knows it won't touch her deeper pain.

As quickly as she appeared, her mother is gone again. Yes, it was Georgie who told her to go, but she wishes everything was different, that her mother was sitting here beside her, helping her.

Except that's not going to happen. In fact, it's as far-fetched as Georgie's childhood fantasies of her mother returning, arms outstretched. A whole lifetime of mistakes stands between those fantasies and the reality of now. And not all of them are Nancy's.

Chapter
Forty-Six

Nancy

Out in the corridor, Nancy presses Dan's car key into his hand. She starts to ask him to write down his mobile number, but then his phone rings and Dan breaks away. He presses one finger into his ear and shouts into his phone – 'I can't hear . . . no, the signal's no good . . . wait' – and then Dan disappears back into the ward.

The stern-looking nurse has come out to make sure they leave, so Nancy, Frank and Irena step into the lift together. As the doors close, Nancy sneaks a look at Frank, still rigid with rage. Then at Irena, who looks surprisingly unperturbed, and Nancy wonders what it's like, being the second Mrs Brown.

She decides to wait in the car park. Dan will come down eventually and she can ask him for his phone number. But of course, his car is parked just behind Frank's shiny Audi and, as the three of them get closer, Frank turns on her.

'What now? Haven't you done enough damage? Take the hint and leave us alone, Nancy.'

'Frank, come on,' she tries. 'Let's talk like reasonable people. That's our first grandchild up there. Can't we be civil, for her sake? For the sake of our own children?'

'No. How dare you do this – breeze back in like you were never away,' he says.

'That's so far from what I'm doing. I didn't even come here on purpose, it was all an accident . . .' She trails off and for the first time in ages she thinks of Bree, her poor dog who she's also let down.

'Nancy, you never took responsibility for what you did. Your deception, your lies. Your infidelity. You were a danger to our children . . .'

'Yes, yes, I know that. And didn't I do what you asked?' Nancy finds she is shaking with anger. All those years she was denied access – she's more than paid for her sins. And Frank is conveniently forgetting what Gerry did. She didn't have the vocabulary for it back then, but Gerry was an abuser. He stalked her, he manipulated her.

'You could have let me back in a long time ago,' she says. 'Would it have killed you to write back yourself? To tell our children where I was?'

Frank hadn't written back, but Irena had. Flimsy blue aerogrammes that Nancy came to crave. Irena told Nancy how her first letters had been forwarded to Redhill, arriving intermittently, sometimes months after the postmark.

Frank hadn't been quick enough to spot her postcards – the ones with the tiger cubs. But after that, he looked out for Nancy's letters and he hid them away. After a while, he didn't bother opening them, simply lit a corner of the envelopes and dropped them into the sink, leaving the soggy ashes for Irena to clear away. So Irena had taken matters into her own hands. She made a point of meeting the postman at the front door and she pocketed any letters from Nancy. And eventually, she had sent Nancy a reply.

Irena steps forward. 'I'm sorry you didn't get the news about Georgie being pregnant. The last address I had was a campsite.'

'That's OK,' Nancy says. 'Yeah, I moved on from Morag's. I should have let you know.'

'Oh, this is wonderful, delightful.' Frank is shaking his head. 'Now I discover the two of you have been penfriends all this time.'

'Well, why not?' says Irena. She looks down at her neat court shoes. 'You have nothing to fear from Nancy. In fact, you owe her an apology.'

'I beg your pardon?'

'Yes,' Irena continues smoothly. Her words come easily, as if she has been storing them up for a long time. 'You acted like the injured party, crying to the children, telling them how their mother had left them. But you never told them about us, did you?'

'Well, there was nothing to tell.'

'Except there was, Frank. Because you and I didn't meet when I came to clean your London home, did we? We met a long time before that.'

Frank is a trapped animal, looking from his wife to Nancy, his hands flexing and clenching into two tight fists. 'Irena, there's no point in this – it was years ago.'

'But Nancy deserves to know the truth.' Irena turns to Nancy. 'I'm sorry, but Frank and I met years before you left. We had an affair. I was working on the bar at the golf club. I knew he was married and had two small children, but, well, I was young and he told me it was all but over.

'He said that you were ill, the two of you were only staying together for the kids, all that stuff.' She looks down at her navy coat, picks a fleck of white dust from its collar. 'I suppose that's why I answered your letters. Because I felt guilty. It was my way of saying sorry.'

Nancy knows she should feel angry. She'd accused Frank of affairs, in her drunken rages. She'd thrown glasses, then grabbed the shards and thrown them at him too. And every time, he said she was delusional. She was mad, she was crazy, she was a drunk. But Nancy is done with anger. Slowly, she lets out a long breath.

'Oh, Frank,' she says. 'What was the point?'

Frank doesn't answer. He's looking down at the ground and he too looks broken.

'All those lies we both told. What was the point? It didn't keep us together and it didn't help our children. I should have told you what Gerry was doing. He terrorised me, Frank. Kept turning up, threatening to tell you things, blackmailing me. I was a bag of nerves. Our marriage was in ruins, Frank. But neither of us could admit it.'

Frank looks up and she sees a flash of the man she fell for. His kind eyes. How he took her by the hand and led her out of that clinic and then, when they broke into a run, the way they couldn't stop laughing. His kisses, planted over her face, her eyes, her open mouth. A glowing certainty that this was it: they would be together and this happy, always.

And then the past vanishes and a far older, angrier Frank is scowling at her. 'How could I trust you, Nancy? I couldn't, and I wanted a proper life for our children. A nice house, a decent life. You were a mess – what could you offer them? And that revolting man. He was a danger and you chose him, not them.'

Nancy is shaking her head. 'I didn't choose him. I didn't have any other option. I needed help before that, Frank. But you just made me feel that I'd failed and I'd let you down. Like I was doing it all wrong.'

Frank hangs his head. 'I just wanted us to be a proper family.' And Nancy almost feels sorry for him.

'But what does that even mean? None of us are perfect. God knows I made some dreadful mistakes, but so did you, Frank. But you never admitted it. You were so . . . so rigid. You couldn't bear anyone to be wrong, not even your own children. Like Georgie – she could never do anything right. You always criticised her. It broke my heart to see you treat her like that.'

Irena has been biding her time, but now she speaks up again. 'Frank, you are still so hard on her. All she wants is you to say "Well done" or "That's great" every now and then. Like you do for Dan.' She looks down at the ground. 'You could say it to me once in a while, too.'

Nancy thinks, if Irena, with her neat court shoes, her handbags and her talent for cleaning still doesn't make Frank happy, *what chance did I have*?

'It's complicated with Georgie,' Frank says in a tight voice. 'You know that as well as I do.'

Nancy sighs. 'It really isn't, Frank. It's very simple. Your daughter, the girl you raised, is over in that hospital, with your grandchild. Just for today, let yourself enjoy that fact. Go back inside and tell her you love her.'

Nancy turns away from Frank. It's up to him now. She will stay close to Dan's old and dusty car and wait for him. Then she will get a bus into town and try and find the address that Sandrine the nurse wrote down, the animal shelter where she hopes she will find out news about her dog, Bree – whether she has been found or if Nancy has lost her, along with everything else that she ever held dear.

259

Chapter Forty-Seven

GEORGIE

Dan rushes back in holding out his phone and Georgie feels a flare of panic.

'It's Wilf, but the line is terrible, it keeps cutting out,' Dan says. He's right, the line is bad, with an echo that makes it sound as if Wilf is standing inside a wind tunnel, but it's enough. She shouts out the important bits: that it's a girl, she's fine, she's right here, feeding. That Georgie went into labour early in the car, but Dan was with her. 'I couldn't have coped without him,' she says.

'I can't believe it. I'm so sorry I wasn't with you, Georgie.'

'When can you be here?'

'Oh God, I never should have left you, Georgie. I don't know. I need to get back to Marrakech and then I'll be on the next flight out.'

'When is . . .' she starts to say, but the line breaks up, fizzes with static and the howl of distant satellite signals.

She catches words: 'Tomorrow . . . find a Jeep . . .' and then the line cuts out.

She didn't have a chance to tell Wilf about today's bedside dramas, but she will. Seeing her mother and father come face to face with each other for the first time in twenty years is a reminder that a relationship can't survive on secrets.

She looks over at Dan, who is gazing out of the window, possibly down to where their mother is waiting, and she feels a rush of love for him. Soon, they will leave this hospital bubble and she worries about what sort of life Dan will return to: no Mandy, no job. But now they've both been honest with each other, Georgie hopes she can help him through.

'I need to go down,' Dan is saying. 'Give her my phone number, so we can keep in touch.'

'Whatever,' Georgie says.

'But they seem to be talking – Nancy and Dad. I can see them from here. Dad's arms are crossed. Now Irena's joining in. It's all very weird.'

All Georgie wants is to be left alone. The baby is feeding but it still hurts like hell – why does nobody tell you these things? She's dizzy with tiredness and her arms and her neck ache from holding this hot, damp bundle in the same position. So much has happened and she can feel herself cracking, breaking into different parts: the Georgie who loves Wilf, Georgie and the tangle of her mother, Georgie and Dan. And now Georgie and her baby – and she doesn't know how to keep them all together.

Dan's still looking out of the window, giving a running commentary. 'OK, Dad and Irena are walking away. No, hang on, Dad's stopped. He's looking up at this window. Maybe he's going to . . . Oh no, he's walking faster now, back to the car. Now he's driving away.'

He turns back to Georgie. 'I'll just nip down anyway. Give Nancy my number.' Good old Dan – he always wants to make everything all right and keep everyone happy. But Georgie's not sure he can pull it off this time.

From outside the ward, Georgie can hear the squeak and roll of a gurney, the cry of a woman in pain. An alarm goes off and, further down the corridor, a phone is ringing. The woman in the bed opposite catches her eye – Georgie has been avoiding her gaze since the Brown family floor show. 'Busy out there,' the woman says. 'Expect I'll be turfed out soon.'

A nurse comes rushing in, flushed and flustered. 'I'm sorry,' she says to the woman opposite. 'We're going to need your bed. I hate to do this but . . .'

'No, no, I get it. I'll ring the husband. Quite fancied another night away from home, but no worries. I was half expecting it.' The woman gets out her mobile.

As the nurse turns around, Georgie gets ready to give her a grateful smile, but her smile fades as the nurse comes closer. Her face has the bloated look of someone who hasn't slept properly in a long time. 'I'm so sorry,' the nurse says. 'I know it's your first, but your baby's a good weight and you're feeding well. We've got three emergencies coming in, so I wondered when you think you'll be ready to go home?'

Her vision of Wilf arriving here isn't going to happen in time – he isn't even close to an airport. The staff here have been so kind, but she's an extra patient they hadn't bargained for and now they need their bed back. She's just absorbing this information when Dan reappears and the bewildered look on his face confirms what she feared might happen.

'She's gone, hasn't she? She didn't wait.'

Dan gives a sharp nod, steps over to the window, as if hoping to spot her from up here. As if there's been some mistake.

But Georgie knows that this reckless journey in search of their mother has come to an end, of sorts. And now that dusty, scratched and impossibly slow car is going to have to make one final journey. All the way back to Devon.

Chapter
Forty-Eight

NANCY

She'd watched as Frank took a few steps towards the hospital building and paused. And then she'd seen Frank spin around and stride purposefully back to his car. He'd considered doing the right thing – returning to his daughter's bedside – but in the end, he couldn't.

Nancy knows all the things she did that ruined their family, but Frank's inflexibility, his inability to see any point of view but his own, also broke them apart. The man is a fool. If she could, she'd rush back to Georgie's bedside in a heartbeat. But she's been told to leave and that's what she'll do.

Nancy walks over to the spot where Frank's car has left black tyre marks on the ground in his rush to leave, jabs at a stippled shape with the end of her stick. She suspects Dan won't come down to give her any phone number. It's too late for that. She had a tantalising glimpse of what could have been – and an intimation of how hard the past twenty years have been for her children.

Yes, her children came looking for her, but it was driven by curiosity, not love. And she can imagine what a disappointment she must be.

Beside the car park, a bus is pulling into a bay and right now it feels like the answer to all this confusion, so Nancy raises her stick in the air, signalling for it to wait.

As the bus pulls out, Nancy feels as if she's settling back in an old rhythm – travelling away from people who know her name and all the things she's done wrong. She has no idea where she'll go next, or if Bree will be by her side, but it's time to move on. She will hold on to that vision of her daughter and granddaughter snuggled together for a while. It will fortify her and it will haunt her. Then, eventually, it will fade.

◆ ◆ ◆

She changes buses and finds the rescue centre, an unprepossessing building off the ring road on the other side of the city. The young woman on the reception desk says she'll check, but there are procedures to be adhered to. 'Even if she's here, we can't just go handing dogs over to anybody, can we? You'll have to fill in the forms. Show proof of ownership.' She sees Nancy's face fall.

'Or a letter from your vet?'

'I haven't ever needed a vet,' Nancy says. 'Please, if you could check if she's been brought in? A collie-cross with a white tail.' She gives her hand a wave, mimicking how Bree holds her tail. 'Even if you can't let me have her, it would mean a lot to know. I'll be able to rest easier tonight.'

The woman does some tip-tapping on the keyboard, then she calls over an older colleague. The women wear green sweatshirts with a logo on the front and they mutter in low voices, heads together. The older woman has cropped hair and a no-nonsense manner and she glares at Nancy suspiciously through the glass. 'Wait here,' she says.

This centre isn't a bit like the ramshackle place where Nancy worked in Ireland, where desperate dogs were kept in sheds and there was no such thing as paperwork.

Nancy feels hollowed out with tiredness. Her ankle hurts now, a steady, throbbing reminder that she has no place to go tonight. She sits and, just for a moment, lets herself give in to the warmth of this waiting room that smells of dog kibble and disinfectant, where people do things in an orderly manner and tick boxes on forms.

A door opens. Then there's a scrabble of claws, a yelp, and all at once the dog is on her, licking her face, nosing her hand, trying to jump into her lap. It's Bree, her Bree, and Nancy can't help it: she lets go of all her held-in sobs – for this scared dog, but also for her children and for herself. She's a mess, wiping away snot and tears with the crusty sleeve of her coat and trying to calm the dog and let her know she's safe.

'She means a lot to you, eh?'

'Yes.' Nancy tries to smile. 'But it's also . . . well, it's been quite a day.'

'Your dog is fine, we've checked her over. Someone found her this morning, hiding under a bush. Took her to their local vet and they only just brought her in. We could tell she wasn't a stray.'

'Thank you. This means so much. I've let everyone down. If I'd done it to Bree too . . .'

But already the woman has turned away and is busying herself, loading sachets of dog food into a carrier bag. 'Strictly speaking, we shouldn't release an animal without proof of ownership. But I don't think there's any doubt this is your dog. She's had a good meal, but this should see you right for a few days.'

Bree keeps jumping up, trying to lick Nancy's face, so it takes them a while to walk back out to the road. It's only just gone 3 p.m. but it's already getting dark, and Nancy can tell it's going to be a cold one tonight. She stands at the bus stop for a bit, the route that will take them back into the city, then she looks across the road, wonders about hitching again.

She looks down and Bree looks back with her trusting brown eyes. 'Where to next, then, girl?'

Chapter
Forty-Nine

GEORGIE

Georgie never thought she'd get back into this wretched car again, yet here she is, opening the passenger door. Bits of the journey return to her like a bad dream: that early tension between her and Dan. The pain of remembering Finn. The dark tunnel of trees leading to Gerry's place and then the terrifying, juddering point of no return as she went into labour – it all comes rushing back.

'You OK?' says Dan, looking at her.

'Yes. Let's just get going.'

Dan had gone to some out-of-town shopping centre to buy a car seat and also found a garage that fixed the flickering headlights. 'Faulty fuses,' he says, as if Georgie has any interest. Once the baby is strapped in safely, Georgie sits in the front, but she can't help turning round every few minutes because it's still hard to believe she has a baby.

A message from Wilf pops up on Dan's phone:

Back in Marrakech. Will try and get on next flight out.
Thanks for photos – she's beautiful. Can't wait. All love
xxx

As the engine roars into life, Georgie feels a lurch in her stomach and a tell-tale spinning in her head. *No, not again*, she thinks. Georgie's body is already seeping and leaking and aching in ways she never knew were possible, and now her brain is also conspiring against her. It must be being back in this car because it feels as if some memory is hovering on the periphery of her mind, then sliding away, out of her grasp. But she lets it go because it's a dark memory, one that has the drag of imminent disaster.

Their old friend the driving app pipes up: 'Nine hours and twelve minutes – you are on the fastest route.'

They are coming to the outskirts of the city when they see her. It's raining and the windscreen wipers are doing their ineffective scraping and it's hard to see out. But still Georgie recognises the lone figure, lopsided because of her crutch, a dog next to her. There's no time to speak, Georgie just raises a finger and points. The two of them exchange looks, Georgie gives the briefest nod and Dan flicks on the indicator and pulls over, bumping the car roughly up on to the kerb.

As Nancy hears the engine, she turns around and there's a look of fear in her face – but it vanishes when she realises it's them. Dan leans across and calls out, 'Where are you going?'

Nancy looks left and right, as if he might be speaking to someone else on this wet, windswept ring road. 'I don't know,' she says. 'I just thought I should leave.'

Dan looks at Georgie again, his eyebrows raised.

Then, before she can speak, Dan is out, trying to work out how to fit Nancy and her dog and her bag into this miniature car. In the end, Georgie moves on to the back seat beside her baby and Nancy and her dog squeeze into the front.

At first, they drive in silence, taking in this new and surprising arrangement. The light is fading, but Georgie can still see the back of her mother's head. She studies the jagged parting that runs through her hair, the layer of grime that's worked into her collar.

She smells it again, the scent of turf and clean air and a hint of the farmyard that seems ingrained into her mother's coat.

She thinks of Nancy's face just now when they drew up alongside her and it reminds her of another time, so long ago. An afternoon when Georgie and her mum were walking along the road in a pretty holiday town in Wales and Gerry's dark-grey van had overtaken them and slowed to a halt. Georgie felt a dread, because she knew how Gerry had found them. But when she glanced up at her mother, she saw raw fear. There is a difference, she is beginning to understand, between running away and running scared.

Up front, Dan is asking Nancy questions about her dog. It's easy, inconsequential chat, the sort you make with a stranger, but it's oddly soothing. And as the bright street lights give way to the black, open lanes of the motorway, Georgie finds that if she rests her head against the car seat, she's almost comfortable. The voices make a pleasant background hum and she's aware, on some level, that this feels like the right thing to do. She thought she'd lost her again, that Nancy had taken her at her word, but this feels like a reprieve. For the first time in twenty years, she knows exactly where her mother is, and they are bringing her home.

They make several stops on the way back. There's a service station where Dan and Nancy go and get cups of tea and sandwiches and Georgie feeds the baby. Then Dan pulls over for a nap and they all try to rest and Georgie feeds again. The car is uncomfortable and the journey is long and Georgie wonders if it will ever end. But she must have fallen asleep because she wakes to the car bumping over the unfinished surface of Orchard Drive.

As each of them steps out of the car, she realises what a motley crew they are: Georgie wearing a top dotted with posset and milk stains; Dan, dishevelled in clothes he's been wearing for four days straight. And Nancy with her long scarf, shedding flakes of dry mud off her boots as she steps out of the car. Then there's the dog, which is running in circles, keeping low to the ground and trying to round them up.

Georgie carries the baby into the house. She drops her keys into the bowl in the hall and hears the familiar chink. Four days ago, she left this house in a mad rush. And now she's back, with a whole new human being – and a mother in tow.

It is 5 a.m. Already Dan is looking in the fridge, asking where he can go and buy some food. 'There's a garage down the road,' she tells him. 'You'd best drive there, though, it's not a very relaxing walk.'

She hears the familiar thrum of the engine start up and fade and then it's just her and Nancy, both looking down at the sleeping baby in the car seat. Then they look at Nancy's dog, which is standing at the bifold doors, looking out intently at the garden.

'Is she all right with children? With babies, specifically.'

Nancy's words are a whisper: 'She's good. Very gentle. We lived on a campsite for a bit – lots of kids there. A baby, too.'

'Sit down, then, put your coat somewhere.'

She watches as Nancy rolls her coat into a ball and sits gingerly on the edge of the sofa, as if trying to take up as little space as possible. Nancy looks up. 'I can't thank you enough for giving me this chance . . .'

'I'm giving you nothing,' Georgie says. 'I need answers, that's all. It was Dan's idea to pick you up.'

'That's fine, I get that. And you deserve answers, you both do. I'm sorry your father didn't give better ones all those years ago. It was unforgivable, the way you both got caught in the middle.'

Georgie looks down at her sleeping baby and she remembers life with Nancy. The shouting. Things being broken. Georgie sitting upstairs in a window seat, looking out at a darkening sky and hearing the crack of plastic bunting. And she realises that was just how it felt – like being suspended between two warring factions, powerless but responsible, too.

Then, today, the sight of her father's tight jaw as he sent Nancy away again and Georgie's own hardened heart, telling her to get out. And she looks down at her baby and she thinks, this has to end, all this blame and anger. If Georgie wants answers, she needs to ask them in the spirit of forgiveness. Feeding the hate and the blame will help no one.

'There's a spare room upstairs. You can put your stuff in there.'

Georgie listens as her mother's uneven footsteps make their way up the stairs, followed by a gentle padding across the floor above. When Nancy comes back down, she avoids looking directly at Georgie. She goes over to the bifold doors and lets herself and the dog out into the back garden. Georgie thinks that in a while her mother will throw a stick for the dog, but Nancy just stands there, looking up at the dark sky.

Chapter Fifty

NANCY

The dog won't settle in this strange house. She keeps getting up, circling around and sniffing the air. Nancy doesn't blame her because she can't get her bearings here either, in this place where even the smallest sound bounces off the hard white walls. When Dan rummages in the cutlery drawer, the clash of metal echoes through to the open-plan living room. When the front door slams, it rattles the back windows.

It's a house that feels clinically modern but has a confusing array of old furniture, as if the wrong people have moved in. The nicest things she can see are some photographs that hang in frames on the wall and Nancy wonders if Georgie took them. There are several bleakly beautiful landscapes and one of a man sitting on a shingle beach. He has tight, closely cropped dark curls and he's smiling at the camera, a warm, easy smile, and she wonders if this is Wilf.

But all in all, it's not a bit like Nancy's bothy, a place where she and the dog had felt safe. They liked how it was just one room with two small windows and a sturdy door that kept the weather and strangers at bay. Here, it's open and noisy and Nancy wishes she could press a button, like the one Dan just used for the TV, to make everything go mute.

Standing out in the garden had eased her nerves for a while, but gradually that outside space began to feel all wrong too. Up close, everything was fake: the grass was an unnatural just-laid green and the stunted shrubs had been shoved into too-dry soil. Instead of the secret rustle of animals, all she could hear was the rumble of a distant road. Above, even the sky looked drained of life.

Dan cooks them all a breakfast of eggs on toast and she feeds her crusts to Bree under the table. They've been driving for so long, but nobody seems ready to sleep – there's a lot to take in, she supposes.

Georgie is feeding the baby and Dan has lit a fire in the fireplace. Here, even the logs don't look natural – they are a uniform size and shade of brown, made from compacted sawdust, apparently. Still, they give a nice enough glow. Nancy sits opposite her children, one hand resting on Bree's head. She knows the time has come.

'I'm wondering where to start,' she says.

'Well, maybe just start at the beginning,' Georgie says.

Nancy wonders where the beginning might be, whether it was when she was a little girl, the lone child of parents who never made her feel welcome. Or whether it was when she arrived at university, believing her real life was about to start – only to meet Frank and Gerry in the same week, two men who trapped her in different ways.

Or maybe the story begins in a clinic in the last term of Nancy's degree, where she realises she's not so clever after all and Frank suggests what feels like the best solution. But, instead, she tells an old story, the one she's sure she's told them before, about the day she and Frank met.

'The first time I met your father, I knew he was a kind man,' she says. 'One of the lecturers made me feel very small and silly and nobody said anything, except Frank. He had a clear idea of right and wrong. It's just that, somewhere along the way, we both lost sight of it. And of each other. Things got harder after we added a baby into the mix . . .'

Nancy chooses her words carefully because here's Georgie, just starting out with her own baby. 'I was so young when I had you, Georgie. I felt very lonely and things were different back then – men weren't expected to help much. So your father couldn't understand what was wrong. But I was twenty-one and I was struggling.'

Georgie nods. 'When I was twenty-one, I was barely capable of looking after myself, let alone a baby.'

'I think I felt like my life was over before it had started. And I suppose that was why I let Gerry visit. I realise what he did would be seen differently now. He was what your generation would call "coercive". He was my lecturer and he abused his power. But, at the time, I was flattered by his attention. He made me feel special. Frank wasn't perfect himself – and clearly we were both lonely – but I never should have let Gerry into our lives. In the end, he was the reason I had to leave.'

'But I don't understand how you could walk out and never come back.' Georgie's brow is furrowed. 'Not even to check on us or say goodbye. Didn't you want to explain things?'

'Well,' Nancy says carefully, 'I suppose you could say I left twice. Once after that terrible holiday in Wales. And then, a few months later. After my visit.'

'What visit?' Georgie is looking confused and Nancy falters, remembering what Dan told her. She has to explain the best she can.

'So, the first time I left, it was just to give me and Frank some breathing space. He was very hurt and angry that Gerry had turned up in Wales. That's when your father got it into his head that I'd been having an affair with Gerry all through our marriage, which wasn't true. That I'd had a baby by him . . .'

Dan stabs the fire with a poker, sends up a flurry of sparks. 'Different stock,' he announces.

There's a silence and Nancy's stomach gives a sickening flip. 'Sorry, what do you mean?'

Dan bashes the log again, then drops the poker with a clatter. 'I mean, if we're doing this – being honest and open for once in our lives – that's what Dad used to say.'

Heart thumping, Nancy looks from Dan to Georgie, whose eyes are wide.

Dan's voice is clipped and hard. 'After you left, Dad used to take me on all these father-and-son jollies. To golf – very boring – or rugby, which I hated too. But fishing trips were the worst because it was just the two of us, for hours on end, sitting in the cold beside a lake.

'And that's when he'd say things like that. The first time, he'd had a few swigs of whisky – he always brought a little silver flask – and he slapped me on the back and said something like, "Son, Danny Boy, we're a team. Georgie's OK, but she's not like us, is she?" And I thought he meant that she was a girl but then he took a few more sips from that silver flask and he said, "Different stock, son. Different gene pool." And when I got home I looked up those words and I started to understand what he meant.'

Nancy raises her eyes to the perfect white of the ceiling, and she wants to let out a howl. *Oh, Frank*, she thinks. *How could you say such a thing? To a child.*

But she's come this far – and now it's time for the lies to stop. She looks at both of her children and she knows there's no easy way out.

'Georgie, Frank got it into his head that he wasn't your father, that your father was Gerry. Even when you were little, he never treated you equally, and it broke my heart seeing that. It was so wrong, but I didn't know how to stop it.'

'What?' Georgie sits forward. 'That creepy man in the woods, with his false teeth and his whiny voice – Gerry is my father?'

'No, he's not.' Nancy runs her hands over her face. This is impossible. 'Georgie, that was never true. Your father is Frank – and shame on him for always treating you like second-best. You're his daughter, for better or for worse.'

Dan butts in, 'But, Dad said, about the gene pool – why would he lie?' His face looks so soft and vulnerable. She can't bear to carry on, but she has to.

'Frank should never have said such a thing. On that holiday in Wales, he asked me if I'd had a child by Gerry and I couldn't deny it. But he had it the wrong way round. It's not Georgie. It's you, Dan. Gerry is your father.'

Dan starts to shake his head, swearing and saying, 'No, no, no,' and Bree leaps to her feet, growling, sensing something is badly wrong.

'I wish it hadn't happened, but it did. Gerry caught me at a difficult time. He told me he would put a word in for me, with a casting agent . . .'

'So it never crossed your mind that I had a right to know? Or that it was wrong to trick Frank into thinking I was his?' Dan shouts. 'That's disgusting. That's immoral.'

She could have left Frank at that point, she supposes, pregnant and with a toddler. Gone back to her parents, begged their forgiveness so she could scrub toilets and serve breakfasts and give her children the same joyless upbringing she'd had. Yes, she could have done that, but she didn't. She swallowed down her secret and continued with the charade of their marriage. For a while, they muddled through. She found a solace of sorts, in drink. Frank found his, with Irena.

But deep down she knew the truth. Just as with Georgie, her body had felt different from the moment she'd fallen pregnant. Because Georgie had been born a couple of weeks early, no one was too surprised when Dan arrived even earlier. Then, as she watched her son grow, her suspicions were confirmed. What most people noticed was how tall Dan was for his age and his sunny nature. Which was just as well because what Nancy saw was how Dan's mannerisms, even his smile, were sometimes an uncanny echo of Gerry's.

She wants to explain all this, but her children won't look at her. Georgie is crying and Dan has moved away, standing at the bifold doors and staring out at the arid garden. 'That man,' he's saying. 'That vile man. And then you let him into our lives again until finally he showed us all what he was capable of. On the bridge. How could you?'

A silence falls and Dan turns, realising, too late, what he's said. And then Georgie says, 'What bridge?'

Chapter Fifty-One

GEORGIE, 2002

'I CAN'T REMEMBER A THING ABOUT IT'

She recognises him immediately. He's standing in front of them, blocking out the sun and getting ready to spoil their fun all over again, like he did in Wales, and it makes her tummy tighten and melt at the same time. Their mum has just bought her and Dan ice creams and Georgie has been eating hers as slowly as she can, taking tiny licks so it lasts longer than her brother's.

At first, it had been weird seeing their mum, but nice too. And now Georgie is just starting to let herself enjoy the fact she's sitting next to her mum and working up the courage to ask if Nancy is feeling better and when she will come home. And that's when it happens: she looks up and sees that man who tricked her into telling him where they were going for their Easter holiday.

Her mum kept muttering 'How?', trying to work out how he'd found them in Tenby, but Georgie knew how. She'd led Gerry to them. And, even worse, then she'd told her dad about seeing him. Frank had bought her a massive bag of sweets and they felt like her reward for answering all his questions and saying, 'Yes, a man called Gerry does visit. And you'll never guess who we bumped into, that day when you went fishing.'

So, now, sitting on a bench on Southbank, eking out those precious last minutes with their mum, Georgie looks up and sees Gerry and she feels an anger well up inside her. That's when she decides. *Right*, she thinks, *I'll show him, this ratty man with his ponytail and his greasy beard, I'll tell him what we think of him.* And when Dan says he needs the loo, she sees her chance. She says she'll stay here, thanks, with this so-called old friend. Because Georgie reckons she can handle him.

It's her idea to go up on the bridge. Her plan is to lead him away from the bench and then tell him where to go. Like the kids at school who tormented the trainee teacher until he went red in the face and had to leave the classroom. Then she'll run back to the bench, where their dad will meet them and they will all go home together and it will be OK.

So she walks ahead of Gerry, swinging her arms. 'Come on, I want to show you something,' she says. 'It's all the way up here. God, you're so slow. Are you too old to keep up?' She's feeling pretty sassy wearing her new cargo pants and her crop top, and her hair looks good too. She likes the swish of it and the way she keeps catching glimpses of that blue twist on one side. The feel of those tiny beads at the end of the braid, tapping her shoulder.

But once they get on to the bridge, Georgie feels less sure. It turns out there are trains running alongside the walkway and their brakes screech and scream and she can see sparks on the tracks, through a grid of metal. But she keeps going, she wants to lead him away and keep her mum safe.

They get to a spot and she thinks, *this'll do*, and she turns to face him, hands on her hips. 'Look . . .' she starts to say. But then her words won't come out. It's as if a switch has been flipped, like stepping from sunlight into shadow. Now she's up here, alone with him, Georgie feels scared. Because Gerry has a weird look on his face, his lips are wet, and when he smiles it makes his moustache move.

'So, you've brought me all the way up here – what's your game?' he says.

Georgie's throat is closing and no words will come out. She is beginning to think she has just done something rather stupid. She looks around, but nobody is taking any notice of a girl and a man on the bridge.

She tries to edge past him so she can get back down to her mum and Dan, but he's too quick and he grabs her from behind, holding her around the waist. Before she realises what's happening, he's hoisted her up to the railings and he's pressing her so that she's leaning over the top, looking down at the water. She can feel his belt buckle, sharp on her bare back. Then she feels his hand between her shoulders, pushing her down. He's got her stomach pinned against the hard metal of the rail, but Georgie's top half is floating, falling.

She's suspended above the brown, roiling waters and the wind is whipping her hair, filling her open mouth. She feels the danger, the expanse of air and nothingness below. Then Gerry leans forward and she thinks it's OK, it's over, his little joke. But it's not. He's doing this so he can talk to her, whisper in her ear.

'You, little miss, think you're so clever. But in my opinion, you need a bit of discipline. If it was up to me, I wouldn't have you wearing this tarty outfit. And I would teach. You. A. Lesson.' With each word, his hand pushes her down a little further. His breath is hot in her ear and she smells tobacco and rotten teeth and now she realises that the way he's pressing down on her means she can't draw breath.

She gasps, tries to suck in air, but her stomach, her lungs are being crushed. She lifts a hand, sees it wave uselessly in the air, hears a train's wheels screech behind her. She catches sight of the blue thread and the beads woven into her hair, the way they flutter innocently in the wind, and she wonders if it's the last thing she'll see. She wishes she hadn't had them put in, because she sees now that it's childish and stupid. But most of all, she wishes she hadn't come up here with Gerry because now she'll never see her mother or anyone again. This is how it will end.

And then she feels his hands move up to her shoulders and he's pulling her back and talking in a different voice, one that's intended for the small crowd that has gathered around them. 'Whoa there, little lady – you were leaning out a bit too far for my liking! Back you come, you're safe now.'

And then there are other hands, ones that feel firm but kind, and she can breathe again. There's the crackle of a walkie-talkie radio and she's shaking and she wants to go down now, away from that man. Except when she turns around to point him out, he's gone. 'That man . . .' is all she can say.

Then she's being taken down some steps and she looks for her mum, but she can't see her. Instead, she sees her dad and she runs to him. She can't bear to tell him what she did – she feels so stupid and she wants to forget this whole afternoon ever happened.

The doctor is kind and the nurses give her stickers, even though she's too old for them. And when they ask what happened, all she can say is, 'I wanted to fix it,' but her words don't make sense to anyone, so they stop asking. And then Georgie stops talking. When she and her dad get home, Granny and Grandpa Brown are there, looking after Dan, but she doesn't talk to them either. She locks the bathroom door and she cuts the blue twist of thread out of her hair so it leaves a prickly stump and then she goes to bed. Later,

Dan creeps in and lies on the floor beside her, but she still doesn't talk, not even to him.

And on Monday morning at school, when Mrs Mendosa asks if Georgie did anything nice at the weekend, Georgie acts like one of the tough girls who sit at the back. She chews her gum and side-eyes her teacher, and she says, 'Naah, nothing. My weekend was so boring, Miss. In fact, I can't remember a thing about it.'

Chapter Fifty-Two

GEORGIE

Her mother is describing an incident on a bridge and as Georgie hears her words, she can picture bits, but they feel like someone else's memories. Like scenes from a film that she doesn't want to watch. Instead, she thinks of the spools of railings and bridges that she glimpsed from the car window and how they brought on that deathly swoon of vertigo.

She's never been good with heights, but it got much worse when she was pregnant. In fact, it was one of her first symptoms: a high-pitched tinnitus and an aversion to going anywhere near bridges. 'Must be your protective instinct kicking in,' Wilf had said.

The first time it happened they were on a day out in Bristol and he'd taken her up to a grassy mound to admire the view over a gorge, with the suspension bridge looming above. Even seeing it from a distance was too much: she'd stood blinking away black dots, sure she was going to vomit. The monumental swoop of iron, the yawning space below – it was too awful to comprehend.

Now, she turns to Dan. 'Is this true? Do you remember this?'

He gives a quick nod.

'You didn't ever speak about what happened,' he says. 'You didn't seem to remember. You had some sessions with a therapist. Me too, because I saw some of it, but only from a distance.'

In fact, Georgie can remember bits of those long, boring afternoons, sitting on bean bags in a stuffy room. Looking at a blank sheet of paper, knowing something was expected of her but unable to draw the right thing. Making an effort, drawing a boat, hoping that was what they wanted. A patient voice asking, *Is that what you saw, Georgie? How does that make you feel, thinking about the boats?* At the time, she thought going to that room with the bean bags was to do with being from a broken home, a way to help reconcile Georgie to the fact that she was so unlovable her mother had left.

But now, Nancy's words are taking her back to Gerry and the bridge. She remembers the immensity of the air around her, the freefall drop of a bad dream, knowing it couldn't be real because when you're this high up, if you fall, you'll certainly die.

'Everyone said that you'd remember in your own time. They told me not to talk about it because, like waking someone who is sleepwalking, the shock would be too much,' Dan says. 'Except you never did remember.'

'Until I got pregnant,' Georgie says. 'And my body remembered.'

Her memories of what happened afterwards are crystal clear: Irena sliding into their lives, first with a yellow duster and then a set of pink suitcases. The jumble of their old house being packed into boxes, never to be seen again. Starting over at a new school and in a new house where Nancy's name – let alone what happened on the bridge – was never mentioned.

But now, through the haze of her tiredness, other fragments of that day start to come back and they are slotting together to make a different picture. She remembers being carried away by her father, but also how she craned her neck, trying to spot Nancy. She wanted to know if her plan had succeeded – if she'd managed to keep her mother safe. But Nancy looked far from safe. The last time she saw her mother wasn't when she waved Georgie off to school. It was that day, when Nancy was a blur of fists and fury, a crazy woman shouting and fighting and being held back by the police. It was a frightening sight. The sort you'd want to forget.

Then she remembers Gerry whispering about teaching Georgie a lesson and she wonders about all the things he might have said and done to Nancy over the years. Georgie's vision of Nancy as a crazy lady who didn't love them is starting to fade. And in her place, a different woman is emerging – one who had been held back and trapped in all sorts of ways. That afternoon by the bridge, Nancy was fighting back, trying to get to her children. It was something any mother would do.

Chapter Fifty-Three

GEORGIE

Wilf phoned as soon as his flight touched down and he's on his way. Georgie's head is thick with tiredness, but she's too wound up to sleep. So to fill the time, she and Dan have offered to take the dog for a walk. The baby is strapped to Georgie's front, bound tightly into a simulacrum of how she was in the womb. Georgie is wearing an old jacket of Wilf's that's big enough to fit around the two of them.

'Good to get out of the house, eh?' Dan says. They are trying to make their way across the muddy field that lies at the end of Orchard Drive. It's not the prettiest walk, but preferable to the other option – slogging along the main road to the village.

Nancy's collie-like hound looks up at them with quizzical brown eyes, as if asking why they are going so slowly, but walking through this sticky sludge is hard work. Georgie is trying not to engage with this dog; she can't help begrudging it the uncomplicated, affectionate bond it shares with Nancy. Is it wrong to be jealous of a dog? Almost certainly.

She looks down at her boots, now claggy with mud, and tries to catch her breath.

'This is crazy, let's go back,' she says.

'Yeah. Maybe this walk is nicer in the summer.'

'Maybe,' Georgie says. She's not so sure the country life agrees with her, or at least this version of it.

'I wanted to say thanks,' she says. 'For everything – for doing the trip and being there for me. For not freaking out when I went into labour by the side of the road.'

Dan gives her a smile.

'And if you want to talk, I'm here for you. Like about Nancy. Or Finn. Or the whole Gerry thing.'

He stops for a moment, tries to dislodge a particularly large clod of mud from his once-white trainer. 'Thanks,' he says. 'Well, going to find Nancy was something we needed to do together.'

They walk on, with difficulty.

'As for the Gerry thing, as you call it, I have no idea what to do with that information. I mean, in a way it doesn't change anything about my everyday life or my relationship with Dad. But it also changes everything.' He shakes his head. 'Talk about kicking a man when he's down.'

'I had no idea,' Georgie says. 'About your job, or that you and Mandy were having problems.'

'Well, I didn't feel I could tell you. Seeing as Finn's death was the trigger. I couldn't face seeing you, full stop. I knew you'd be grieving, missing him too.'

Georgie can't meet his eyes, so she looks down at the dog instead.

Dan continues. 'So, yeah, Mandy and I will probably sell the house, go our separate ways. As you know, I need the money. Need to get those loans sorted. But, once that's done, I'm thinking of a career change. I'm not cut out for that financial world. Plus, all the new kids are already whizzing up on the inside.'

He stops, scans the endless brown horizon.

'And now, this news about Gerry. I mean, do I tell Dad? Should Nancy tell Dad? Is there anything to be gained from doing that?'

'If this week has taught me anything, it's that a family can't survive if it's built on secrets,' Georgie says. 'But the same goes for me. If I tell Dad, "Hey, actually I'm your birth child, not Dan", how is that going to help any of us? The time for me and Dad to build a bond has passed. I'll carry on visiting him and Irena for high days and holidays. I suspect he'll continue to be distant and polite; we'll muddle along, as we always have.'

They've barely been out ten minutes, but Georgie can feel the baby stirring in her tight cocoon, starting to root. 'I need to go back and feed her,' she says.

'I guess I'll keep walking. Give the dog some exercise,' Dan says forlornly.

Georgie pats the baby's back and sways from side to side to buy some time. She knows she has to speak now, because it will be too painful to dig into this wound again for a while. 'I just need to say – Finn's death was a terrible waste of a life. It was a tragedy, for him and his family. But both of us have been torturing ourselves, taking the blame. And after this week, I don't think blame helps, does it? Nobody wins a moral victory or feels better in the end.'

These words need to come out, so she keeps going. 'Finn dying was no single person's fault. It wasn't mine, or the person who sold him the drugs or the barman who served him more drinks. It wasn't yours, or the woman on the station platform who couldn't stop him, and it wasn't the train driver's. It wasn't even Finn's fault, not really. With a different set of circumstances, he could have made it home and fallen into bed with me at two a.m. But then he might have gone out and done it all again the next Friday, no matter how much we wanted to save him. Do you see what I'm saying?'

Dan gives a small nod, runs a hand over the rough twist of the dog's lead.

Georgie has reached a point beyond tiredness, where her mind feels crisp and lucid. 'It's like Mum and Dad and Gerry – who was the most to blame? I mean, yes, Gerry did some truly terrible, abusive things. But in the end, it was a set of people and events who came together at exactly the wrong time. One person made a mistake, then someone else did, and so it continued. But no single person is to blame, and no one is completely blameless. Life isn't like that.'

Dan takes a step towards her. Because of the baby in the sling, he can't hug her properly, so they settle for a sideways shoulder squeeze. They must look funny, Georgie thinks – two people standing side by side, arms wrapped around each other's shoulders in the middle of a muddy field – and she lets out a sound that's half laugh, half sob. She's so glad they have each other.

Chapter Fifty-Four

GEORGIE

Back inside the house, Georgie lays the baby on the sofa while she shucks off Wilf's jacket. She can see her mother is outside on the patio again, gazing up at the sky as if she's hungry for the air. She looks like a zoo animal, craving freedom. When the baby starts to cry, Nancy turns around, guiltily. 'Oh, sorry, I'm letting all the heat out. I just needed . . .'

She comes back inside, fiddles with the fancy kitchen tap until she figures it out, then she brings Georgie a glass of water. Georgie nods towards the armchair, a flowery cast-off from Wilf's parents. 'Sit, would you, you're making me nervous.'

She's just easing into the feed, swallowing down the first stab of pain, when she hears the sound she's been anticipating for so long: the scrape of Wilf's key in the lock.

Wilf rushes in and then he's there, his face down close to hers, taking her in, then the baby. He seems larger than life, from a different world. His clothes smell of stale plane-cabin air and coffee and she can't take him in at first, just bits of him: his eyes, his chin, his slender cheeks. And then his lips as he kisses her, then the baby, gently on her head.

Barely looking down, Georgie slides a finger into the corner of her baby's mouth, feels her warm gums loosen, and then she holds the baby in her arms so Wilf can see her properly.

He sits down beside her, strokes the baby's cheek. 'Wow,' he says. 'You did it, all by yourself. This is incredible.'

'Well, there were a couple of midwives helping. And Dan wasn't in the room, but he helped me before. And actually, Nancy gave me a bit of encouragement, too . . .'

She looks over to Nancy and smiles. Neither of them has mentioned this yet, that strange half-meeting they had in some hospital cubicles hundreds of miles from here. Wilf looks up, does a double take at this woman in a ratty sweater, who seems to be trying to shrink into a chair in his living room. Her plaits are coming undone, her trousers are worn at the knees and her ruckled socks are dark with dirt. Georgie sees how Nancy might look to a stranger and it makes her feel oddly protective.

'Wilf, this is Nancy,' she says firmly.

'Hi,' he says, standing up. He goes over and Nancy gets to her feet. 'Really good to meet you.'

Then he turns back to Georgie, looking a little confused.

Georgie takes a deep breath. 'Wilf, when you met Irena I should have explained that she's my stepmother. Nancy is my birth mother. She's been living up in Scotland. We met up in Yorkshire. In the hospital.' Georgie quite likes the way this sounds – almost reasonable.

'Well, it's great to meet you,' Wilf says, barely missing a beat. 'You must be very proud of Georgie. And your new granddaughter.' He shakes her hand warmly.

'Yes. Yes, I am.' Nancy gives a tentative smile, then disappears upstairs, so Georgie and Wilf can talk.

First, Georgie tells him about the birth – how she thought the contractions were just Braxton Hicks and then how she lost her phone in the panic, then the hospital and the pain that was an unstoppable force. The incredible rush of the baby when she arrived. The midwife lifting her on to Georgie's chest, remarking on the short umbilical cord. 'There are photos,' she says, 'but they are on Dan's phone and he's out walking the dog.'

'Dan your brother?'

'Yes.'

'And he has a dog?'

'No, the dog is Nancy's. My mum's.'

Wilf is looking even more confused.

'I'm sorry, there's a lot for you to catch up on. Things that have happened in the past few days, but also things that I've never told you. Because my family is far from perfect, Wilf. I didn't want to tell you, because I thought you'd run a mile.'

'I'm not going to do that, Georgie.'

'I know. But the past felt like some kind of darkness inside me – something I had to hide. Then I got scared it was going to come out anyway.'

Wilf doesn't say a word, he just rests his head against hers. And it feels so good, she wants to stay like this forever.

'You're always so positive,' she says. 'I don't know how you do it. It overwhelms me, sometimes. Like I'll never be as happy and bright and breezy. That's just not me.'

'Oh, Georgie. Don't ever pretend anything.'

And then she carries the baby upstairs and she sleeps and the baby sleeps and when she wakes Wilf is there lying beside her, gazing at them both.

'I'm sorry I wasn't with you,' he says. 'Truly sorry. If I'd known, I never would have gone. You, us, the baby. That's what's important. Everything else comes second.'

'I know. She came early – you weren't to know. Neither was I.'

'But to be there – cut the cord, all of that.'

He looks so sad that all her frustration and fear dissipates. 'Wilf, I wish you'd been there too. But will it matter in a few years' time? When this little one is running around and we're busy living our lives? It'll be about playing with her and her learning to talk and helping her make friends – all that stuff. There's more to being a dad than being there at the birth. It's what comes afterwards that really matters.'

When they come downstairs, the dog is lying in front of the eco-log fire and Dan and Nancy are discussing what sort of meal they can cobble together. Georgie has lost track of whether it's lunch or dinner, but she knows she's hungry. She introduces Wilf and Dan and then watches as Wilf does what comes naturally to him – he chats and puts people at ease.

He shows Dan where to find the saucepans and then he stands at the worktop beside Nancy, chopping onions. He asks her what she liked best about living in Scotland and then she talks about a farm she lived on in Ireland, and Georgie sees how Wilf has managed to home in on the bits of Nancy's life that she feels comfortable talking about.

Soon, Nancy is stirring a sauce in a big pan. She's adding herbs and a sprinkle of salt and as Georgie smells the onions and garlic, she remembers how it used to be. Back in the kitchen at St Luke's Road, there would be music playing on the radio. Their mother would sing along as she moved back and forth, getting things out of the fridge and nudging the door shut with her hip. Then she'd be back to chopping vegetables and chucking them into a big pan.

On evenings like that, Georgie would sit at the kitchen table drawing and Dan would be making something complicated out of Lego. Outside it would be dark, but inside it would be bright and friendly and warm. Those were the good times, ones that Georgie would love to recreate one day, in her own home for her own daughter.

And now, as she watches her mother cook, her fluid movements are so familiar that Georgie has to gulp down a sob for all the years they have missed out on. And for the times she'd cursed and hated this woman, never stopping to wonder if she knew Nancy's whole story.

Wilf sees Georgie watching, comes over and strokes the baby's back. 'I can see the resemblance, you know.'

'The baby? Yes, she has my nose, I think,' Georgie says.

'Well, yes. Your nose, I hope. And she'll probably have your hair. But really, I was talking about you and Nancy.' He nods over to the kitchen, where Nancy is absorbed in her task. Every now and then, she reaches up to tuck an imaginary strand of hair behind her ear. 'You do that, too,' Wilf says.

Georgie knows she does. And as she watches, she thinks that maybe being a little bit like her mother is OK. It's not necessarily a bad thing. In fact, it's something she can grow to love.

Chapter Fifty-Five

Nancy, six months later

Nancy is sitting on the log bench outside her front door. Dusk isn't far off and, from here, she can see swallows doing their nightly flit, as if making the most of the wide sky before darkness falls. When that time comes, they will break apart and then, in twos and threes, they will head for the old barn, dip under the overhang of the roof and stay there until morning. Below the sky, the marshlands are aglow, hazy with sea lavender, shot with heads of golden samphire.

The landscape here took a bit of getting used to – it was so flat compared to the hills and crags she had come to love in Scotland. But now she sees the raw beauty of this part of Kent. If you know where to look, the place is teeming with hidden wildlife – dragonflies zip across the ponds and the long grasses hum with insects.

In the distance, there's a power station and soon the floodlights will come on. All night they give out their orange glow and, when the wind changes, Nancy can hear the distant hum of machinery, of civilisation.

Sometimes, visitors are taken aback when they arrive and see those tall chimneys. They come in search of lapwings and owls and lolloping hares, not signs of industry. But Nancy rather likes its ugly presence. It's a reminder that this is a place where humans have tried to make their mark, but nature continues to grow back around it. It is a place for those who have survived.

Her home-to-be isn't much to look at right now – just a plasterboard shack that needs fixing up – but it's all hers and it's perfect. Two rooms, a porch and a view of the salt marshes. It used to be a store for farm machinery and still has an oily, metallic smell about it, but Nancy likes that too. It makes the place feel honest, hard-working. It's tucked away from the prettier buildings, where guests stay.

This place of marshes and winding waterways used to be a farm with livestock, but then the farmer diversified and turned it into a nature reserve. Now twitchers come for the day, carrying hefty binoculars and tiny notebooks, and at the weekend couples arrive. They wear Hunter boots and walk arm in arm along the tamped-down trails before retiring to their shepherd huts and bothies for the night.

When Nancy saw the nature reserve's version of a bothy, she had to smile because it was nothing like her old place. It had feathery pillows, a power shower and a bean-to-cup coffee machine. Still, the weekenders seem to love the idea of a rustic hideaway, although Nancy can't imagine what they need to escape from.

Six months ago, Nancy thought she needed to keep running, but now she knows she was doing it out of habit. Like an animal, she was following an old path that she'd made for herself, one that had become deeper and more worn every time she ran. But she's not scared of that man any more. Right now, Gerry is the one who is worried about Nancy and what her fancy lawyer might do next.

Dan had been right when he'd seen through Gerry's bluster. He was never capable of coming to find her – he's practically a recluse, by all accounts. Nancy's lawyer – hired by Dan, who also got Frank to foot the bill – served an injunction on him anyway.

She made a statement to West Yorkshire police about historic crimes, including all the things he stole from his grandmother's house and sold. They were honest with her – said it was unlikely any charges would ever be brought as none of his family want any dealings with him – but it was good to have him on their radar.

Then she and Georgie made another set of statements to the Metropolitan Police, clarifying his actions on the bridge, which amounted to child cruelty. Again, nothing will happen, but it is a matter of record and, for now, that feels like enough for them.

She stayed with Georgie and Wilf for a while longer and this gave her and Georgie a chance to start getting to know each other. She knows it'll take time to regain Georgie's trust, but already they have started to talk. Georgie confirmed what Nancy had long suspected – how, all those years ago, Gerry had stalked her twelve-year-old daughter and extracted information about where they were going on their family holiday. The worst part was hearing how Georgie had blamed herself. 'Absolutely not. None of it was your fault,' Nancy had said. 'And even in the darkest moments, I never stopped loving you both.'

She moved in with Dan for a bit, kept him company as the For Sale sign went up and new, shinier versions of Dan and Mandy marched around his house, tapping walls and talking about knocking through and extensions and letting in the light.

He and Mandy are getting divorced, but it's all very civilised. Who knew you could have an amicable divorce? Not Nancy. Mandy even told Dan about an organisation that helps people manage their debts and deal with unscrupulous loan sharks.

And it was Mandy who told her about this nature reserve. It's run by a client of hers who mentioned they needed someone reliable who loves the land and works hard. Nancy got to work right away, mending fences and staking footpath signs, and when spring came, she and Bree worked together to bring in the sheep. Nancy watched each one being shorn, their fleeces peeled off like too-heavy overcoats. She liked the way the sheep shook themselves afterwards, as if they felt unburdened, lighter – because Nancy was starting to feel the same way.

Dogs aren't usually allowed on the reserve but they made an exception for Bree because she's a worker, not a pet. Well, until the end of the day. That's when Bree jumps up on Nancy's bed and curls into a ball, as she always has.

The best thing about this place that feels so remote and other-worldly is that it is only two hours from London, where Georgie and Dan live. They each have a flat in north-west London, only about twenty minutes from St Luke's Road, where they grew up.

Georgie says she loves being back in the city: she's already met lots of other parents and she's gone back to work part-time. Yes, she even likes the noise and the dirt, she says, after her taste of country life. Nancy tells Georgie that Orchard Drive was never the real countryside and she knows that as Georgie spends more time here, she'll understand what Nancy means.

Georgie and Wilf have named the baby Lily. It's an old-fashioned name, but not one that runs in either family and Georgie says that's the whole point. 'She will be her own person – not an echo of someone who came before her.'

A baby and another house move, all in the space of six months – it's been a lot for Georgie and Wilf. But they seem to be coping. Like Nancy and Frank, they are having a baby early on in their relationship, but Georgie says it's going well. They are talking, sharing things, and Nancy is quietly optimistic that they will make it.

Dan's coming down next weekend to help Nancy start fixing this place up. He's never going back to his old job, or anything like it. 'Now it's time to do what I want,' he says – and he's retraining to be a carpenter.

Nancy is more than happy for him to hone his carpentry skills by helping her do up this place. She knows how she wants it to look – the inside lined with old planks, so it feels like a secret cabin. A bit like her old bothy, if she's honest.

Now the sun is dipping down and Bree is yawning, wondering if it's time to go inside. But today was such a good day that Nancy wants to sit here a little longer and savour the memory of it.

Georgie and Wilf brought Lily for a visit, and in the afternoon Wilf suggested he and Georgie could take a walk and explore the nature trails. He said Georgie could take some more photos for the series of landscapes she's putting together for a solo exhibition. But Georgie looked uncomfortable, said she wasn't sure.

Nancy looked away; she could tell Georgie didn't want to leave Lily alone with her and she understood why. But then Wilf said, 'Ah, come on, Georgie, it's gorgeous out there. Let's make the most of having a babysitter – Lily will be fine.' And so they went, leaving Lily with Nancy.

At first, she carried the baby around the small patch of earth that she intends to make into her garden, talking to her about all the things she wants to plant. But inside, Nancy was a bundle of nerves because it was the first time she'd been left alone with her granddaughter. Lily must have picked up on her tension, or maybe she was just tired, because soon she was turning her head, crying out and looking for her mother.

So then Nancy sang her a nursery rhyme, one she used to sing to her own children. She never knew the proper words back then and she still doesn't. And as Nancy sang, she felt Lily starting to quieten and sink into her, despite the warmth of the day.

And Nancy sang to her grandchild about mockingbirds and diamond rings until they saw Georgie and Wilf walking back and she went out to meet them on the cinder path. As they got closer, Nancy waited for Georgie to reach for her baby, or for Lily to reach out for her mother. But neither did. Lily stayed tucked up against Nancy until they got home and every step of the way, the heft of her little body, the brush of her hair against Nancy's cheek – it felt like a gift.

ACKNOWLEDGEMENTS

First of all, a huge thank you to you, the reader, for choosing this book or e-book. I hope *The Last Time I Saw You* has meant something to you, whether it got you thinking about relationships, families and motherhood or because you enjoyed the story.

Huge thanks to my lovely husband, daughter and son (and Lottie the dog), who I had to ignore for long stretches of time while I wrote, rewrote and edited this book.

I am indebted to my editors Kasim Mohammed and Sophie Wilson, who came up with brilliant suggestions when I was struggling to get to grips with the story. Kasim, you are the best, most supportive editor I could have – thank you so much.

Thank you to copy editor Jenni Davis, who polished and honed my words sensitively, and Sadie Mayne, who was the proofreader.

I'm very grateful to the whole Amazon Publishing team and the PR team at FMcM, who have helped to get my books in front of so many readers and reviewers.

For the cover, thank you to Emma Rogers who has done it again with another beautiful design.

My sincere thanks to editor Julia Cremer and her team at Droemer Knaur in Germany, who I feel very privileged to work with.

Finally, a heartfelt thank you to my fantastic agent Hayley Steed, whose faith in me has never wavered. I could not hope for a better champion for my work.

Thank you to writing tutors Claire Fuller and Jarred McGinnis and my fellow writers on an Arvon course I took in October 2022. I arrived with the bare bones of this story and came away feeling inspired – and with lots of great memories.

Thank you to the supportive and friendly fellow writers in my Debut group, my fellow Lake Union writers and to novelist (and former midwife) Jessica Ryn for answering my questions.

Being interviewed by Zoe Ball for the Radio 2 Book Club was a real pinch-me moment that helped get my first novel, *Tell Me How This Ends,* into the hands of thousands of readers. Zoe, you are an absolute star and I will always be grateful. To the librarians with The Reading Agency who help select the BBC Radio 2 Book Club picks – a thousand thank yous. Librarians are the best people.

To the many book bloggers, podcasters, book groups, journalists and reviewers who have been so welcoming and asked such interesting questions, a huge thank you. You are the quiet stars of the publishing industry. Many thanks to Heron Books in Bristol for your support.

Thank you to every single reader who has got in touch, particularly those who have shared their own stories. For me, books have always been about a sense of connection, of recognising your own experience or empathising with someone else's, and I look forward to chatting to lots of readers old and new about this book.

My friends and wider family have been so supportive. Special thanks to Nick, Sarah, Philip and Joanna, who have always been there for me.

Caroline S, Alison C and Caroline G, thank you for being the best group of 'mum' friends ever. We were brought together by our children, but our friendships thrived far beyond. Here's to those TP nights – the very best times.

A special mention for my friend Helen Westgate (née Barnard), who always filled my life with colour.

The setting for the final chapter was inspired by a trip I took to Elmley Nature Reserve. I could instantly imagine Nancy there amid its raw, uncompromising beauty. Other places mentioned in the book are a mix of real and imagined. The Scottish island, St Luke's Road, Orchard Drive, The Beaufort, Skipley and Hoyton Beck are made-up places.

AUTHOR Q&A

How would you sum up *The Last Time I Saw You*?

It's a story of a mother, a daughter and the secrets they both carry. When we meet Georgie, she is desperate to leave behind a troubled past and make a fresh start – which includes having a baby. When she and her brother set off on a journey to find their missing mother, they also discover long-buried family secrets. It's a book that explores our deepest bonds – and how, in order to move forward, we sometimes have to look back at our pasts with an unflinching eye.

Where did the idea for *The Last Time I Saw You* come from?

When I was growing up, a new girl joined my primary school. Her family was unusual because she and her brothers were brought up solo by their dad. He swiftly became a bit of a local hero, admired by the other mums for doing it all on his own. The rumour was that the mother had 'done a runner', but nobody knew when or where she'd gone . . . or dared to ask why.

Years later, when I had my first baby, I remembered that girl and her absent mother and I began to question what was really going on back then. Was her father, this larger-than-life character, really Super Dad? Or had something happened to make the mother leave? It felt wrong that nobody ever got to hear the mother's side of the story.

Families come in all shapes and sizes. They can be blended or include adopted or fostered children. They can include step-parents, single parents, cousins and grandparents. This book does not suggest that any shape is 'better' than another, but I did want to explore the scenario of a mother leaving without trace. Then I wondered, what might happen if a mother who had disappeared many years ago suddenly reappeared? What emotions would that stir up – and what family secrets might also come floating to the surface?

Were you making a wider social statement too?
I definitely feel that society would judge a woman who had left her children more harshly than a man. I think it's somehow seen as 'unnatural' and I was interested in how this might translate to a sense of shame that's also internalised by the daughter and son that Nancy leaves behind. When Georgie and Dan move to a new area, they are faced with a choice: do they tell their new neighbours and schoolfriends the truth or start living a lie?

When they choose the latter, covering things up becomes 'a family tradition' and this leads to issues for them both further down the line.

What made you want to write about the 1980s?
I started to write Nancy's 1980s and 1990s timeline to gradually reveal her backstory, which had been hidden from her children. Like Nancy, I went to university in the 1980s. I never had a relationship with a lecturer, but I saw it go on. Back then, similarly unequal relationships between teachers and sixth-form students were not unknown. For context, this was the era when The Police had a number one hit with a song about a teacher asking a schoolgirl not

to stand so close, lest he give in to temptation or frustration – and we all merrily sang along.

The climate now, post #MeToo, is so different. Not perfect, by any means, but there are better safeguards in place and I hope someone in Nancy's position would be more aware of the power imbalance at play.

What do you think the book says about motherhood?

After writing about grief and the end of life in *Tell Me How This Ends*, I had a strong desire to write about birth and the beginning of new lives. Through Georgie, I wanted to convey not only the intense experience of birth, but the enduring emotional bond that comes with becoming a parent.

Then, through Nancy, I wanted to explore the pressures that can come with motherhood. The moment a woman becomes a mother, it changes not only her world view, but how the world views her. It alters her career prospects (this was even more true in the 1980s), her relationship and her sense of self. When Nancy became a mother, she had barely formed her own identity, so she feels these pressures even more keenly.

I hope that the overall message about motherhood is that it can be the most rewarding and fundamental relationship, where an unqualified love flows in both directions.

SOME SUGGESTED QUESTIONS
FOR YOUR BOOK CLUB

At the start of the book, Georgie and Dan know very little about their mother or her life. Do you think Nancy was right to hide certain things from her children?

When Nancy leaves, she talks about her sense of shame. But does society judge a mother differently for leaving her children than a father?

The first time Georgie meets Finn he says, 'Rescue me'. Why do you think this chimed with Georgie – and could she ever have succeeded?

When we meet Georgie, she has moved to the country to leave her past behind. How well has she succeeded? Has this changed by the end of the book?

If Georgie had ignored the news story and not gone in search of Nancy, how might her life have unfolded? Might her relationship with Wilf have been different?

At the start and the end of the novel, Nancy is living in remote places, close to nature. Why might she have been drawn to such places?

How does the sibling relationship between Georgie and Dan change over the course of the story?

Gerry acts in a way that would be considered inappropriate by our modern standards. Do you think the same behaviour could happen today?

Nancy talks about feeling ill-equipped to be a mother. How much did her own upbringing help or hinder her mothering skills?

Towards the end of the book, Georgie tells Dan, 'It was a set of people and events who came together at exactly the wrong time . . . No single person is to blame.' Do you agree with this statement?

How do you imagine Nancy's relationship with her children might progress after the novel ends?

A secret lay at the heart of Nancy and Frank's marriage. But could their marriage have been saved?

How much sympathy do you have for Frank?

ABOUT THE AUTHOR

Photo © 2022, Charlotte Gray

Jo Leevers grew up in London and began writing fiction after a career in magazine journalism. Her bestselling debut, *Tell Me How This Ends*, was a BBC Radio 2 Book Club choice. Whether writing fiction or interviewing people for articles, she is fascinated by the stories and secrets that we all carry with us. She has two grown-up children and lives with her husband and their wayward dog, Lottie, in Bristol.

Follow the Author on Amazon

If you enjoyed this book, follow Jo Leevers on Amazon to be notified when the author releases a new book!

To do this, please follow these instructions:

Desktop:

1) Search for the author's name on Amazon or in the Amazon App.
2) Click on the author's name to arrive on their Amazon page.
3) Click the 'Follow' button.

Mobile and Tablet:

1) Search for the author's name on Amazon or in the Amazon App.
2) Click on one of the author's books.
3) Click on the author's name to arrive on their Amazon page.
4) Click the 'Follow' button.

Kindle eReader and Kindle App:

If you enjoyed this book on a Kindle eReader or in the Kindle App, you will find the author 'Follow' button after the last page.